Highly recommended! A hard-edged and well-crafted novel, with surreptitiously smart prose, confident plotting, and characters you feel you know.

MICHELLE BURFORD, founding senior features editor of *O, the Oprah Magazine*

*Feast for Thieves* is smart, gritty, and unforgettable. Filled with calamity and humor, this book is a hands-down winner. It's about time veteran writer Marcus Brotherton added his powerful voice to fiction. His writing voice is superb.

TOSCA LEE, *New York Times* bestselling coauthor of the Book of Mortals series.

An exhilarating story told in a neo-Western genre, of all things. Masterful and riveting, humorous yet poignant. Anyone who enjoys books by Ted Dekker, Randy Alcorn, or Leif Enger will enjoy every story woven by Marcus Brotherton. This unique and page-turning adventure will harvest a whole new fold of fans.

JULIE CANTRELL, *New York Times* bestselling author of *Into the Free*

Part *Band of Brothers*, part *True Grit*, this is the rollicking tale of a wartime hero's fight to find his place in a post-war world. Rich with action, *Feast for Thieves* is cinematic storytelling at its best.

ADAM MAKOS, *New York Times* bestselling author of *A Higher Call*

As a great admirer of Marcus Brotherton's nonfiction work, I was eager to dive into his debut novel. *Feast for Thieves* does not disappoint. From the first page, Rowdy Slater emerges as a character to root for, complete with flaws, charm, and an unshakeable conscience. I enjoyed this story from beginning to end, a wonderful tale of redemption that will leave readers hoping for a sequel.

KRISTINA MCMORRIS, bestselling author of *The Pieces We Keep*

A gutsy, never-preachy story filled with massive redemptive undercurrents. Why read this? Ultimately it's a book of hope, and it shows how anyone's heart can be changed.

MATT CARTER, lead pastor, Austin Stone Community Church, Texas, and coauthor of *The Real Win*

Marcus Brotherton has crafted more than a rousing story here. He's created characters who leap off the page and a small corner of the world you can lose yourself inside, all held together with stirring prose. I really enjoyed this book.

BILLY COFFEY, bestselling author of *The Devil Walks in Mattingly*

This story is a delight. There is a strong sense of literary quality here, combined with a remarkably unique redemptive message. The characters are real, the descriptions potent, and the force of a good story well told is strong throughout. Highly recommended.

DAVIS BUNN, bestselling novelist, writer-in-residence at Regent's Park College, Oxford University

A ROWDY SLATER NOVEL

# FEAST FOR THIEVES

MARCUS BROTHERTON

*Marcus Brotherton*

**MOODY PUBLISHERS**
CHICAGO

The author is represented by the literary agency of WordServe Literary Group (www. wordserveliterary.com).

Edited by Pam Pugh
Interior design: Ragont Design
Cover design: Erik M. Peterson
Cover photo of man in water: copyright © by Pearl/Lightstock. All rights reserved.
Cover photo of landscape: copyright © by Im Perfect Lazybones/Shutterstock. All rights reserved.
Picture of paratrooper on back cover, courtesy the family of Joe Toye

Library of Congress Cataloging-in-Publication Data

Brotherton, Marcus.
    Feast for thieves : a Rowdy Slater novel / Marcus Brotherton.
        pages cm
    Summary: "Sergeant Rowdy Slater is the most skilled-and most incorrigible-soldier in Dog Company, 506th PIR, 101st Airborne, an elite group of paratroopers fighting for the world's freedom in World War II. Through a bizarre set of circumstances, Rowdy returns to the States after the war, turns his life around, and falls into the only job he can find-preacher at the sparsely populated community church in Cut Eye, Texas, a dusty highway town situated at the midpoint of nowhere and emptiness. The town's lawman, suspicious that Rowdy has changed his ways only as a cover up, gives an ultimatum: Rowdy must survive one complete year as Cut Eye's new minister or end up in jail. At first Rowdy thinks the job will be easy, particularly because he's taking over for a young female missionary who's held the church together while the men were at war. But when a dark-hearted acquaintance from Rowdy's past shows up with a plan to make some quick cash, Rowdy becomes ensnared due to an irrevocable favor, and life turns decidedly difficult"-- Provided by publisher.
    ISBN 978-0-8024-1213-3 (paperback)
    1. World War, 1939-1945--Veterans--Fiction. 2. Life change events--Fiction. I. Title.
    PS3602.R64798F43 2014
    813'.6--dc23
                                    2014002536

We hope you enjoy this book from River North Fiction by Moody Publishers. Our goal is to provide high-quality, thought provoking books and products that connect truth to your real needs and challenges. For more information on other books and products go to www. moodypublishers.com or write to:

River North Fiction
Imprint of Moody Publishers
820 N. LaSalle Boulevard
Chicago, IL 60610


1 3 5 7 9 10 8 6 4 2

*Printed in the United States of America*

For the hungry and thirsty.

— **Part 1** —

# ONE

March 1946

W hen it came to robbing the bank, we wasn't polished or nothing. We just set the old truck's hand brake and jigged out the side while the motor was still running, shrugged off the rain while throwing sacks over our heads to hide our faces, and bustled straight up the middle with our rifles aimed forward. Shoot, I never would have hurt nobody innocent. I just needed money real bad, like anyone does if he's spent time in the clink and nobody will give him a job once he gets out.

Right through the front door, Crazy Ake walloped the guard over the back of the head and he went down like a sack of peas thrown on a stock house pallet, which I felt sorry about, but not much blood was coming out, so I ran to the counter and stuck my rifle up in the clerk's skinny face so the man could see I wasn't fooling. We was only carrying one sack to fill—mine—so as one partner could be more of the muscle if folks decided to fight back. Besides, it was a big sack, and the clerk stuffed it full while Crazy Ake strode back and forth up there on the countertop yelling about how he was the fires of hell and was pouring down wrath on the town.

All that yelling may not have been simple scare tactics with Crazy Ake. He was foaming around the edges of his mouth where the sack was cut for an airhole, and cursing a blue streak, and he looked genuinely like his finger might twitch tight against the trigger and blow some man's head away if aggravated enough. Yes sir, that worried me a might. It did. But I didn't offer much time to my worrying because once my sack was good and full we ordered the folks to lay down on the tile and count backward from five hundred to one while we skedaddled out the door and back to the truck for our getaway.

Dang that rain. Our old truck's motor coughed its last revolution just as Crazy Ake slid behind the wheel and I slid in the other side. He stomped on the starter but the wetness must have already slunk into the wiring because the motor sputtered and growled, but no life came. It never rains in West Texas, least never when I was growing up near here, and I don't know why we picked this day of all days to commit a crime. Sure enough, the rooftop gutters on the adobe bank were full and overflowing, and muddy rivers were flashing up and rolling down the streets already. Crazy Ake slugged me hard in the shoulder as if the truck's dead motor was my fault. I moved to paste him back when I thought smarter and hollered instead, "Run!"

The bank sits square on Main Street, right across the way from the sheriff's office and jail. We sprinted east a block, hooked south onto Highway 2, and kept running. Far in the distance we could see our goal. There ain't but one stretch of two-lane in and out of the town of Cut Eye, Texas, and if we'd had more time we would have done smart to hide somewhere. But since we could already hear a siren starting up from back of the sheriff's house, we kept running, hoping to get lost in the wide section of bunch grass and mesquite trees out of town.

We passed by the café and mercantile, the tavern and pool hall with its shady rooms on top, and pushed ourselves hard past the Cut Eye grade school, a red-and-white brick building that squats direct across the street from the tavern. I reckoned city planners wanted their children to grow up seeing the evils of strong drink up close, which made me laugh, though by the time we reached the far edge of the school's baseball field the thought of the school's ill location flitted out of my head. Except for a few scattered houses, the town of Cut Eye was finished. Crazy Ake and I were running free.

That's when a bullet zinged behind my ear. I jagged to the right and Crazy Ake jagged to the left. Another bullet rang out and thudded into the mud on the highway's gravel shoulder five yards in front of us. That sheriff behind us was never a military man, I reckoned, to shoot so far away from his target such as he was doing. Or maybe he was simply a man of mercy and wanted to catch his criminals before frying them in the chair.

I glanced back and saw the long snout of the car's hood gaining on us. No way we could outrun it no how, and I could already see the narrowed eyes of the two men inside. By the cut of the man's uniform in the driver's seat, I knew it wasn't the sheriff but only a deputy. He shot out of the window of the squad car with one hand on the wheel and another on his gun. That meant he was shooting left-handed and squirrely, though a bullet is a bullet any way you look at it. Another man in regular clothes sat beside him, just some hayseed in overalls who probably had money in the bank, so I knew he weren't the sheriff neither, which further relieved me a might.

Even so, I sprinted harder and jagged off-kilter again so the next bullet would be just as hard-pressed to find the back of my head. Sure enough two more shots thudded into the blacktop near my feet, and then a fifth and a sixth. I noticed the deputy shot with a Smith & Wesson square-butt military and police revolver, a real gem of a weapon that's warmed the hearts of thousands of men in authority across the country. So with six shots fired, that meant he needed to pause and reload. That gave me a moment to hatch a plan.

A hundred yards ahead lay the bridge across the river. Crazy Ake and I jagged closer together and kept sprinting forward. The squad car pulled in close and breathed on our heels; it's a wonder the deputy didn't accelerate and run us over. Wasn't much of a plan, I knew even in the moment, but I dropped my rifle to the pavement, lashed my gunnysack to my belt while still on the run, and hollered, "Jump in the river! Swim with the current!"

Our boots clattered on the edge of the bridge's grating just as two more bullets whizzed over our heads. Crazy Ake didn't answer at first. Then he yelled, "That's my money! You remember that, Rowdy Slater!" And he leaped over the guardrail and dived into the water faster than you could yell jackrabbit.

I jumped after him and counted on the long way down. *One Mississippi. Two Mississippi. Three Mississippi. Four*—and sucked in a quick lungful of air right before I hit. The shock of cold water smacking my body flattened me out. It was all mountain runoff, and I burbled underneath the black river that raced along now in flood proportions from today's heavy rainstorm. Immediately something hard struck me from behind and scraped its way along the top of my head. I fought against the current and scrambled to reach the surface, but no surface could be found. I pushed and shoved with my hands and arms, kicking with my legs so as not to go deeper under. Whatever was blocking me rolled and turned this way and that. I was stuck.

From its feel, the blockage seemed to be the stump of a tree trunk caught over my head. The deadwood washed its way down river same speed as me, except now I was tangled in the bare branches on the stump's other end. I kept counting, all the while struggling to break free. *Thirty Mississippi. Thirty-one Mississippi. Thirty-two*—I clawed and pushed against the branches. Nothing would budge. I couldn't bounce upright and I couldn't clear myself away. *Hundred-and-one Mississippi. Hundred-and-two Mississippi* — my lungs pounded in my chest. The tree became my lawman, judge, and jury, and was trying me for my crimes, finding me guilty, holding me under. *Two-hundred-and-fifty Mississippi. Two-hundred-and-fifty-one Mississippi*—my hands flailed against the branches above. Air trickled out of my nose. My lungs emptied and I fought a strong urge to gasp.

Strange how a man is racing along under the surface of a rain-swollen river, he's but a moment away from death, and he takes a split second to take stock of his life. Maybe the thought rushes at him because he can't help himself. I knew I was about to die and I wasn't afraid. No, it honestly wasn't fear. Last December 1944 I'd survived the artillery blasts of the Battle of the Bulge. For two months I'd slept in a foxhole during Belgium's coldest winter in thirty years. We were outgunned and outmanned with no proper winter clothing or supplies. We ate thin brown bean soup with maggots in it and peed on our hands to warm them before pulling the trigger against our enemies. No, it wasn't fear.

'Twas regret. That was the thought that rushed at me. *All that scrapping around I done. All that getting loaded. All that visiting the shady rooms above taverns.* My C.O. once called me "the most incorrigible man in Dog Company," and considering we were a combat-hardened group of paratroopers who brawled, drank, and visited brothels every chance we got, that was paying me no compliment indeed. Shoot—I was the worst of the lot. From a hundred yards away I could fire my M1 and hit the wings off a fly, and that's the only thing that saved me. My skill as a sharpshooter won their respect. My ability saved their lives. My knack with a rifle saved me from going to the clink before I did, even though I undoubtedly deserved it way ahead of time.

The thought raced away from me as quick as it came, and I continued to fight. Raging water surrounded me. I began to black out. Still I fought, but still the branches wouldn't come loose. My chest sunk flat and a pressure caved the insides of me. I inhaled a lungful of muddy water, and then another. The river swirled into me like a bullet from a Nazi's rifle, choking my insides, filling tight my lungs.

That's when I heard him. I swear I did. The man spoke loud, although I couldn't tell from what direction his voice came. Some man I didn't recognize, maybe a lawman who sprinted alongside the riverbank. He shouted at me the same clear way I'd shouted at Crazy Ake exactly eight minutes and thirty-eight seconds earlier by my count of Mississippis.

"Hey fella!" came the voice. "You want to live?"

How that man's voice was reaching me so far under the water, I couldn't rightly fathom, but there under the river, caught as I was and speeding along in the current of destruction, I nodded my head and hoped a saving rope would soon follow.

"Then find the good meal and eat your fill," it said. "Swear you'll do that?"

I nodded again. *What a crazy thing for the man to say*, I thought. Maybe I was going unconscious, but just then the tree broke loose like a strong hand moved it, the tangle of branches passed over my head, and I shot to the surface. A moment later my knees scraped gravel on a shallow section of riverbed. I stumbled forward out of the river, walked three steps onto dry ground, and vomited a bellyful of muddy water.

No one was around. I flopped down on my side and stayed flat against the cold river stones for some time, panting. I could see the river bent right where I washed up. The river's force must have propelled me to safe ground, and the lawman, whoever had yelled at me, was lost in the dusk. Maybe passed by on the bank.

Little by little, the rain let up. Somewhere a coyote howled. Crazy Ake was nowhere to be seen, same as the deputy and the fella in the overalls chasing me in their car. The sack of money was still tied to my belt. After a time, I stood and walked to the river's edge. I washed away the vomit's slime from my mouth, then scrambled a mile or two more downstream on my feet, all the while taking stock of what to do next. I found a thicket to hide myself and waded into the midst of the trees. Again I listened carefully. No sirens. No dogs in the distance. If the shouting lawman had been near he would have caught me by now. I didn't know exactly how far I'd traveled, but I might be ten miles away from Cut Eye now at the rate that river raced.

A piece of flint lay in my jacket pocket, same as I always carried it, so I gathered some brushwood, lit a tiny flame so as not to be seen, and set about drying the chill out of my wet clothes. The thicket covered me well enough, so in stealth I counted out the cash, ventilating stacks of bills in the heat of the flame so they wouldn't stay wet and grow moldy, and saw we'd bounced out of the bank with exactly $18,549. That amount of money would solve any man's aggravations, I knew, including mine. But when I stared at the loot it looked oddly tarnished, as decaying as an enemy corpse found in the woods. As impossible as it seemed for someone like me, I actually whispered out loud, "I don't want it."

'Course, I didn't know what to do with the money neither. A man can't be roaming around the Texas countryside with fifteen years' wages stuffed in a gunnysack. I clambered halfway up the bank, far enough so high water would never touch the mark, and eyed out a location at the base of a tree. I scraped out a hole, lined it with rocks to prevent rot, and buried the money still in the sack.

My stomach rumbled. The adrenaline buzz of nearly dying gave me the shakes, and I reckoned some food might do me good. After making it up the rest of the bank, I stopped, momentarily mesmerized by the clearing of the clouds. The wind blew storm-like, except the storm was leaving, not coming, and high in the night sky as far as I could see was a breathtaking blue and black. Below that were the ends of a sunset, the purples and reds, and low against the horizon were the last oranges and yellows, all fire and brilliant, an absolute pure light.

I didn't want to leave this sight of wonderment but I knew a criminal needs to make haste. In front of me lay thin growths of tussock and salt grass. One lone juniper tree stood tall in the dark. I wondered what distant land I might run to now, far away from Cut Eye, Texas, and the law. There came another rumble deep in my gut, one I couldn't shake no matter how hard I tried, and I recognized it as the kind of ache that brings about death if a man ignores it long enough. I wondered how I might find that good meal, the one the voice was talking about, and eat my fill.

# TWO

They say the town of Cut Eye sits halfway between nowhere and emptiness. It's been around for some one hundred and thirty years, ever since the days of the Wild West. The only highway for two hundred miles in any direction is Highway 2, which passes right through Cut Eye, and I knew if I didn't find that highway, I'd be wandering around in the sagebrush until the buzzards ate me.

So I left the riverbank, pointed myself southeast, and started walking. What I hoped to do was flag down a long-haul trucker, a man passing through who had no knowledge of the events that transpired the late afternoon before. What I didn't want was any locals to come along and get suspicious of a man standing beside the side of the road with his thumb sticking out, someone they didn't recognize straightaway.

It took me most of the night to find my way back to the blacktop. I hid in the ditch while a car or two passed. When a tanker truck loomed in the distance I took a risk and stepped up. Morning sun was just beginning to show, and on the truck's side was painted "Kansas City Southern Lines: *For the Duration*," so I knew he was hauling for the railroad, most likely out of Shreveport or Lake Charles. Sure enough, he pulled to the shoulder and I ran to the cab.

"Where headed?" He was a colored man, which didn't bother me none, and although he was leaned over so as he could speak to me, I could still see a shotgun resting across his legs pointing my direction.

"Next town ahead."

"You drifting?" He wasn't smiling.

I paused before answering truthfully. "Yeah."

He looked me up and down as if weighing his options. "Lots of fellas drifting these days. A man of your height and build surely saw some action. What branch?"

"101st Airborne."

"I was Red Ball Express. We hauled your sorry butts up to Bastogne. You fellas had it tough up there, fighting surrounded like you were. Good thing Patton broke through the lines to save y'all."

I coughed and muttered, "Patton might have broken through, but he sure didn't *save* us."

The trucker launched into a big grin, then laughed and set the shotgun back on the rack behind him. "Hop in. I can always use someone's ear to bend on these long empty roads."

I climbed aboard and the trucker took off at a slow crawl, working through the gears, gradually gaining speed.

"I've always wondered what kind of courage it takes for a man to jump out of a perfectly good airplane," he said. "How many campaigns was that for you, anyway—Normandy, Market Garden, Belgium? You make it into Germany too?"

I shook my head. "Belgium but not Germany."

"So what now? Headed for the oil fields? That's some hard labor, but a man can make a buck at it if he puts his back into it."

"Not me." I was still telling the truth. Two months ago I spent a week working for a rig. Every day we worked from dawn to dusk, slippery crude covering us 'til we was black as darkness. But late one evening at a bar, I was drunk and punched out some yahoo who ratted on me to the company's manager. The manager became mistrustful and asked to see my papers, which he'd overlooked at first. When he saw my dishonorable discharge, well, I was out on my ear. It wasn't a new story.

"Farmhand then?" the trucker asked. "Ranch hand? Lumber-yard? Trucker like me? A man returns from war and he's got to find his trade."

I shook my head and kept silent. I'd tried all those. Applied, anyway. With all the servicemen spilling home from overseas, there weren't hardly no jobs to be had. The rare openings that came up, I was always last in line. Time after time they checked my papers and I heard the same thing: "Keep moving, boy." I knew who I was.

The trucker kept talking without seeking much feedback from me, and I let my mind wander. I guess I even dozed a bit because next thing I knew the sunrise was over and a city was upon us. He pulled to the side of the highway and motioned to the door with his head. "I can take you farther, but you said 'next town.' This is it." He held out his hand. "You best be finding your purpose soon, friend. A man with no purpose is a man who don't last long in this world."

I shook the trucker's hand and climbed out. The truck growled and headed away down the highway. I took stock of my surround-ings. Last meal I'd eaten was yesterday morning. Crazy Ake had a biscuit in his pocket and we'd split it between us. My pockets were bare of cash like usual. I hadn't taken a dime off the loot we'd heisted. Somehow it just didn't seem right.

A diner sat on the edge of town and I walked around back of it and tried their garbage cans but they were empty still in the morning, so I kept walking up the road. In front of me was a bright neon sign that said "Union Gospel Mission of Texas—free meals." I didn't cater much to religion, but a man on the run can't be choosy. The door listed open and I walked inside the entryway where a man behind the desk told me to sign in and join the line that was forming through the main door.

"You gotta hear the preacher first," the man said. "That's rules. Breakfast is served afterward."

Well, that seemed like a raw deal to me, but I wasn't arguing with my stomach growling like it was. I filed into the chapel, sat on the back bench, and leaned back with my eyes closed. I could use another thirty minutes of sleep.

"Hear now the words of Isaiah." The minister took his stand, flopped open his Bible on the pulpit, and cleared his throat. He was an older fella with a thin, sharp face and round wire-rimmed glasses. His suit was starched and clean-pressed and he looked to me more like a fella in an advertisement for the Arthur A. Everts jewelery company than any preacher I ever knowed.

"'Come now, and let us reason together, saith the Lord.'" The preacher began to read. "'Though your sins be as scarlet, they shall be as white as snow; though they be red like crimson, they shall be as wool.'" The preacher looked up, paused for effect, and added in his own words, "I wonder if there's a man out there this morning who knows what this passage from God's Word means?"

Men were still filing into the room, knocking over chairs, sitting down hard. I glanced around. Most were winos, bums who'd never seen an honest day's work in their lives. A few of the younger men looked sober, men simply out of work like me. Most still wore bits and pieces of their war uniforms.

"It means that God is in the business of giving men second chances," the preacher said. "It's true your sins are reprehensible to God. You might be an adulterer or a reprobate, a slanderer or a gossip." He cleared his throat again. "You might even be a murderer or a thief, but God's Word declares there isn't any sin that can't be forgiven."

Well, when he said that bit about being a thief, I was listening.

"Isaiah continues," the preacher said, "and he offers us this warning as well as an encouragement. 'If ye be willing and obedient, ye shall eat the good of the land: But if ye refuse and rebel, ye shall be devoured with the sword.'"

Well, now that preacher had my full attention. I was willing and obedient. I'd always been a soldier who followed orders. And there was that mention of eating from the good of the land. I wondered if that had anything to do with what the lawman beside the river shouted at me.

"With God's help, any man can change his ways," the preacher said. "You may be lost and without direction. You might have led a life with a complete lack of purposefulness. You might be drifting forsaken through this world same as many of you are drifting through Texas right now, but the shed blood of Jesus Christ can make you a new man. When Jesus was crucified on the cross, two thieves were crucified along with him. Both men deserved death. The man on one side cursed Jesus and went to his condemnation. But the man on his other side asked to be remembered. Some consider that one of the first churches, a congregation of thieves, and Jesus extended mercy to that second thief and said to him, 'Today, you will be with me in paradise.'"

The man was preaching straight at me, I knew, and I respected him for it. He wasn't fiddling around with his words or trying to sugarcoat the facts. There was a heaven and a hell, and I was bound for hell. I knew that. That preacher was to the point and he was calling out my life as he saw it.

I stood to my feet.

"Rev'rund," I said. "Are you for real?"

The minister looked jolted for a moment, like he wasn't used to outbursts in the middle of his sermons. "Come forward and receive salvation," he said. "You'll know this is no lie."

That plank-hardened room was swimming in scent, I tell you. Something lay in the air of the room, and it wasn't the smell of the winos. It was the good smell of bacon and eggs. The bacon was frying up crispy and golden; I could almost taste it on my tongue. Those eggs were real, not powdered, the kind a man didn't need to pour ketchup on in the mess hall. I'd put salt and pepper on them. Maybe some chili sauce if they had it. And the smell of that breakfast cooking worked its way through my nose and down into my gut.

"I'm saved!" I cried out. "Let's eat!"

The preacher's eyebrows lowered. "Blasphemer!" He reared back like he was getting ready to shout out a mouthful, and sure enough it came forth mightily: "What right have you to partake of the kingdom of God?! If all you came for is a free meal, then out with you. Go out into the byways and highways, and let God have mercy on your soul!" He pointed at two burly looking types standing in the wings. Then strode over to me and grabbed me by the arms.

"C'mon fella," one of them said. "Time for you to leave."

I shook off his grip. "I ain't leaving without a meal!" I shouted. "I sat through the sermon. Now I'm saved. Time to eat!"

The other fella started shoving my shoulders, pushing me toward the side door. I hate to be shoved. He dropped his chin like he was getting ready to be rougher with me, and before he could move again I slugged him across the jaw. He went down into a million glass pieces, and the other fella jumped on my back and started whaling on my head with his fists. I crashed over backward on him to break his grip, leaped up in case he beat me to it, and another man's fist came from out of nowhere and popped me in the eye. One of the out-of-work servicemen joined in. I walloped him back, and the room erupted. Men who'd previously sat together hearing the holy Word of God busted each other's chins, broke chairs over each other's heads, and knocked each other on the nose.

A hard-backed Bible flew my direction. I ducked its sharp edges just in time, hit the deck, and crawled toward the door. Over the years I've learned the floor's the safest place in any large fight.

Not that I was always seeking a safe place mind you, but I figured the law would be called soon, and a man such as me would be wise to take an opportunity in the chaos to beat a hasty retreat.

The sunlight streamed against my face and I slammed the mission's door behind me. I ran across the street, spotted another trucker bearing down on me, and flagged him down.

"You sticking around this joint long?" I asked as soon as he opened the door.

"Driving straight through."

"Good enough." I climbed aboard before he could say otherwise.

A siren sounded in the distance, and a sheriff's car appeared heading toward us. It roared by and kept going, headed straight for the brawl at the mission.

"Wonder what all that was about?" the trucker asked.

I shook my head. "You know those church folks. Always squabbling about something."

# THREE

We was two hundred miles south of the mission before I asked the truck driver to pull over and let me out.

"Here?" He kept his hands on the wheel. "It's middle of nowhere."

"I'm heading the wrong direction," I said. "There's something I need to take care of up north."

The driver shrugged, geared down, and pulled to the side of the highway. The sun was high overhead when I climbed out. I crossed over the highway behind the truck and stood on the other side of the blacktop.

After the truck left, everything felt desolate for some time. I kicked at a creosote bush and nibbled on the end of a blade of buffalo grass. Far in the distance lay a ridge of low hills covered in tarbush with some burro and salt grasses. Around me was wide wasteland. The sun beat down on my head. I stunk of sweat.

I was actually listening to that preacher. I'm not exactly sure what got into me when I jumped up like that. I had in mind to come forward and ask him some more questions about the changes stirring in me, but the good smell of that bacon nearly drove me mad with hunger, it rightly did, and then when that fella started shoving me, well, that was enough aggression to cause a man like me to snap and lash out. The thought of that missed meal kept floating through my mind, and I thought, *Wow, what I wouldn't give for a plate of bacon right now.*

It was nearly an hour of waiting before a trucker picked me up and we started heading north again. Briefly I considered stopping back at the mission and seeing if I couldn't make things square with the preacher, but I shook the thought from my mind and continued on with my other plan.

We drove all the rest of that afternoon and into the night. I'd marked the spot where I first hitched a ride, and when the spot was reached I asked to be let out, then found my way back to the thicket, to the tree halfway up the riverbank where I'd stashed the loot. It proved straightforward to find again, and the sack came up real easy. I dusted off the dirt, counted the money to reassure myself it was all still there, and hiked back to the highway again just as the sun was coming up. It was now two full days since my last meal.

The fella who picked me up this time drove a battered Ford pickup, and he eyed my gunnysack with a face full of suspicion until I explained it was some laundry I was taking into town to have cleaned. He squinted in disbelief but wisely kept his mouth shut until we were back in Cut Eye when he said, "This is the place, right?"

I nodded. The pickup slowed to a stop, and I climbed out without a word. I squared my shoulders, walked north a block past the school and the tavern and café and swung left when I got to Main Street. I knew exactly where I was headed. The sheriff's office sat right on the corner. The front door faced Main. The bank was across the street and one lot farther down, although I noticed a big "closed" sign out in front.

I stopped walking, inhaled sharply, and eyed the sheriff's office again. It stood directly before me now, and I shaded the sun from my eyes. I nodded, found my feet, walked up the cement steps, and opened the door to the jail.

Behind the front desk sat a young woman who kept her eyes focused on her work, even when I approached and cleared my throat. No one else on duty looked to be in sight. I could tell by the shape of her dress she was willowy underneath but I wasn't here for womanizing, not this place. I cleared my throat again.

"Hang on a minute," she said. "What rhymes with 'luminous'?"

I furrowed my brow. "Not sure what you're getting at ma'am."

She frowned, exasperated. "*Where she had at one time descended into an aureole of light luminous*—it's my poem, see? I'm almost finished, but this last line needs a rhyme."

"Well, I'm here to see the sheriff." My voice was curt, and I glanced about the room. Two closed doors on the left led into what I guessed to be offices. Behind the girl sat a row of four jail cells. One was occupied by six sleeping drunks. In the other, five wide-eyed men paced, all muttering to themselves. A third cell was packed so full I couldn't tell how many men were inside, all yelling and hollering general deviances. The fourth held two women of ill repute. One was sitting with her head in her hands. The other raised her eyebrows and whistled my direction.

The girl sighed over the noise and frowned again. "Well, the sheriff's not here. You'll need to wait."

"Thank you, ma'am. Can you tell me how long he'll be?"

The girl looked up for the first time, rankled her nose, then closed her eyes. "*Their hands united like a raven in flight, where she had at one time descended into an aureole of luminous light.* There— that's all I needed to do, reverse the words." She opened her eyes again. "Now, what were you asking?"

I tapped my foot. "You got too many beats in your last line."

"No I don't."

"Sure you do. Count it out."

"It's perfect the way it is."

"Look, lady," I said, "if you're so smart, how come you asked for my help in the first place?"

"Look mister—" The girl folded her arms. "I don't know you, but if you don't like my poetry, then you're no friend of mine." She pointed to a hard-backed seat against the far wall. "You can sit over there. The sheriff will be here when he gets here." She paused, glared, and added, "Will there be anything else?"

I glared back at her. "You're plumb full of sassafras, aren't you?" I judged her to be eighteen. Maybe nineteen. Without waiting for her to answer, I walked to the chair, sat down, and set my left boot on my right knee.

Just then the front door opened and a man I reckoned to be the sheriff walked in. He was mustached, tall and barrel-chested, and wore a black three-piece suit with a thin matching black bow tie. His hands were big, his face jowly but muscular, and he wore a white Stetson tilted rakishly to one side.

"Any calls?" he asked.

The young woman shook her head. "All was quiet on the Western Front. Deuce Gibbons passed out cold and hit his head in cell three, but I called the doc, who says he's okay. Oh—and this fella's in a hurry to see you." She nodded toward me with a scowl.

"Cup of coffee first. Have him follow me in." He motioned to one of the closed office doors.

The young woman looked my direction and gave a half snicker. "You want coffee too? Help yourself."

"Not when it's mixed with arsenic," I muttered, and followed the sheriff inside his office.

"Close the door." He motioned to a chair. "Why you here?"

I set the gunnysack on his desk and sat down.

He untied the top, stared inside, smelled the bills, and let out a low whistle. He closed the bag up, sat back in his chair, and draped his left arm on the cabinet behind him, his right arm on his knee near his revolver where I couldn't see the fingers. For a moment he grinned, studying my face. Then his smile faded and his eyes became stern.

"You listen to me good, boy. From here on out I'm asking the questions. You will not say another word unless I tell you to speak. You got that?"

I nodded.

A knock came at the door and the young woman poked her head inside. "Sheriff, what rhymes with horizon, as in *They watched the sun set as it disappeared on the horizon . . .*"

The sheriff studied the girl a moment. "Prison. Hellion. Rebellion. Brazen. Emblazon. Liaison. Raisin. Crimson." He scratched his head. "Bunion . . . Does that help? Oh wait—" He motioned to the gunnysack. "Take this out of sight and count it for me, will ya?"

The girl smiled at him, took the sack, and closed the door behind her.

"Now—" He returned his attention to me. "I've been a lawman for a lot of years, and the way I figure it, there are only two reasons why a man walks into a jailhouse with a sack full of money, which creates a powerful dilemma for me. One, the man has found the money and is returning it for a reward. Since I've never seen you around town, and the reward money hasn't been posted in the newspapers yet, I'd be hard-pressed to understand where a man such as yourself heard about any reward. That primes me to think you fall into the second category." His voice trailed off and we sat in silence at least two full minutes. All the time he studied my face.

Another knock sounded on the door and the young woman appeared. "Total comes to $18,549. You need anything else, Sheriff? Another cup of coffee?"

"Nah—thanks." He nodded toward the door. The girl disappeared again. The sheriff opened a folder on a desk, checked a figure, then closed the folder and sat in quietness again, studying me intently. At least five more minutes passed. We could hear the prisoners shouting through the walls.

"Sir." I broke silence. "You mentioned a second reason, sir?"

The sheriff flushed and slammed his hand on the cabinet. "You will not speak unless spoken to!"

I nodded.

The red drained from his face and he leaned back again, although I could tell he was still tense. "First question: where'd you serve, son?"

"Sir, Dog Company, 506th Parachute Infantry Regiment, 101st Airborne, sir."

The sheriff nodded but remained otherwise expressionless. "506th, eh? One of Colonel Sink's boys. Name and rank?"

"Sergeant Zearl Slater, sir. Actually . . . uh . . . my last rank was private."

"Zearl?" The sheriff's eyebrows raised. "Your name is Zearl?"

"Sir, it was the name my father gave me, but, yeah, everybody calls me Rowdy."

"Well, Private Rowdy Slater who used to be a sergeant—" he drummed the fingers of his left hand on the cabinet. "Don't move." He hit a buzzer near his desk phone. The young woman appeared again. "Get Martha on the switchboard," he said. "Have her connect you to West Point. Let 'em know who's calling and that I want to speak with Five-Oh-Sink—they'll connect you. He's now assistant division commander of the 101st last I heard."

The girl nodded and went to her desk. Three minutes later she stuck her head back inside the door. "Colonel Robert Sink is on the line."

"Bob!" the sheriff said. "Halligan Barker out in Texas. Yeah—I know, far too long." He laughed. "Look, Bob, we'll catch up on small talk another time. Right now I've got a fella in my office says he was one of your boys. What can you tell me about Zearl Slater? Dog Company." The sheriff went silent as he listened. A few times he nodded. A few times he said, "Is that so?" All the while he kept his eyes on me. He wasn't smiling. "Thanks, Bob," he said at last and hung up the phone.

I shifted uncomfortably in my chair.

"So you spent time in military prison."

"Sir, yes sir." My voice was low.

"Why?"

"A bar fight in Mourmelon, sir. I got drunk and busted a guy's head in. Turns out he was a major."

"How long he spend in the hospital?"

"Long enough to give me six months."

"Anything else I should know about that?"

"Sir, that's about it, sir."

The sheriff pursed his lips. "Ever wounded?"

"Took a bullet in my side during Operation Market Garden. Passed clean through and I was able to rejoin my unit soon."

"Anything else about that story?"

"Sir, that's about it, sir."

The sheriff took a sip of coffee and cleared his throat again. "According to my talk with the colonel, there are a few details you're leaving out, Private Rowdy Slater, which brings me to reason number two why a man would walk into a jailhouse with a sack full of money. It's because the man committed the crime himself, is now remorseful, and wants to change his ways."

I opened my mouth, but the sheriff abruptly held up his hand. "Keep your mouth shut, boy. That's an order." The man's eyes were firmly set.

I nodded.

He leaned forward in his chair. "What the colonel said was that the major you busted in the head had it coming. Seemed he got fresh with a French civilian, a married woman, and you stepped in and defended her honor. The major swung wide, fell down like a sack of horse hockey, and hit his head against the bar—that's the only reason he got hurt so bad. Four paratroopers, a tank commander, and the bartender all signed affidavits at your court martial swearing that's how it happened. But because of your past record of carousing, the judge advocate thought it best to teach you a lesson. Is that how you remember the story?"

I swallowed. "That's what they say, sir."

The sheriff was on a roll. "Colonel Sink also informed me that after you got wounded back in Holland, you had a golden ticket home if you wanted it, but you broke out of the hospital and rejoined your unit. You weren't even healed yet, but you chose to keep doing your duty because you didn't want to leave your brothers alone on the line. When a man doesn't tell such things about himself, then that tells me something about the man's character. Understand what I'm saying Private Slater?"

"I don't think so, sir. Not exactly."

The sheriff wouldn't stop. "The colonel furthermore informed me you helped silence the guns at Brecourt Manor. That action saved a heap of men's lives down on the Normandy beaches. You received the Bronze Star for valor, and in Carentan you pulled three wounded men to safety while a German sniper rained down a hailstorm of lead. After the men were safe, you went back and took out the sniper. You killed at least twenty-three enemy due to your sharpshooting ability, and twenty of those occurred in the most harrowing and dangerous battle situations. So my conclusion is you're a scrupled man who doesn't fear death, although you've made some mistakes, Private Rowdy Slater, and that's what brings me back to my dilemma. Any clue what that might be? Answer if you know."

"Sir, no sir."

The sheriff inhaled sharply and held his breath until I thought he was going to explode. Then he released it and the words rushed out of him angrily. "It means next election I lose votes. If you found the stolen money, then the bankers' committee needs to pay you a reward, which makes them aggravated and they campaign against me next November. But if you stole the money in the first place and returned it because your conscience grew heavy, then I send you to the Texas Department of Criminal Justice, and those boys hate it when an attempted murder of a public safety officer is involved—which is how they'll see it because the bank guard got walloped over the head." He paused just long enough to breathe. "The state factors in your prior criminal record, and then they get itchy to send you to Huntsville. Other states send you to the chair only for capital murder, but in Texas we fry you for a whole host of felonies, providing you don't get lynched first. Big case like this costs big taxpayer money, and that means I get an angry call from the governor who riles up folks to campaign against me. You'd think folks would be happy because the money's been found, but that's the hard-luck life of the sheriff in Cut Eye. You tracking with me? Powerful folks get aggravated and I lose votes, and then Mayor Oris Floyd pushes through the man he wants into office, and I most definitely do not want that to happen! Savvy what I'm saying? Answer me, boy. Do you?"

I swallowed dryly and nodded.

"So here's how this is going to work." The sheriff moved his right hand to his hip, looked me straight in the eyes, and unlatched his holster. "In a minute you and I are going to take a drive. My secretary's going to come along as a witness because my deputy is so straightlaced he won't understand why a man of justice needs to take this sort of action. And since I don't know for sure whether you're a criminal or a hero, I'm going to be polite to an American citizen and pose it as a question—are you coming or not?—and since I'm the man with his hand on the gun, that means you're gonna say yes."

# FOUR

The backseat of the sheriff's car smelled like old winos. I wasn't handcuffed, but the doors were locked. The sheriff drove and the secretary sat in the passenger's seat.

We headed east on Main, turned south onto Highway 2, and followed it past the baseball fields where we turned right onto Lost Truck Road and drove for another mile. The sheriff slowed the car and turned left onto a rutted dirt road overgrown by bushes. In half a mile the road ended.

"Get out," he said.

Wasn't nobody around. The sun was hitting its afternoon stride and the sky was cloudless, the air hot. A trail lay before us bordered by tall grass, and the sheriff motioned for me to walk ahead of him. His secretary followed, still with a scowl on her face. The sheriff brought up the rear.

Within two hundred yards we reached the river, although this looked more like a fork off the main branch. A swath of land flattened out halfway across the flowing water and a pool had formed in the eddy on the other side. Pine trees and high grasses ringed most of the pool. If my heart hadn't been pounding in my chest, I would have looked upon the area as scenic. We stopped by the water's edge. The sheriff's right hand hovered near his holster, and the three of us shivered in silence a few minutes; at least that's the way my nerves felt. Finally the sheriff spoke.

"You know how Cut Eye sprung into existence, boy? Answer if you know."

I shook my head.

He glanced around at the pond and sniffed. "It's because men on Highway 2 needed a watering hole between destinations. You're no stranger to watering holes, I guess, so you know what kind of business it is that money-loving men put on top of taverns." He glanced at his secretary, then glanced away.

I kept silent and studied the pond. It appeared deep enough, cold and quiet, and I wondered if they'd ever find my body once the sheriff finished with me.

"That's right, boy, all other businesses in my town sprung from the first watering hole and the place of ill repute that still sits on top today," the sheriff said. "My town is founded on a lack of scruples, I admit, and it's grown up hard and fast with iniquity ever in mind. These days, two miles northeast of Cut Eye, there's a branch of the Murray Company that runs a plant for gas-fired floor furnaces. It's honest work, heavy labor, and fairly mindless. Couple hundred fellas from Cut Eye work there, although mostly women did during the war, and the rest of my town is populated by ranchers, oilmen, drifters, and other rough-hewn men. Every mother's son is looking to fight and drink and spend his money on a good time, and those roustabouts are exactly what I deal with every day in my line of work—men making my life hard as sheriff. You were born in a small town, yes, Private Slater?"

"Yes sir. Denim. About two hundred and thirty miles from here."

"I know where it lies. Your folks still living?"

"No sir, both dead."

"Any other kin?"

I collected my thoughts before answering. "A niece, sir. Uh ... age four. She's an orphan too, boards with a family in Rancho Springs. She needs—"

"That's all I need to know." The sheriff's voice was brusque and he tapped me on the shoulder. It felt like a shove. "Strip to your briefs and wade to your waist in the pond."

I glanced at the secretary. My heart was nearly pounding through the lining of my chest now. Her face remained motionless, her eyes focused at the sky.

"Go on," the sheriff said. "There's an easy way and a hard way. Your choice."

I took off my jacket and shirt, my boots, socks, and pants. My dog tags jangled in the wind. Don't know why I still wore them. Maybe I always felt naked without. The pond water was mountain cold as I waded forward, and my skin rippled with goose pimples. No sense looking back. No sense trying to intimidate a man with a revolver when all you got is your stare.

"Far enough," the sheriff called. "Turn around and look at me."

I obeyed. His hand still wisped against his revolver but he hadn't yet drawn. For a moment I considered making a run for it. I knew I wouldn't get far.

"You grew up in a small town, Private Slater—so you were taught to fear Jesus. That the case? Answer."

"Sir, I went to Sunday school as a child."

"So you fear God today, even though you've led a wayward life? Answer."

"I guess so, sir. As of yesterday—"

"Your mouth is shut!" the sheriff shouted. "We ain't here for testimony."

The secretary watched me now. All this time she hadn't uttered a word, but now she tapped the sheriff on the arm and said, "I'd like to say something before it occurs."

He nodded.

The secretary took two steps forward on the beach and raised her head slightly. Her nose looked too far in the air for my asking.

"One of my inspirations, the great poetess Ella Wheeler Wilcox, spoke of a burial for her dead," the secretary began. "Missus Wilcox didn't have a shroud or coffin, no prayers uttered or tears shed. Only a picture turned against the wall. In moments where life and death is pictured, I prefer Psalm 23—'Yea, though I walk through the valley of the shadow of death, I will fear no evil' . . ." Her voice trailed off. A small, reddish dabbling duck flew in and skidded onto the pond between me and the shore.

The sheriff grunted at her finish and called my direction, "Dunk yourself then, Private. We don't have all day."

I stared confounded at the man. "Sir?"

"You heard right. Get your hair wet. I don't think it's official unless your hair's wet. I'd come out there and do it myself, but I fought the flu this winter. The girl would do it, but I don't condone mixed bathing. Go on. Get yourself under."

I kept my eyes on the sheriff, sunk myself down in the water, and stood up again.

"Back to shore now," the sheriff called. "Plenty of work to do." He turned to his secretary and gave her a pat on the shoulder. "Sit in the car for a bit, will ya, sweetie. Write another of your poems. No sense you being here for the rest of this."

She nodded, smiled at him, and headed back up the trail.

Everything became clear in an instant and I waded back to shore in a huff. My nervousness fled. I saw straight through the sheriff and his cowardly ways, and my blood bristled. Three yards south of him, I squared off, the cold river water dripping off my body. His hand was still a flea speck away from his holster.

"You baptize a man before you kill him, that your game?" I said. "Clear conscience before murder—you aiming for that? If you were half a man you'd throw me a rifle and settle this fairly."

The sheriff looked startled a moment, then broke into a low chuckle. He bent at the waist and gave a good hee-haw, straightened up, and laughed again. "Look, Private—you're the one who walked into a jailhouse carrying a sack full of stolen money." He wiped the tears from his eyes. "You're right, I was baptizing you, but I ain't here to fight, Rowdy. I'm here to offer you a job."

"A job?"

"You're a man of scruples who isn't afraid of death. You can fight. You can speak. Can you study a book?"

"Yes sir."

"For what I've got in mind, those are the only skills needed."

"I got no idea what you're talking about, Sheriff."

"If a man's truly changed, then his change is shown by his actions." The sheriff dug into the shore with the toe of his boot. "I've got a hunch you're a changed man. Or at least you're beginning that direction." He looked me over from head to toe. "Dry yourself off with your shirt and put your clothes back on. Let me see if I can explain the bigger picture."

He took off his Stetson, wiped his head with his handkerchief, and a faraway look came to his eye. "Around 1900, a hardy band of women from the Texas Missionary Society opened the Cut Eye Community Church. It's been sparsely attended ever since, mostly by the wives of the town's business owners and a few old ranchers. These days, come Saturday night, most men in my town are atop the Cut Eye tavern. Their actions spill over during the week. Families are falling apart and my jail's full to capacity. The last preacher we had didn't last long, sorry to say. While the war was on, a missionary held the church together but is heading overseas soon and doesn't want the job permanently."

"A preaching job?" My eyes were round.

"Hiring and firing is up to me. I'm head of the church's deacon board. Job comes with all your meals taken at Cisco Wayman's café, a rickety parsonage that's ready to topple over, and ten dollars spending cash per month. You'll need a truck too, and we'll scrounge up something to drive until you can afford your own. It ain't much compensation, I know, and the job also comes with one unbendable condition. You following me boy?"

I nodded, now speechless.

"I'm a fellow veteran myself, fought and bled under General John Monash in the trenches of the Somme, so I can empathize with a fellow veteran who's down on his luck, particularly since this is the great state of Texas where men are allowed to be a little rough around the edges." The sheriff turned his head, scowled, and sniffed all at the same time. "It's true—I want a new minister more than I want a crime confessed to. So here's the condition: the real test of your changed ways will be to stick it out for a solid year. Twelve months of preaching in Cut Eye. Can you do that, boy?"

"Thanks much, Sheriff." I found my voice. "But I don't know nothing about being a preacher."

"Actually, I ain't offering you the job, son. It's an order. I want this town cleaned up, and cleaned up good. A preacher who's been an elite paratrooper is exactly the strong man to do it. It's true I'm suspicious of a fella who arrives in a jailhouse with a sack of money, so this is your ultimatum: you take the job, or you go to jail right now. And if you don't last the year, then my hunch will be correct—you robbed the bank—and I'll hunt you down and crush you with the full weight of the law. But—" he cleared his throat, "belly chains and leg irons seem like an awful waste of a man with your potential for success."

The wind rustled through the pines. My stomach growled and I found I was out of arguments except to mumble, "Like I say, sir, I don't know nothing about being a preacher."

The sheriff flushed with sternness. "Well, this is how I see it. In a moment we're going to hike to the car and drive back to Cut Eye. My secretary will return the money to the bank and tell the examiner I found it, which ain't a lie because it appeared on my desk. Meanwhile, you and I are going to walk around the corner to the Pine Oak Café where Cisco Wayman's wife serves up the best peach cobbler this side of the Missouri. Once we sit down and begin eating, I'm going to tell you more about what comes next for you, Rev'rund Rowdy Slater." He held out his revolver hand as if to shake.

A dry swallow slid down my throat, and I stared at the sheriff's outstretched hand. *Rev'rund Rowdy Slater*—I had no idea what to think of that title.

"That's my offer, boy—one solid year of preaching in Cut Eye." The sheriff grinned, his hand still outstretched. "You take this job and you do it right." He winked. "Or else you die."

# FIVE

She called it Peach-Lime Cornmeal Shortcake, and she described the ingredients in the same easygoing motion as she laid down a plateful in front of the sheriff, another plateful in front of me. "Four cups fresh peaches—canned if it's all you can muster." She dabbed her forehead with the corner of a serving towel. "One tablespoon fresh lime juice. One cup cold heavy cream."

Her words flitted through my head loosely, mind you. Both my eyes stared transfixed on that plateful of glory while I licked my lips in cautious hope. Out of my periphery I saw the sheriff remove his Stetson, pick up his fork, and dive in. Right away I got busy with my teeth. The shortcake flaked in all the right places, still warm from the oven. The peaches dripped over the side, serious in their syrup. Another layer of fruit followed underneath with cream so buttery I swear it came straight from the cow that morning. Another solid foundation of shortcake held it in place from the bottom up. I cleaned my plate and hoped more would soon follow. Maybe even a whole meal.

"The name's Augusta Wayman—and don't call me Mrs. Wayman either—it's always just Augusta." The cook spoke with brightness in her voice, but there was a sadness hiding behind her words too—some hidden story of loss she couldn't bury deep enough. She poured me a cup of coffee and added, "Cisco's my husband. He works the breakfast rush only and ain't here just now.

Together we own this place, the Pine Oak Café, the only respectable eatery in town. Oh, a fella could choke down a hamburger along with his whiskey next door at the tavern, but the grease they use in their deep fryer is so dirty it would lower the price of a used Studebaker." She was plump with gray hair wisping out from beneath her kerchief, and she snorted in disgust as she said the last words. The phone rang and she walked toward the kitchen to answer it.

"It's for you, Sheriff," Augusta said. "Martha at the switchboard says to come quick."

The sheriff stood with a start, headed for the phone on the side wall, and took the receiver. "This is Halligan." He listened a moment. "How bad?" His voice was flat. "Be right down."

"Quick piece of pie for the road?" Augusta called over the counter.

"No time. Much obliged." He grabbed his hat, made for the door, and pointed his thumb at me to follow. My visions of more food evaporated in the warm café air. The sheriff slid behind the wheel and motioned for me to sit up front in the passenger's seat next to him this time. The siren let out a wail. He tore up the street out of town, the blue and red overhead lights flashing.

"One of your duties is to be chaplain of the sheriff's department," he explained. "When we get to where we're going, you stay out of the way and let me and my deputy handle business. Comfort the grieving. Notify next of kin if they can be found. Savvy?"

I started to say something but I could tell the sheriff wouldn't be listening to nothing I might say just now. He wore a look of uncommon seriousness, and I watched the speedometer inch past 85. The force of the wind against the car made me brace my feet against the floorboards, one hand holding steady to the door. Two miles up, a sign flashed by us that read, "Murray Plant 500 yards," with an arrow pointing to the left. The sheriff slowed to 65 and kept his course northward. Traffic was stopped ahead of us. He pumped the brakes as we came closer, made for the left-hand lane, and inched by the row of idling trucks and cars. "This is gonna be a real mess," he said.

Sure enough, twenty yards ahead a semitrailer lay on its side. The driver was already out, fuming at the wreck. His truck was jackknifed across the road, blocking both lanes of traffic, and the sheriff stopped the squad car and set the brake. We both jumped out and started jogging toward the accident. Off to the side in the field lay a Packard Custom Super Eight crumpled on its roof, all its window glass shattered. Whoever had driven that car needed to have some big money to own a piece of fine automotive craftsmanship such as that. A woman stood near the car, pacing. Her hands were balled up in fists, blood matted on one side of her head, her nose looked broken, and she was hollering in screams, letting loose one long wail after another. The sheriff's deputy was already on the scene—I could tell by his uniform, the same fella who'd shot at me after Crazy Ake and me robbed the bank. The deputy was crouched on his knees next to the Packard, peering inside. The sheriff made for the ditch.

"Roy?" A tremor shook in the sheriff's voice.

"Truck driver's okay," the deputy answered. "Just a cut across the forehead." He rose from his crouch, turned and faced us gravely. "That's more than I can say for Ridge Hackathorn, though." He motioned toward the Packard. "I'm sorry, Sheriff. I know he was close to you."

The sheriff's eyes narrowed shut. He paused a minute, swayed slightly, then swallowed hoarsely. "Emma been notified?"

"I had Martha give her a call. She'll be here shortly."

"You told her to leave the children at home, I hope."

The deputy inhaled harshly. "No sir. I figured they had a right to know."

A fighting man is trained to know when another man will make his move. For a split second I thought the sheriff was going to haul off and swing at the deputy. Instead, he changed course and glared hard at the other lawman, then motioned toward the hollering woman who stood nearer the road.

"Anyone coming for Luna-Mae?"

"No sir. She's okay, despite the look of her wounds. I had Martha notify Ava-Louise at the tavern. She said to call an ambulance and that Oris Floyd would pick up the cost."

"Oh! That's mighty Christian of him." The sheriff spat the words.

I glanced again at the hollering woman and noticed for the first time how shapely she was in spite of her ailments. Her dress was torn at the shoulder and I wondered if the sheriff's friend might have had something to do with that. I was beginning to piece together the story.

"You called Gummer for the tow truck?" the sheriff asked. "Gotta get this traffic moving soon."

The deputy nodded.

"Well, not much to do until he arrives." The sheriff turned to me and motioned to his deputy. "Roy, you should know Rowdy Slater. He'll be the new preacher in town. Reverend Rowdy, you should know Deputy Roy Malwae. He's law and order through and through."

We shook hands. Roy was a skinny fella, all bone and gristle, and his hand was soft as a woman's. He eyed me suspiciously and asked, "Have we met somewhere before?"

I shook my head and glanced away. The sheriff stepped between us. "Rowdy, go see if you can calm Luna-Mae down. She helped land herself into this mess I wouldn't doubt, but that doesn't mean she doesn't need a charitable hand."

I glanced toward the hollering woman and hesitated. I didn't want to stay close to the deputy's prying eyes, but I wasn't known much for calming women down neither.

"Go on." The sheriff gave me a firm pat on the shoulder. "It's your job."

I climbed the bank of the ditch and walked toward the woman. Her nose was broken all right, and one eye was puffy and swollen. I'd seen enough black eyes in my time to know it wasn't due to the traffic accident.

"Ma'am?"

The woman stared at me and hollered but said nothing.

"You going to be okay?" I asked.

She stopped hollering long enough to sniff. "Does it look so?"

"Just trying to help, that's all. I'll check the bleeding on your head if you want."

"Deputy already did that. I'll be fine. Sheriff say anything about me?"

"Only that you might need help. Maybe you can sit down somewhere? Find some shade out of this sun."

She hollered again, then laughed. It was a cold laugh, death-scared like someone unused to public speaking gives at the start of a talk. "You best be prepared to take a hike, mister, unless you want your nose smashed. A fight's going to break out any moment, and it ain't going to be pretty."

"You threatening to hit me?"

She laughed again. "No, not you, mister. Do I need to spell it out? Within the next thirty seconds, the wife of Ridge Hackathorn's going to come screeching down this road. She's going to see her husband lying with his neck broke in that Packard over yonder, then take one look at me and finally figure out what's been going on these past six months. That's when the fight's going to break out. If she don't kill me first, then the sheriff will soon enough."

I stayed silent a moment, not understanding the breadth of her words. The woman hollered again. I'd been around enough medics to press the ailment issue again if all else was failing, so I asked, "Mr. Hackathorn do that to your eye? We can find some cool water somewhere. Press it over the eye."

The woman stopped hollering, sniffed again, and gave a snort of repulsion. "Yeah. It was him all right. But forget the cool water—it's too late for that. My nose broke in the crash. Same with my head. Cut's not deep, I can tell. Shoot—the way I look now, I ain't going to be able to work for weeks."

This time I kept my mouth shut. It wasn't the first occasion I'd been around women such as Luna-Mae, although usually I was buying such a woman a drink, helping her get comfortable before heading upstairs hand in hand.

She looked toward the mesquite grass of the field and changed her tone. "Last week he told me he loved me. What an idiot I am. He promised he was leaving his wife and told me to meet him at the plant today where he's the foreman and we'd head out together. Well, I met him as agreed, and we started driving up the road, see? I had my suitcase with me, stupid as anything, and when he asked what it was for, I reminded him of his promise and he broke out laughing." She hollered a blue streak again, a nervous laugh of hilarity, like her mind was churning on something big and it had no place to land.

"You ain't stupid, ma'am." I wished I had a handkerchief to give her.

Her tone turned stern again. "'No man loves a whore.' That's what Ridge Hackathorn reminded me of, his exact words, and when I got angry at him is when he blackened my eye. I told him to let me out by the side of the road—I didn't even care about the money this time. Well, he got in such a huff that when he turned the corner from the Plant Road onto Highway 2, he lost control of the steering wheel just as that truck was coming straight toward us. Poor fool swerved a couple times, the truck jackknifed, and we went over onto our roof into the other ditch. Snapped his neck like a twig. So now you know the whole story. You a deputy too? You sure don't look like one."

"Not a deputy, ma'am, no."

"What then? Why ain't you writing any of this down? You work for the mayor—he's already got all I own. You can tell him off for me, too. I don't care anymore."

My mind was reeling, and I wasn't sure how to answer the woman—not about trying to help her, and not about what I did and why I was there. I sure didn't feel like any reverend. I was still wearing the only clothes I owned, the clothes worn into the river—so I reckoned I didn't look like a reverend neither. Fortunately just then a Mercury station wagon pulled up behind the sheriff's car so I didn't need to answer. I swallowed dryly and we both looked at the car. A woman climbed out along with four kids. Luna-Mae groaned, "Oooooh, here it comes."

The woman climbing out was a few years older than me, I guessed, maybe twenty-nine or thirty. She was pretty and her hair was neatly done and she wore a yellow dress with a flowered pattern running lengthwise. The oldest child, a boy, looked maybe nine or ten. A girl followed in age, then another two younger boys. The smallest looked about four or five, I reckoned, about the same age as my niece.

Sure enough, Mrs. Emma Hackathorn glanced at the smashed Packard lying out in the field and let out a yell. Sheriff Barker sprinted up and was at her side in a jiffy while Deputy Roy stayed with the body in the car. The sheriff spoke low to the woman, laying his hand on her shoulder. She broke down in tears and collapsed in a ball on the pavement. He crouched down along with her and gathered her in his arms, holding her close, then gathered the children to him and hugged the family together. The oldest boy wouldn't come over, and stood by himself. I found it strange that the sheriff would hold one of the townspeople in such a familiar manner. She was sobbing on his chest now, long impassioned cries, and I thought the woman might die from her wailing, I rightly did.

From the other direction came an ambulance. It drove slowly along the shoulder and stopped behind the overturned semitrailer.

"This would be my ride." Luna-Mae quickly turned to go. She dried her tears, tried to smile, and added, "Stop by the tavern and say hello whenever you get a chance, whoever you are."

She was working again, I could tell by her words, trying to survive, trying to make a dollar, and I stood on the road smack dab in the middle of this unraveling tale of confusion—one unloved woman climbing in an ambulance, another unloved woman huddled in a ball of tears in the sheriff's arms. I stood there on the shoulder of Highway 2, not knowing anything else to do, and so I simply let time pass.

By and by another car drove along the shoulder and another woman got out along with a woman I recognized to be the sheriff's secretary. The secretary glanced my direction, then rushed over to Mrs. Hackathorn, gave her a long hug, and helped her stand. The secretary and the other woman helped Mrs. Hackathorn and the children get in the second car. The secretary drove off back toward town with the woman and her children while the friend drove Mrs. Hackathorn's Mercury following.

Ten minutes later a fella I guessed to be Gummer came with the tow truck. He worked for the next three hours to get the jackknifed truck pulled upright and off to the shoulder. I found some motion to my feet, introduced myself to Gummer by my first name only and helped him wrestle with the semitrailer, then I went back to the shoulder by myself and stood. Deputy Roy directed traffic while a hearse came to collect the body of Ridge Hackathorn. I didn't walk near to the proceedings—I'd seen enough dead men in my day to last a lifetime—but I wondered more of who this man was. I knew he was once the proud foreman at the Murray plant, a man wealthy enough to buy a Packard and support a family. He was once the loving husband of Emma Hackathorn—at least he loved her enough once to marry her. He was once the father of four young children, three boys and one girl. That counted for much in my book. Much indeed.

The sheriff talked to the mortician for a long time. I saw him signing papers. Then he climbed up the ditch and stood next to me. He shuffled his feet in the dirt of the highway's shoulder. When he found his voice, he was all business.

"I got to head over to Rancho Springs and handle some more paperwork tonight. Deputy Roy will take you back to Cut Eye. It's too late to get you settled at the parsonage, so we got a closet in the jailhouse with a cot in it. Stay there tonight and head back over to the café for breakfast. Sorry for not getting you any supper. You must be hungry."

"I'm okay. Thanks for thinking of me, sir."

"I'll be tied up all tomorrow too. Lots to do to close this file. Deputy will take you over to the church after breakfast. Secretary will show you around and then you get to work. Understand what I'm saying? You better not skip town, that's what I mean in plainest terms."

"No sir. I understand, sir."

The sheriff turned toward the field and stared at the Packard in the ditch. I turned around with him, and we stood without saying anything more, the sheriff and me. Maybe half an hour passed. Maybe forty-five minutes. He just kept staring at the waste of a wrecked car. His eyes were steeled with intent, the way a man's eyes look when he's lost someone he cares about. I'd seen that look in soldiers before. I'd felt the same look in my own eyes more than once myself. I decided to speak first.

"You knew this man, then—this Ridge Hackathorn? Deputy said he was your friend. You play cards together or something?"

It might have been another twenty minutes passed and still the sheriff didn't say a word. Finally he spoke. He said one sentence, his voice staunch and unbendable.

"He was my son-in-law."

In the dusk, a bird flew overhead. It flew not more than ten yards in front of us, and I recognized the breed at once due to its great concentrations in west Texas. It's classed as a game bird, and it's widely hunted in these parts. The bird was a mourning dove, and the sheriff said one more sentence, his voice just as resolute.

"This is why we need a preacher in this town."

Sheriff Halligan Barker turned, walked wordlessly to his squad car, and drove into the night.

# SIX

Texas, land of abundance, is a self-sufficient inland empire. Folks from Montana with their wheat fields and folks from Iowa with their corn might disagree on this point, but I don't give a hoot nor a holler. Not only does Texas feed much of the nation and the world, but it also provides its native sons and daughters with all the fruits of Mother Earth in plentiful profusion. Frankly, we're big eaters in this state. We like our bellies round. And we've got the cattle, sheep, goats, hogs, and poultry to prove it—they're known far and wide for their savor and quality. We've also got fresh fruits and vegetables—peas, beans, squash, carrots, radishes, tomatoes, apples, oranges, peaches, blueberries, melons—anything a mouth could want, all grown under balmy Texas skies, and all recognized for their topflight quality and deliciousness.

That's why at 6:20 the next morning I was already lined up outside the Pine Oak Café with at least two hundred other hungry fellas ready for Cisco Wayman to open the door at 6:30. They was all plant workers mostly, I could tell by their uniforms, lucky fellas with jobs living in the apartments and plant housing down the street. The Murray's first shift started at 8 a.m., I ascertained by their talk, and the fellas would have plenty of time to eat up and drive up the road for the day's work.

Sure enough, a man I guessed to be Cisco opened the door at the crack of half past the hour, and all us boys piled through in a rush. My stomach was growling something fierce and I just had time to glimpse the all-you-can-eat breakfast buffet laid out along tables in the middle of the café—piles of hickory smoked bacon, flapjacks and johnnycakes with their rich cornmeal texture; succulent eggs; warm buttermilk biscuits; tender waffles; steaming apple pork sausage links and mounds of honey hams; a hot roast beef ready for carving; uncountable platters of fried country-cut potatoes and onions; bowls of grilled mushrooms, ripe avocado, creamy coleslaw, and fried grits; dishes of butter; jugs of syrup; milk, coffee, and orange juice; oranges, apples, bananas, and grapes; barbecue sauce, salsa, ketchup, and pepper sauce—yes sir, I saw it all in one clear and glorious picture. It was how I imagined a feast in heaven might look, if a man such as myself would be permitted to enter, and I ain't a man for crying but I do admit the sight of such Texas culinary profusion was just about enough to make this hungry man blubber like a baby.

"Hold on, fella, where do you think you're going?" A powerful hand gripped my collar and jerked me out of line.

It was Cisco Wayman. He was tall and broad in the shoulders. As big as me but gray-haired and slower on his feet, I reckoned, if it came to blows.

"My name's Rowdy. Rowdy Slater. I ate here yesterday along with the sheriff. Augusta served us."

"That's Mrs. Wayman to you." He glared into my face. "I ain't never seen you around these parts. You a drifter? We don't feed drifters here. If you want to eat like all these other fellas, you need a job."

"I got a job."

"Where?" He looked me up and down. "Don't see your plant uniform. I know every man in town. Who you work for, and why didn't he tell me he hired you on before sending you over?"

I swallowed. "The sheriff hired me, sir. He needed to go out of town today, on account of last night's traffic accident."

Cisco's eyebrows lowered. He was an angry man in general, I gathered, and with the heap of good cooking he'd done before dawn, he was making sure nobody ate for free. "You a deputy then?" he asked. "I didn't hear nothing about Roy needing help."

"No sir."

"What then?"

"Well . . ." It was time for the first public declaration of my new profession. I wasn't sure how the words would come out of my mouth. I decided to blurt. The blurting wasn't about courage. It was about needing to eat, and I said it all in a jumble—"Sir, I'm the new preacher at the Cut Eye Community Church."

The whole café hushed. A lone fork clattered on the tile floor. The silence was flagrant. Other men gawked my direction, their hungry mouths hanging open. Far in the back of the room, a snicker broke. Another followed, and the whole room erupted in laughter. Men clapped and whistled, hollered out catcalls, and blew raspberries with their tongues. "Give us a sermon!" someone yelled. None of the rattle was charitable, I gathered.

Cisco held up his right hand and the room shut up. With his left he grabbed the front of my collar and twisted the fabric. "You listen to me, and you listen good. The town of Cut Eye don't need a new preacher. And even if we did, you don't look like a man of the cloth. Any fella who comes into my joint lying to my face is a fella who needs a fist smashed into his. So you got five seconds to clear out. One . . . two . . ."

"Look mister," I interrupted. "I don't want to fight you, but I will if need be. You can telephone over to the sheriff's office if you'd like. They told me all my meals came with the job, and I'm ready to eat."

"Three . . . four . . ." Cisco kept counting.

I sighed. The big man wasn't backing down. I knew I could take him if I fought him alone, but as he arrived at the count of five, at least ten other men stepped in a circle behind him. They folded their arms across their chests, burly fellas all, and I reckoned that might be too many to handle at one wallop.

"All right! All right!" I said with a sneer. "I'm leaving. But I'll be back for lunch. Augusta knows me. We'll settle up then—"

"That's Mrs. Wayman to you!" Cisco roared, and shoved me out the door onto the street. A chorus of guffaws swelled behind me.

Well now, I took stock of my situation. My pockets were empty, as empty as my stomach. It'd been days since I'd eaten much of anything. I wandered back over to the sheriff's office, stuck my head inside the front door, then meandered out onto the front patch of grass to wait for Deputy Roy to come by and take me over to the church building. I thought about having somebody from the sheriff's office telephone over to the café and vouch for me, but Sheriff Barker wasn't in, of course, and his secretary wasn't there this morning neither. In her chair sat an older gal with thick reading glasses, and I doubted if reports of my new job had been relayed to her already. My eating breakfast was a losing proposition any way I examined the matter.

Half an hour went by and I stood and waited. I paced around and whistled a few tunes, killing time. I cranked out a few sets of pushups on the patch of grass. A gamble quail scuttled across the road. Its color, like that of the scaled quail, is bluish-ash, but it has that plume of soft curved feathers on its head that gives its subspecies away every time. My stomach rumbled.

Deputy Roy pulled up precisely at seven a.m. with the passenger window of his car already rolled down. "Get in," he said, and I obliged.

We drove east on Main Street and turned the corner south onto Highway 2. It was the same route Crazy Ake and I had run only a few days ago. We passed the café and the mercantile, the tavern and pool hall south of that, the school with its baseball field, and then we were out of town. The wind whistled through my open window. I hadn't closed it on purpose of the way I stunk. There was no shower in the jail where I overnighted, although I tried to wash up as best I could in the bathroom sink. My clothes were a mess. That don't matter much if you're lying in a foxhole for days on end, but for a man on his first official day of work, I felt a might ashamed of my condition, even if I was only stinking for Deputy Roy.

"You been to the church building yet?" he asked.

"No sir."

"Just so you're oriented correctly as to the lay of the land, we take a right on the Lost Truck Road just before we hit the bridge over the river. Church is down that road on the left. You from these parts?"

"Grew up in Denim." Him nosing around my past made me antsy, and the specific whereabouts on the highway were looking all too familiar. This was the very same stretch of blacktop he'd shot at me.

"Denim, huh. We used to play them in baseball. What year did you graduate?"

"Finished tenth grade then went into the CCCs."

"Digging ditches for President Roosevelt, eh. I've never gone out for that unskilled manual labor myself, and I don't cater much to public relief programs. Yet I'm curious about your ministerial training. Where'd you say you went to seminary?"

"I didn't."

"Correspondence courses?"

I shook my head.

"You trained as a chaplain then? What branch of the service? I would have liked to serve our country myself, but I was 4-F on account of my flat feet."

"No sir. Wasn't a chaplain."

The deputy slowed the car and stopped. He didn't pull over to the shoulder even. It was right in the middle of the highway.

No other cars were around, and we both sat there, neither of us saying a word. Finally he spoke. "Engine's running a might warm today, Rowdy. Be a pal and pop the hood for me. I want to let it cool a spell."

The engine was still running. I knew he was testing me. He wanted to see me stand in front of his patrol car, to gauge my height and build against his memory. The color of my jacket. The way the back of my head looked through his windshield.

"Go on," he said. "Get out and pop the hood."

"Seems to be running fine." My voice was low. As low as I could make it while still being heard. My heart pounded in my chest. I didn't want to need to kill a man this morning, and I didn't want to get shot at neither.

"No, you're wrong. Engine's hot. Needs to cool off. I'll just sit here if that's okay. My back's been out of sorts lately."

The deputy wasn't relenting, and I knew the man wouldn't until he got his way. Slowly I eased open the door. Slowly I walked to the front of the car, reached down while keeping my eyes on the deputy, and fiddled with the hood latch. It popped and I opened the hood. I stayed standing where I was, not even looking at the engine. It was a typical Ford Flathead V8, and it wasn't steaming, I knew that much—not steaming in the least. I counted three hundred Mississippis in my mind until I was certain five solid minutes passed. All this time the deputy kept the engine running. I closed the hood, making sure it latched firm again, slowly walked around to the passenger door again, opened it, and slid in.

"Seems to be cooler now," the deputy said.

I nodded.

"Thanks, Reverend. That was kind of you."

I nodded again.

The deputy put it in gear and started down the road. My heart was still pounding, but nothing more was said between us. I didn't know precisely where this man stood. He catered to the letter of the law, so I knew his mind worked on suspicion. But he didn't have nothing solid on me other than his hunch. It had been raining thickly that day of the robbery, and a man shooting at another man will often not look closely at his features if he's not trained to do so, which I doubted this fella was.

The deputy pulled up in front of an old white-boarded building and let me out.

"Welcome to the Cut Eye Community Church, Reverend Slater." The deputy coughed slightly. "A man of your background and training should surely enjoy your time here." He coughed again, this time louder.

I looked at him through the open passenger window and touched two fingers to my forehead lightly in an even-tempered salute goodbye. "Deputy," I said. "Thank you kindly for the ride."

He smiled broadly. Too broadly. "Reverend Slater, be warned that some in this congregation may call into account your background and training, but I am not a man to question the Lord's anointed. The test of any true preacher comes by fire and the blood. So I'll be praying for your sermon this Sunday—that it would be delivered with power and might and real conviction. Yes sir, I will be praying for you. Be praying for your soul."

I did not want to turn my back on him, even to walk away, and so I eyed him without gesture, as one might eye a cougar in a tree. The deputy put the car in gear and drove away into the dust.

# SEVEN

The building needed paint, I saw that right off. I doubt if it had seen a brush with color since it opened in 1900. The roof was missing shingles. One of the two windows in front was boarded up. A bell tower sat to the right. The wood siding was peeled, the rope to the bell had long since rotted away, and when I gazed up into the cup-shaped hollow, the clapper was rusty—an indication that the church bell hadn't been rung in years. Parked sideways in the gravel was a dusty 1934 Plymouth, the world's lowest priced car, so somebody was inside the church building, undoubtedly waiting for me to show.

I ambled up the steps to the church's front door. It was unlocked and I poked my head inside, looked around, and called out a long, "Hello-o-o-o." The room smelled musty and needed a thorough cleaning. Rain from a leak in the roof had colored brown the ceiling in the far corner, and the hymnbooks in the backs of each pew looked worn and frayed. I counted ten rows of seats with an aisle down the middle and reckoned the building held a hundred and twenty folks in a pinch. A large stump of a pulpit stood at the far end and an old black pump organ squatted to its right side. One bare lightbulb hung limp from a cord on the ceiling. I tried the light switch but it didn't turn on. Those were the church's only furnishings.

"You're late!"

A voice from behind made me start and turn. It was brittle

and loud, and the woman who spoke was thin-faced and in her late sixties, I guessed. She stood with a stoop, but her back looked sturdy, like she was no stranger to hard work.

"Come 'round to the side door where the office is," she bellowed. "You don't look like much, but we'll get you settled away quick."

I obeyed. Nailed to the left-hand side of the church was a rickety annex built onto the main building. Four doors ran lengthwise of the annex and each opened to the outside. "General office is closest to the road." The woman pointed. "Pastor's study is the second door. Sunday school classroom is the third. Furnace room is in the fourth—although if you ask me, coal is a waste of money when we've got a perfectly good stand of trees right next door."

"You're the church secretary?"

"You expecting somebody else? Name's Myrtle Cahoon, but everybody calls me Mert. I've been administrating this office now for eighteen years, but you'll only find me in this place an hour each day. Time's wasting and I also sell eggs and put up fruit and deliver mail to a rural route and drive the school bus mornings and afternoons. My husband, Clay, is a kindhearted dirt farmer, the purest man you'll ever meet. He's ailing with fevers, can't work anymore, and needs medication, and medicine ain't cheap. You got any more smart questions?"

I shrugged. "I suppose you could show me around."

"Nothing to see. This here's the church building. Out back are the privies, a bar of soap, and a faucet for washing hands. There's a toolshed with a ladder in it, and next door is the parsonage where you'll stay. To the west lies a hundred and eighty acres of slash pine forest deeded by the church board, and you'll need to start now to put in a winter's stock of firewood if you want to stay warm next cold spell. You're also welcome to chop and sell all you want for your personal savings, and if you ask me, a strong fella such as yourself would be a fool not to spend every waking minute doing exactly that. I left two keys for you on my desk—one for the parsonage, one for the church. Reverend Bobby will be dropping by in an hour to explain more of the job. Have I left anything out?"

"Reverend Bobby?"

"The missionary who's been holding the church together during the war. Didn't the sheriff explain anything?"

"Not much, no."

"Well, the expectations are straightforward. No smoking, drinking, drunkenness, chaw, gambling, movie going, dancing, loud music, novel reading, gum chewing, card playing of any sort, or unchaperoned visits with ladies in the parsonage. You'll work more than a full day and receive lower than normal wages, but since it's a preaching job that's to be expected. Consider yourself lucky to have a job. The church will need to know your whereabouts at all times, so leave a note on my desk each morning with your schedule as you know it. The phone rings in my office and it's rigged to a bell in the parsonage, so you'll know it when you hear it. May sound obvious, but be sure to answer the phone whenever it rings. The car you drive must be nice enough to look presentable, but not so nice as to put on airs. Same goes with your clothes. Wear a shirt with a collar at all times and a suit jacket with a tie when making pastoral calls. Make sure your shirt is well ironed. Have I forgotten anything?"

I stood silent, letting it sink in. I had no idea the scope of expectations placed on preachers.

Mert pointed to her car. "I best be off. The cleaning supplies are in the furnace room. You'll want to get started on the sanctuary—this being Friday, Sunday's coming quick. Where's your books and things—they still being shipped?"

"Something like that, yeah."

"Well, we should get along fine, Reverend Slater. I'm firm but I'm fair, and as long as you preach the gospel, keep your sermons short, and don't cross me, you'll have nothing to worry about."

"Worry about? What do you mean?"

She held out her hand and we shook. "I sign your checks."

———————

It was only eight o'clock in the morning yet the sun was already hot. I wandered behind the church, scoped out the fuller layout of the property, then ambled over to the parsonage front door and peeked inside. It wasn't locked neither, and inside was a living area with a stone fireplace, an old couch, and one hard-backed chair. A kitchen lay beyond it with a table and the other three chairs along with a sink, stove, and fridge. To the right lay a bedroom with a bare closet and a double bed. To the front of the house lay a second bedroom with a baby crib and two cots nearby, about the right size for children.

The water was on when I tried it from the kitchen faucet and it ran cold and clear, but there was no indoor bathroom and no shower. A washtub lay to one side on the kitchen floor, and I reckoned that's what a fella and his family bathed in, respectively, if he so had one. The entire parsonage was maybe five hundred square feet. It was budget-built and not maintained well. The floorboards were warped. The outside walls had been tar papered for insulation, but the paper was ripped and worn. In places I could see straight through the walls to the outside. This ceiling, too, was brown from water damage, and the entire place stunk of not being used. I wondered what sort of a man this Reverend Bobby might be if he didn't care for his living quarters. Maybe he stayed someplace else.

I walked outside, saw the firewood area to the right side of the building under a wood awning, and noticed the wood was down to almost nothing. An axe sat near one pole with a whetstone nearby for sharpening. I decided to make good use of my time while waiting for my predecessor to come and show me the ropes.

First things first. I tested the corner of the firewood cover, saw it was strong enough, and cranked out a few sets of overhand pull-ups from a dead hang. A man's got to stay in shape every chance he gets, and I liked to do a hundred each morning whenever I got the chance. Next I grabbed the axe, chopped kindling, lit a fire in the kitchen stove with my flint piece, and got it blazing. Underneath the sink lay a large pot, and I heated water on the stove and ladled it into the wash tub until full. The bar of soap from the church outhouses was weighty, thick, and a good sort of brown. It plopped nicely into my tub. My filthy clothes I shucked off in a jiffy and I climbed in and settled down for a good scrub. I hadn't bathed since being baptized, and that was just a scant dunk in the river.

My, but the morning was warm. A hint of breeze flitted through the open kitchen window. My eyes closed and it got downright dreamy. Outside, a vehicle pulled up. I'd recognize that familiar rumble anywhere—the unmistakable chug of an army jeep. At least Reverend Bobby had good taste in vehicles, I thought, to locate such a find on surplus.

"In here!" I called. "Be with you in a minute."

The front door to the parsonage opened. I heard a gasp. "Reverend Slater!"

My eyes flew open.

It was the sheriff's willowy secretary. Never did catch her name. With a rush I sat forward in the waters to cover my unmentionables.

"I'm sorry, ma'am. Really I am. I thought you were Reverend Bobby."

The secretary stood by the front door, not moving. She glanced away and then glanced back, not in a salacious way but only curious, like she hadn't any brothers to grow up with. She glanced away again and this time I stared at her then glanced away myself, noticing in a flash her curves through her dress—all set in place by the good Lord in all the right places—and I wondered if she was going to be so ornery to me this time.

She cleared her throat. "But I am Reverend Bobbie."

# EIGHT

Texas wildflowers were beginning to bloom across the road. I sat next to her on the steps outside the parsonage and ran my hand through my wet hair.

"Well," I said, "I expected Reverend Bobby to have broader shoulders."

"From what?" retorted the girl. "Gripping the pulpit?" She wrinkled her nose my direction and took a sniff. "You might throw your clothes in that wash basin along with you next time."

"Relax," I said. "It's not the first time you've seen me dunked. I don't know why you're so worked up now."

"I am not worked up. You're the one who called me inside while you were taking a bath."

"I didn't call you inside. I only let you know of my presence as to not alarm you. Besides, I didn't think a girl would be driving a jeep."

"It's my daddy's jeep, and I've got no problem with the human form. None of the world's greatest artists are upset by naked-ness as long as nakedness is kept in its proper place. *O to bathe in the swimming-bath. To splash the water! To walk ankle-deep, or race naked along the shore.*" She looked straight ahead. "Walt Whit-man—'A Song of Joys.'"

"Oh, you got an answer for everything."

"And you, sir, stink like the earth." She pursed her lips and stood up in a huff. "Let's take a walk. I can recount what I need to more easily if I don't smell you."

I harrumphed but stood anyway and followed her. She led the way behind the church to a trailhead between the trees and followed it southeast back toward the dirt road that traversed south from Lost Truck Road to the river. The sunshine was bright for the morning, and the asters and goldenrods were already out. I spotted some buffalo clover and wolf flower and redbud with its brilliant pink of early spring.

"Your name is Bobby? Spelled b-o-b-b-y?"

"No, spelled with an 'i-e'—short for Roberta. Bobbie Barker. I'm surprised nobody told you my full name before now."

"So you're Halligan Barker's daughter—the sheriff's?!"

Bobbie smiled, then her lips quivered. She quickly pushed away her family's grief. "Emma Hackathorn is my older sister— she's the woman who came to the accident last night. Our mama's been gone for five years now, so it's just Daddy and us and Emma's four children. That's our whole family. You?"

I sidestepped the question and asked instead, "I thought you worked the front desk at the jail. How come you're the minister?"

Bobbie nodded. "I fill in at the jail from time to time. That's what I was doing that morning you showed up. As for my job in the ministry, you ever heard of Rosie the Riveter? That happened in churches, too. All the men were away at war. The ones left in Cut Eye weren't fit to run a church, except maybe my daddy, and he already had a job."

"You trained formally to do this then? You can't be more than eighteen."

"I'm twenty-one. After I graduated high school I took three years of free correspondence courses from the university in Dallas. Their programs were subsidized through the government throughout the war effort. I've already got my associates degree. I'm heading for the mission field just as soon as I can gather the money."

There came that upturned nose again, at the mention of a college degree, but I said nothing in return. We pushed out of the trees, navigated through tall grasses, and hit a secondary trail and followed it. I recognized this trail. The flowers on the catclaw weren't out yet, though the bees were already getting interested in the huajillo, the flower of origins that furnishes honey for most of the state.

"Ah," she said. "Here again at last."

In front of us lay the swath of land that flattened out halfway across the flowing water, the one where a pool had formed in the eddy on the other side. It was the place of my baptism, and the area today, I admitted, looked downright scenic—particularly since I had less threat of getting shot. We stopped by the water's edge. Pine trees and high grasses ringed most of the pool.

*"He carried her toward the Atlantic ocean, cradling her like a shepherd would embrace a newborn lamb. The cool nocturnal air mixed with the salty sprays of the sea, and the sand shifted under the clams."* The girl looked downright triumphant.

"I ain't so sure *lamb* fits that well with *clams*," I said. "Seems a sense of elegance that's missing."

"Elegance?" Now it was her turn to harrumph. "What do you know about elegance? Why do I bother quoting my poems if they're not appreciated? It's like casting pearls before swine."

"Who you calling swine?" I raised an eyebrow.

"Well, if the shoe fits . . ."

"That's another cliché. You might want to study up on your literature some more if you're so intent of writing poetry all the time."

"Literature. What do you know about literature? I bet all you ever read are Dick Tracy comic books and the *National Police Gazette*."

"I read . . . I read plenty." The end of my words trailed up and off.

"Yeah? Exactly what do you read? Name some titles. What was the last book you ever read?"

I kept my mouth shut on purpose. We had a guy in my squad who went to university before enlisting. He kept a library of sorts, paperbacks stuffed into his musette bag that he'd loan out to the fellas. The last book of his I read was *Lady Chatterley's Lover.*

"Just like I thought," Bobbie said. "This was such a mistake. Here I was trying to be kind, but I declare I've never met a man as unwashed and as barbaric as you. We're heading back to the church."

The girl turned around and headed back up the trail. Again I followed her. We walked past the trees and bushes and wildflowers and we were both quiet until we reached the building. The girl and I stood out front near the road and looked at the structure. I sensed a strong need to switch directions conversationally, cleared my throat, and asked, "So you held the church together for a couple of years in your spare time. How'd that go for you?"

Again she was silent for a time, then she said, "You don't realize how patronizing that is, do you?"

"What are you talking about?"

"The sentence that just came from your lips. My ministry at the church was not part-time, even though I was doing my schooling simultaneously. I worked my tail off. And I did more than just hold this church together, too. Don't look so surprised, because the church will expect more from you than you can ever deliver."

I might have been insulted at the remark, but instead I stifled a snicker and said, "Look, I appreciate you taking the time to show me the ropes today, but I don't want to keep you from whatever else you got to do. If I can parachute into Normandy, then I can do this. How hard can this job be anyway? All a preacher ever does is work one day a week."

The girl stopped breathing. I'm sure she did. Her ears turned red and I caught the clue too late. She found her breath in a jiffy and exploded.

"One day a week? One day a week!? You have a pencil on you?"

I shook my head.

"Into the office!" It was an order, and she pointed toward the annex. "You're going to want to take notes on this."

I followed her inside. She dug out a pad of paper and a pencil from Mert's desk and handed them to me.

"Your week will begin Tuesday morning at seven-thirty a.m. with a staff meeting," she said. "It'll only be you and Mert, but she'll demand a full account of your previous week, including all attendance figures and a complete list of who *wasn't* there on Sunday—which is the much harder list to generate, you'll soon learn. You'll go over the list and see what needs are evident in the congregation, needs you'll have to address throughout the week. That list will comprise the bulk of people you call on pastorally to see how they're faring."

"So I visit a few people. Okay. Duly noted." I sat down in Mert's chair and swiveled to the side.

"You're not taking notes." Bobbie pointed at me. "You better start taking notes, because I haven't begun to get started. Following the staff meeting you'll prepare your sermon for the following Sunday morning. Always be thinking ahead. A good sermon takes at least eight hours to prepare. Usually more, but you won't have time for more. Your day on Tuesday, like any weekday, will be broken up with people dropping in to the office. They'll say the same thing you did—that a preacher only works one day a week, and then they'll chat away and eat up hours of your time. These are well-meaning folks, mind you, and the conversations will be important parts of your ministry. But each day and every day, a few people will drop in, and that adds up. Soon enough it's past supper on Tuesday and time for the deacons' meeting. That begins at seven p.m. and will sometimes last until midnight, depending on how much church business and praying you need to attend to."

I stopped swiveling in the chair. "Church business? What kind of business happens at a church?"

"Deacons' meeting is always a full agenda. You worry over how to replace the leaking roof when there's no money. You debate how to encourage more people to come to services. You squabble with each other because two people want to be married at the church but they have no good reason to get married and folks think it's a bad idea, so the deacons need to get involved. Catch my drift?"

"Okay, you have some business talk. I gather that." I swiveled some more, then started to take a few notes.

"Then comes Wednesday. On Wednesday morning you'll meet with the deacon board again during breakfast. They'll want to go over any points they missed in the agenda the night before. After that you'll come back to the church and prepare your Wednesday night devotional, the one you'll give for prayer meeting that night."

"Devotional?" I stopped writing. "What's a devotional?"

She gave me a cold stare. "It's like a sermon only shorter. But don't let that fool you. You still need to prepare. Devotionals don't grow on trees."

"That's a cliché again," I foolishly said.

She sat down on the edge of Mert's desk. A cruel smile began to form at the edges of her lips. "After lunch on Wednesday you'll begin your visitation rounds. You'll visit homes in the area until dinnertime, then come back to the church for the prayer meeting. Only five people have been coming to the prayer meeting, but they expect you to be well prepared. You begin at seven p.m., give your devotional, and then pray as a group for the next forty-five minutes about any needs in the community. You should finish your day by eight p.m. unless you're called to counsel afterward."

"Counsel? Who do I got to counsel?" My pencil was dull, and

I shaved it on the top of the paper to sharpen the point.

"Lots of folks. When you're a preacher, people talk to you about their problems. You're their sounding board. They vent to you. Cry to you. Unburden the loads on their backs. You listen. And listen, and listen, and listen. Very rarely do you speak. I realize that's going to be hard for you." She laughed an ornery laugh. "You should be home by midnight."

"Okay. Another long day. I can handle long days."

"Oh, it isn't the long hours." Her nostrils flared. "It's the mental load that will get to you before long. Being a pastor isn't like chopping wood all day. You got to bear people's burdens and then put those burdens somewhere so you can sort them out yourself. I've seen men stronger than yourself crack under the pressure."

I stood and started pacing.

Bobbie continued. "On Thursdays you'll hold a men's Bible study during breakfast. I never held this myself, but it will be an expectation that you begin one, for sure. Somewhere along the line you'll need to prepare for that, but you'll need to cram that into your schedule somehow yourself. After breakfast, come back to the church. You and Mert have another staff meeting, this one briefer, where you go over your plans for Sunday and she makes up the bulletin. Included in this meeting, you'll give her a list of all the hymns you want sung on the upcoming Sunday, any special music from soloists that might be sung, any Scripture passages you want read apart from the sermon, and any notices of special events that folks might need to have publicized in the bulletin."

"Special events?" I was trying to slow her down, but the girl was on a roll.

"At least one a month. Sometimes more. Fall Harvest potluck. Thanksgiving service. Veterans Day honor service. The whole Christmas hullabaloo. New Year's watch-night service. Valentine Mothers' luncheon. Spring cleanup days. Summer barbecues. As a rule, church folks like to meet and eat, and they expect you do the same. You'll figure that out as you go. If you don't, Mert will be sure to remind you. Where was I in the weekly schedule?"

"Thursday afternoon."

"Right. On Thursday afternoon, the women's committees meet. All these special events take a whole host of volunteering to staff. You won't need to lead each committee meeting necessarily, but the volunteers will expect to see your presence when they gather. If they're working at the church building, then they figure you should be working at the building too. Then, on Thursday night the young people meet. We only have a handful of youths, the ones who come anyway, and the church will expect you to build this group up. This age will tell you exactly what they think of you. They say it straight to your face, and it's seldom complimentary. Give them messages that they can relate to, and get used to being called names. Listen to their problems. Encourage them. Help them along. Your day will end about ten p.m."

"I'm sensing a pattern here." I was scribbling faster now, still pacing behind the desk.

"On Fridays you'll want to get to the office early so you can prepare your Sunday evening sermon."

"There are two sermons?"

"Sunday morning and Sunday night. Sunday night is the more sparsely attended service. Maybe eight or nine people instead of the regular twenty or so. But the folks who come are all die-hard churchgoers. There's no way you could ever cancel the Sunday night service. Besides, it does a might of good."

"I believe it." My pencil broke and I hurriedly stuck it into the sharpener on Mert's desk and turned the handle.

"Friday after lunch you'll do more visitation, schedule any special counseling appointments that need to happen—marriage counseling, funeral preparation, baby dedications, meetings with the sheriff to discuss the jail ministry."

"Jail ministry?"

"Friday nights you go down to the jail and meet with the prisoners. Give them a short devotional if any will listen. Talk to them about why they're in jail and try and help them along. That brings us to Saturday."

"Day off?"

"Nothing doing. Three out of four Saturdays per month will be filled with a special event. Maybe an apple-picking party with the young people. A fund-raiser for the women's mission society. You can always catch up on your visitation if there's no event. That brings us to Sunday."

"The one workday?"

"Yeah. The one workday. You get up early and spend an hour in prayer. Trust me, you'll need it. After that you'll clean the church sanctuary from top to bottom including the outhouses. On cold mornings you'll shovel enough coal into the furnace to last until afternoon, and again in the afternoon to last until evening. If there are leaves to be raked, you'll rake them. If there's snow to be shoveled, that's your job too. Make sure the building looks presentable—and I confess that's an area I could have done better in. A man with your skills could surely organize a work party to fix the roof, paint the walls, thatch the grass. You teach a Sunday school class for the children, then preach in the morning, visit in the afternoon, preach again in the evening, and then you'll be done for the week, which brings us to Monday."

"My one day off." I was scribbling furiously again.

"Yes, your one day off. One day per week, and only one day, and usually not even that. Folks won't understand you taking Monday off, because it's a regular workday for them. So they'll want to get together and talk about church matters. They'll get huffy if you say you need one day when you don't talk to people and just go fishing or cut firewood for yourself. So that's something you learn to deal with, too—huffiness. You'd think church folks would have their act figured out when it comes to forbearance, but they're the same as everybody else. At least once a week you'll have somebody mad at you. They'll have high expectations that you won't possibly be able to fulfill. Be prepared to be hated on a regular basis. No, it's not parachuting into Normandy, Reverend Slater, but I can assure you that being a minister is no walk in the park."

She stood and pushed Mert's chair back toward the desk to straighten it. By then I'd fallen silent.

"I understand your belongings will be shipped later," Bobbie added. "You have a study Bible you can use until then?"

I shook my head.

"There's an old pulpit Bible in your bottom desk drawer. It's as big as three phone books stuck together and has been in the church for decades, but it'll work in a pinch. Any questions?"

Again, I shook my head.

"Good, then I can drive you over to the café. It's almost time for lunch. Or maybe you'd rather walk?"

# NINE

It was only 11 a.m. by the time we drove back to the Pine Oak Café, but Bobbie Barker was tasked to bring me back for lunch, and I could tell she didn't care to spend any more time with me than absolutely needed. She dropped me off in front of the eatery, emphasized her need to go home and wait for a long-distance phone call from her beau (some pencil-necked jasper who used too much Brylcreem I wouldn't doubt), then stuck her jeep in gear and drove off in a huff. She was a spunky one, I'll give her that. Tackling a job fit for a man like she'd done.

Augusta Wayman met me at the door even before I could set foot inside.

"Reverend Slater—I am so sorry for what happened this morning with my husband," she said. "You must be starving. Come right in and let me fix you something to eat."

Well, I liked the sound of that. Just the same, I gave a careful glance around the inside of the joint to make sure Cisco wasn't hiding with a shotgun, waiting for my return. Augusta hustled me over to the lunch counter and plopped me down.

"Cisco isn't normally like that," she said. "He's just been so angry lately." Here she paused. It seemed calculated, like she had much to say about the matter but was purposely containing herself.

"It's all been squared away then?"

She nodded. "Sal from the sheriff's office phoned over saying

70

that Sheriff Barker had phoned from Rancho Springs midmorning to make sure somebody filled us in. Cisco took the call, so he understands who you are now. I'm sorry again, Reverend Slater, for the both of us. You're such a nice young man. So nice indeed. Won't you stay a bit and eat an extra helping, just for me?"

An extra helping? She hadn't fed me anything yet, but my quizzical stare was short-lived. They were odd ducks, those Waymans, but any woman offering me food would get no argument my direction. I nodded.

She smiled, all teeth. "Now then, here's what I propose. We have a lunch and dinner menu here, but a young man who's a reverend is family to us at the Pine Oak Café. If it's all the same with you, then don't give a passing thought to the menu. Let me cook special for you each meal—it'll be something different each day, and you won't be disappointed. I had plenty of brothers growing up, and me and Cisco have a boy of our own. He's about your age. Same build, same shock of unruly hair." She reached over and tousled the top of my head.

I smiled quickly to show my concurrence. I reckoned once Augusta Wayman got a plan in mind, she wasn't easily dissuaded. Besides, based on the quality of the peach shortcake I'd eaten the day before, I was sure whatever grub was coming my direction would be just fine.

"Oh-h-h-h good," she said. "I'll be right back. How hungry are you, anyway?"

It was a question without the requirement of an answer. Augusta was already gone before the question was fully out of her mouth. She hightailed into the kitchen, and I heard knives clattering and pots clanging, doors opening and banging shut. The lunch crowd hadn't arrived yet, and I was the only eater in the joint.

First to come my way was a big glass of milk. Seemed like something a mother would bring her twelve-year-old son, but

I wasn't complaining. Next, Augusta returned with more manly fare. On the first platter sat two large pulled pork sandwiches with a heap of golden-fried potatoes on the side. The buns looked fresh baked, the barbecue sauce from the pork oozed out the sides, and the good smell wafting off the plate beckoned to me with more pull than a pretty woman's perfume. Augusta garnished the meat itself with coleslaw. The creamy slaw sat right in the sandwich, between the meat and the bun, which I'd never seen before, but one bite in and I was a believer. My eyes rolled in delight, and Augusta let out a tiny squeal. The woman kept her eyes glued to me as I polished off the first sandwich—it didn't take more than a moment before I dived into the second.

"The special ingredient you're tasting is root beer," she whispered under her gaze. "Back when I was pregnant, I'd eat those sandwiches every night, right up until the day I gave birth."

She scampered back to the kitchen while I polished off the fried potatoes, then she emerged with another platter, this one laden with deep-fried hardboiled eggs. Those eggs were rolled in bread crumbs, and each tasted delectably crunchy. I cleaned the plate. Again she watched me closely, then left and returned again with a dish of meat rollups. *Braciole*—she called them, though I'd never heard the word before. I bit deeply into the first and sighed.

"You like?" Augusta asked. "I take boneless pork cutlets, beef cutlets, thinly sliced Genoa salami, garlic, flat-leaf parsley, and Romano cheese—roll them all up together in a flour tortilla, and there you have it."

In no time flat I had eaten six. There were four more on the plate and I showed no sign of slowing down. She brought me another glass of milk and poured me a cup of coffee to further wash it down.

"Feel like some dessert?" she asked.

I sighed, fondly remembering the day before.

She whisked behind the counter, pulled out a plate of lemon

round cake, and cut me off a quarter section.

"There's lemon pudding inside," she whispered. "You like lemon pudding? Makes it go down smoo-oo-ooth."

I grinned pure bliss and swallowed the quarter cake.

She returned in a jiffy with half an apple pie. I ate it in a wink.

Three freshly baked chocolate donuts followed. They jumped into my mouth and were gone with a lick.

"Lunch rush will be here shortly," Augusta said wistfully. "I need to jig. Can I get you anything else?"

I was beginning to feel full, but I didn't want to press my luck—neither with her generosity nor with my stomach, which was unaccustomed to feeling anything but empty. I politely assured her of my satisfaction.

"We'll see you at dinner then. Oh—" She turned toward the kitchen, stopped, and reached into her pocket for a scrap of paper. "I nearly forgot to give you a message. Sal said the sheriff called over to the mercantile and set up a line of credit for you there. Figured you might be needing a few personal things until your belongings arrived. After that, you're supposed to go see Gummer at the filling station. He's working on getting a vehicle running for you."

I nodded again. "Much obliged, ma'am. Thank you."

"Go directly across the street for the mercantile, Reverend Slater. See you in a few hours."

"Please, ma'am, just call me Rowdy."

"Rowdy," she said. "Reverend Rowdy." Her eyes moistened.

I started to say something, but she was away in a flash. The whole interaction with her perplexed me a might, as much as her feeding me so delighted my innards. It was noon and folks were pouring through the door now, bustling in, calling out orders. I decided to check out the mercantile. I needed to begin work on a sermon if I was to have anything at all to say on Sunday, but that could wait for a spell. My belly was much too full for my mind to work properly, and I needed to walk carefully to balance all that food and not let it spill over into queasiness.

The mercantile looked like any old basic building in Cut Eye. The outside walls were unpainted red brick, and a lone lamppost sat outside. There was no awning nor window decoration, and the store looked altogether unimaginative. The sign overtop read simply, "Texas Goods," and the bell jingled when I walked inside. Behind the counter, the owner looked withered and frail. He mumbled a fast hello, but I could hardly hear him, his voice was so quiet and quick. I walked to the counter and shook his hand when he outstretched it.

"Name's Rowdy Slater," I said. "You got a line of credit established for me."

"I know who you are," the man whispered with a flicker. "Name's Woburn Jones. I'm one of the deacons at the church. Twenty dollar limit."

Twenty dollars, I thought, well that was two months' salary as a preacher, but at least that would buy me a suit, shirt, tie, and pair of shoes. I nodded and looked around the store. A half gallon of bleach cost 21 cents. Two boxes of cornflakes were 35 cents. Three cans of tomato soup cost a quarter.

"Where's your suits, Mr. Jones?" I called out.

"Ain't mmmph shonnn." The shopkeeper mumbled the last two words.

"What'd you say, friend?" I walked back to the counter. "Sounded like you ain't got none."

"Correct. No men's clothes, no. No clothes at all. We got socks and T-shirts and underwear but that's it. That's it completely." He was still mumbling his words in a fast string.

"How come?"

"All the men returning from the war, that's how come. Throughout the nation, all men's clothing is on back order now. Same with cars. Same with houses. Too many men want the same thing all at the same time. I'm sorry I can't help you. Really am. I'll put you on the waiting list."

I stepped back and stared at him, not knowing how to proceed, then pointed to what I was wearing—my army jacket with the patches removed, a dirty V-neck T-shirt, dungarees, and boots. "But this is all I got."

He picked up a pencil and nibbled it nervously. "Try Augusta Wayman at the café. She might have something that fits you." He looked away. For a moment I thought I saw his eyes grow soggy, then he cleared his throat quickly. "I'm sorry I can't help you more. Really I am."

I exhaled, wandered back to the aisles, picked out a pair of boxer shorts, a T-shirt, a pair of socks, a razor and shaving soap, a toothbrush and box of toothpaste, and some Arrid Underarm Cream Deodorant, and came back to the counter. I noticed by a sign overhead that the mercantile also offered cremation services. *Every detail is taken care of according to the most scientific principles that comfort and reassure,* it read. I filed that in mind. Mr. Jones added up my purchases, put them in a brown paper sack, assured me they were on my tab, and wished me good day. I ambled outside.

Well now, what was I going to do with this predicament?

Gummer would be at lunch. Augusta would be busy for an hour. I sat and waited, found a patch of grass and did a few sets of pushups, then waited some more. When the hour was over I decided to try Augusta first and walked back to the café. The lunch crowd was dwindling. I saw she had some waitressing help and another cook in back. It wasn't Cisco, which I was fine with. Augusta greeted me with a warm embrace.

"Back so soon?" she asked. "Another cup of coffee maybe?"

"Afternoon, ma'am," I said, and motioned down the street with a tilt of my head. "Woburn Jones at the mercantile said you might know another place in town I can find some men's clothes. He's plumb out."

The woman twitched at the question. Not unkindly, only like she didn't see the question coming. She twisted her mouth into a thinking pose and stood quiet for a moment. "You need them today?"

"Right away, ma'am, if you can."

She blinked a few times, looked at the floor, then glanced at me, but it was an offset glance, like something powerful churned within her. "Cisco likes to sleep after his morning rush is over. He gets up so early, you know, and never sleeps well at night. But if you'd come upstairs with me, I'm sure we'll find you something that fits."

I broke into a grin. "Well that would solve a heap of my problems, ma'am. Thank you."

She wiped her hands on a dish towel. "Come along. Just please be quiet once we're up in the apartment. I truly don't want to wake Cisco. He's so tired."

I nodded. She led the way through the back of the kitchen and up a flight of stairs up to their living quarters. A door to the left was shut. I guessed that was their bedroom by the blare of snores coming from its direction. There was a kitchenette, a living area, a bathroom, and another closed door off to the right.

"Wait here," Augusta said, and went into the other closed door.

She was gone a full twenty minutes. Maybe more like twenty-five. I began to think she'd forgotten about me or maybe fallen asleep herself, but finally she returned carrying a man's black suit, a white collared shirt, a gray tie, and a pair of black leather shoes.

"Your feet about size 9?" she asked.

"Same as everybody."

She sniffed and pointed to the bathroom. "Change in there. See if it all fits. If they don't, I'm handy with needle and thread. Go on, now." The floorboards creaked where she stood.

I went into the bathroom, shucked off my dirty clothes, and

changed into my new, fine apparel. It had been years since I'd worn fancy duds. In school it was all bibbed overalls and flannel shirts. In the Conservation Corps it was standard issue clothing. When we were garrisoned during the service, I hated to change into my dress uniform. Then, in prison, well, no man thinks of wearing nice clothes then. A mirror stood over the sink and I looked myself up and down. The shirt and jacket fit well in the shoulders. The shoes were snug but hardly used—they'd break in soon. The pants were a little short in the leg, but they'd be an easy fix. The floorboards squeaked again. Then, outside the door, it sounded quiet. Too quiet. I opened the bathroom door, still dressed in my new suit and shoes. Without looking up first, I said, "What do you think?"

Cisco Wayman stood directly before me. He was dressed in his bathrobe, rubbing sleep out of his eyes, and appeared in that halfway state between dreaming and wakefulness. His mouth dropped open when he glimpsed me, and a smile crept up on the edges of his mouth.

"Danny," he whispered. "You're alive."

# TEN

I was a deer in his headlights, and the hurtful knowledge of what I'd done rushed at me like it was perched on the front of a speeding semitruck.

"I'm sorry, Mr. Wayman," I whispered. "I'm so, so sorry. If I'd known, I never would have asked."

His smile faded, and tears filled his eyes. His wife was crying too—standing three steps away from him.

"The boy needed some clothes to do his job," Augusta said to her husband. "He was a perfect fit."

In another flash Cisco's eyes narrowed. He pointed at the door and yelled, "Get out of my house! You come into my restaurant without a job, and you come into my home and try on my boy's clothes. You're nothing but a drifter. I want you out this minute!"

"The boy didn't know, Cisco. Be merciful on him. He just didn't know." Augusta was pleading now, hanging on the end of his arm. He brushed her aside, grabbed me by the front of the suit's lapels, stood to his full height, and yanked me within an inch of my face. The blood rushed into his eyes and a vein throbbed deep in his forehead. I didn't want to defend myself against a man who was grieving so hard, but I clenched my fists just in case he decided to whale on his wife instead of me. He held those lapels in his hands. His fingers twitched, at first involuntarily, it looked. But then I knew he was fingering the cloth on purpose, running his thumbs over the familiar texture. The anger fled from his face and he began to sob. To my complete surprise, he buried his head on my shoulder and hugged me tight with both arms. "Ah Danny," he cried. "My Danny . . . my Danny . . . my Danny."

Augusta was all business now. Her own tears dried, as if this wasn't the first time she'd seen her husband's mind snap. She helped loosen his arms from around me and guided him to the living area. All the while he kept sobbing. The man lay fully on the floor. He huddled his arms to his knees and kept sobbing. Augusta covered him with a blanket, stroked his forehead, gave him a small hug, then broke herself away. She came over to where I stood.

"Keep those clothes," she said. "Keep them and do some living in them." She patted my arm and tried to smile.

"I'm so sorry, Mrs. Wayman," I said. "So, so sorry."

She hugged me, the purest touch she'd presented my direction since I'd first met her, then backed away and looked me in the eyes. "You've got to help my husband through his grieving, Reverend Slater. He's been like this ever since we got the telegram from the war department. He has his good days and his bad days. Most of the time, when he's not fixing breakfast for the café, he just sleeps. I have my times when it all feels unreal, like Danny's still coming back, then the grief hits me all over again and I have a good cry. But my husband—there's something unnatural about his grieving. You got to help him, Reverend Rowdy. I'll be praying for you. I'm at my wits end, but the good Lord will show you what to do."

The door was opened for me. Augusta put my old clothes and boots in a paper sack and handed them over. There was nothing more to do for the time being, I gathered. Augusta led me downstairs and out the kitchen's back door. "We'll see you at dinner," she said, and gave me a kiss on the cheek, quickly turned, and went inside.

Well, I felt a might rattled by the whole experience. It was careless of me and where I'd been for not putting two and two together sooner. In the past few years, plenty of families across the country had lost sons my age. I didn't know how to help Cisco through his grieving. Shoot, heaps of times I'd seen men get shot in the chest, their legs blown away, their arms ripped off. These were my friends, the men on the line next to me. I never considered the lengthier process of grieving, about what a father might do when his son didn't return home. Any time I lost a friend there was no time for a man to think. You shouldered your weapon and kept firing at the enemy. On reserve you gathered the men in your squad still left and drank to the dead man's honor. Afterward you buried your pain deep in the bed of a woman, a woman you'd hired for that exact purpose, although it never brought joy to do so. And then your orders came again, so you shouldered your rifle again, and the next day you got up and marched to your place on the line. How was I supposed to be a church minister to a man such as Cisco Wayman? What did God ever know about losing a son?

I walked far down the street and over to the baseball fields. A bell rang right as I walked up. School let out, and all the young folks of Cut Eye streamed out of the building with a holler. A few of the older ones quick got up a game. One boy took a bat, another took the mound, and another went to the field. The pitch was tossed, the batter swung wide, and the ball clattered against the metal backstop. The batter ran and got the ball, tossed it back to the pitcher on the mound, and stepped to the plate again. This time a fastball zipped in. The batter eyed it closely and walloped it with a solid thwack. The ball soared high over the head of the outfielder, and the runner ran around the bases and back to home.

I watched that game. Those boys so full of life. That was all I did for some time. I just watched that game. While I was watching I shook those troubling thoughts out of my head, those thoughts for which I had no place to secure.

---

The game was over, and I figured I had more work to do—at least to complete my day. So I walked up the street to Gummer's filling station. A big sign in the window featured a grinning fella in a Humble Oil & Refining hat and read, *Buy War Bonds: it's my job to serve your essential wartime needs today to hasten your motoring pleasures of tomorrow.* The sign next to it celebrated the sixtieth anniversary of Dr. Pepper. The small print read, *Delicious, nutritious, it helps when you're hungry, thirsty, or tired. First introduced in 1885 by a Waco, Texas, druggist who had a penchant for experimenting with new flavors at his fountain.*

Nobody looked to be around, and before I could pop inside the garage to see if anybody was there, a fella ambled out of the door, stuck his hands in his pockets, and exclaimed, "Mother of Jehoshaphat! You are just the fella I want to see."

"Nice to see you again, Gummer." I held out my hand.

"Thank you for the help the other night at the accident, señor," Gummer said. "I would have been out there all night trying to get that truck righted if you had not come along." Way back, he came from Mexico, I gathered, or at least his great-grandparents did, by the way he talked English so good yet with a clip. He was thick-necked and strong, about a head shorter than me, and his eyes looked like they were permanently half closed. He wore pants but no shirt.

"It ain't nothing," I said.

He spit a wad of chaw on the dirt. "Come around out back, Reverend. I have been getting ready your buggy."

I nodded. "Sheriff said you might be able to get me a pickup truck. I understand there's a bit of driving involved in this job."

"That, I could not do, amigo." Gummer reached into his back pocket, took out another wad of chaw, and stuffed it in his mouth. He held it out to me. I'd been known to dip on one or more occasions, but I remembered Mert's words and thought best not to test a preacher's expectations just yet.

"What were you able to find then?"

"Oh." Gummer's word took much longer time to say than it should have.

"You found me a truck, didn't you?"

"Oh." Gummer was twisting in his trousers, the man truly was, and he coughed before saying, "Well, I did get you a truck of some sorts or another." He cleared his throat, chewed twice, spit a stream, then added, "What is good to remember is that the job comes with all the gasoline a man could ever use. It is only twenty-one cents a gallon anyway, and this is Texas where we have oil in every backyard ditch."

"Show me the vehicle."

He winced and pointed the way behind the garage.

I blinked twice when I rounded the corner. It's hard to de-scribe such a vehicle if you've never seen one up close. Oh, you see them in newspapers making amphibious landings on beaches in the Pacific. In pictures, they've got a soldier up top, and sometimes another twenty men in the rear. I gave a low whistle. "Where did you ever find such a brute?"

"Army surplus. You may have heard we have a shortage of cars in the country right now. Some roads you need a wide load permit just to drive this thing down, but not around here. Just make sure you stay well to the right shoulder whenever another car passes your direction."

The army called it DUKW. It was pronounced "duck," just like the web-footed fowl. "D" was the letter the army gave to a vehicle built in 1942. "U" stood for "utility." "K" meant power was sent to the front wheels. And "W" meant it had two powered rear axles. Put it together and in front of me squatted a huge, green, six-wheel-drive truck that weighed seven-and-a-half tons. It was built with an up-sloped front end, and the machine's body looked like a boat and could float like a boat. With it, a fella could drive at sea, navigate floodwaters with ease, or drive up on a sandy beach and not get stuck. The DUKW was pure vehicular beast, and this one was all mine.

"Runs on regular gasoline," Gummer said. "Tank holds forty gallons. Get about six miles per gallon on land. Maybe four on water. I welded an extra gas tank to the rear, so your range will be nearly five hundred miles between fill-ups. That should get you anywhere you need to go around these parts. Ever driven one before?"

I grinned. I had friends in the motor pool. "Ten speeds forward. Two in reverse. Top speed fifty miles per hour."

Gummer grinned right back.

I climbed up to the steering box, sat behind the steering wheel, and ran my hand along the dash. The DUKW was as ugly as the back end of a longhorn cow, but it would get any man where he needed to go, and my mind was already hatching a plan. "It's a beaut, Gummer. Both tanks full?"

"I filled them both this morning. Stop by anytime for more. Driving is part of your job. If I am not around, just fill it up yourself. Oh, we will find you a more respectable vehicle one of these days. But for now, consider this your new ride, Reverend Rowdy."

I climbed down again and slapped his shoulder. "Thanks, Gummer. Say, I'll be back in a bit. I got some more business in town. You don't mind if I pick it up whenever?"

"Whenever you wish."

I grinned again, shook his hand, and walked back through town. If you're coming into Cut Eye from the north, Gummer's filling station is the second building in past the laundry mat and the hardware store and lumber emporium. He also sells life insurance if you should ever want some. On the other side of Gummer's is the city hall with the barbershop in back, then you cross Main Street, and then you're at the mercantile again. I walked inside and shook hands with the mumbling clerk.

"Say, Mr. Jones, how much left on my credit line?" I asked.

He checked his figures. "Fourteen dollars and thirty-three cents."

"You do cash advances?"

"On occasion."

"I'll take ten dollars then." I pointed to the shelf behind him. "How about a half yard of that yellow ribbon." I pointed underneath the counter. "And maybe a dime's worth of those red licorice whips."

He looked confused at my choice of purchases, but I wasn't explaining myself.

With my cash in my pocket, my packages under my arm, and a fresh plan in my head, I strode back to Gummer's, checked both ways to see if anyone was watching, fired up the DUKW, and started lumbering north up the highway out of town. I knew it would be difficult to escape Cut Eye—a man driving a vehicle like this wouldn't be hard to track down. But the DUKW didn't need to take me clear across America. It just needed to take me north to the next city, Rancho Springs. My plan was a long shot, but it was the only plan I could think of.

Truth be told, I was still mighty unsettled at the thought of becoming a preacher. If I had my druthers, I wanted out. Already I felt trapped in this new role. Spending my days caring for a community filled with grieving men such as Cisco Wayman, sharp-edged church secretaries like Mert Cahoon, a jailhouse full of drunks, a tavern full of prostitutes, the married men who frequented their services, the widows they left behind from their car accidents, and uppity young women such as Bobbie Barker wasn't my idea of how to best spend my next large chunk of time. I knew the sheriff would hunt me down like a dog if I tried to escape. I also knew that when I reached Rancho Springs night would be falling. From there I could stash the DUKW in a grove of trees, put my ten dollars to good use, and see if there was a better way forward.

First off, when I reached Rancho Springs, I needed to take care of some long-standing business. It was urgent business. Mighty urgent.

In fact 'twas why I robbed the bank.

# ELEVEN

I t was 3:30 p.m. when I left Cut Eye. The afternoon sun was powerful warm. Heat shimmered off the blacktop, and I removed my suit jacket and tie, loosened the neck, rolled my shirt at the sleeves, and roared up the highway in the DUKW at a cool 45 m.p.h.

By 8 p.m. the outskirts of Rancho Springs were in sight. The town of Denim where I'd grown up was only thirty miles away to the northeast, and when I came to a regrettably familiar dirt road, I pulled off the highway, found a thicket of trees, hid my vehicle, and set out walking. I'd only gone about ten yards before I tensed and stopped fast. Beady eyes blinked at me from out of the dusk. The eyes moved, and I realized it was only a possum scuttling across the driveway. I kept walking.

For where I was going, I wished I'd brought a gun. Back in Bastogne I'd popped a Nazi officer at two hundred yards and liberated his Luger. It was a honey of a sidearm and a real trophy for any allied soldier, but just before I went into the clink I gave it to my platoon's second lieutenant. He was a regular fella and never had nothing bad to say about any man. His feet got nearly frozen black from the Belgian cold, and I reckoned the gift would cheer his recovery while he convalesced in Mourmelon.

Fifty yards in front of me lay my destination. In the quiet of my mind, I called it the devil's house. It was a ramshackle old pigsty that sat on about twenty acres, and a long dirt driveway gave the occupants a clear view of anyone approaching. I hated this place, but it was part of me, too. As much as I wanted never to set foot through its doors again, it'd be some time still before it was cleared of my life for good. I walked straight up the driveway, rumbled across the wide porch that surrounded the face of the house, and knocked loud at the front door.

Minutes went by and nobody showed. Hanging from the side wall was the pelt of a badger. The porch light flickered, but that came as no surprise. I could hear rustling inside and could smell the occupants' smoky presence seeping out the siding. I knocked again, this time louder. The front door cracked and a shotgun barrel appeared in the gloom.

"What you want?"

"Sally Jo Chicory—that you? It's Rowdy Slater. Open up."

The crack widened and a swatch of a woman's housedress appeared. She was a few years older than me, as wide as she was tall, and kept the door safely between her and me. She looked me up and down, shooed a fly away from her face, and scratched her hip. "You got money?" she said, opening the door wider.

"I reckon I'll talk to your man about that."

She sniffed, turned, and hollered, "Rance! The hero's here."

I waited on the porch while she rummaged around for her man. My eyes stayed fixed on the open door's darkness. Before long a fella's frame showed. He shoved the woman out of the way, opened the main door fully, kept the screen door between us, and let out an oily chuckle.

"Back so soon, Rowdy? Well, absence builds motivation in a man—that's good for what I'm running here."

"I want to see her."

"You bring money?"

"Ten dollars."

He exhaled in disgust, his breath like canned tuna. "That ain't much."

"Reckon it's good for half an hour."

"Yeah, but it ain't paying your bill in full. Times are hard, Rowdy. Ringtail brings less than two dollars a pelt these days. Gray fox is only ninety cents. Shoot, I brought in two dozen rabbit last week and the fella only gave me six cents apiece."

"Well, I got a new proposition for you, Rance. More money— lots more than trapping. You're gonna like it." I held my breath, waiting for him to bite.

The fella opened the door and stepped outside. He was barefoot, the heat spilled off him, and his gut flapped over his dungarees. I could see the unmistakable bulge of a Colt .45 strapped to his hip. "You're always one for deals, Rowdy." He let loose with a long angry laugh from beneath his whiskers. "Look where the last one got you. What's your deal this time?"

That was exactly what I wanted him to ask. I knew him accepting this new deal would be unlikely, but I reckoned the more intrigued he got, the more willing he'd be to bite.

"Let me see her first," I said. "Then I'll lay out the plan."

He scratched behind his ear. "Gimme your ten dollars. You can visit half an hour. Sit on the porch, just like last time. Don't think I can't see you if you run."

I nodded and forked over my cash.

He hollered over his shoulder. "Sally Jo! Find the rat!" Rance jiggled the porch lightbulb so it stopped flickering, motioned for me to sit on the steps, then disappeared inside into the darkness. I could see an eyeball through the window watching me from the shadows.

Two minutes later, Sally Jo swung open the screen door and pushed a figure toward me. "Time's ticking, Rowdy. She needs to go to bed." Sally Jo let the screen door slam behind her. I wouldn't be surprised if she and her shotgun kept watch on me too.

I stared in her direction. Toward the small figure, I mean. Her hair was the color of honey. Her skin like a peach. She was quizzical and wide-eyed and grubby and stunk of cow manure. She was the most beautiful thing I'd ever seen.

"You remember me, sweetheart?" I asked. My voice grew gentle.

The child nodded.

"You remember my name?"

The girl shook her head no.

"I'm your Uncle Rowdy. You remember how I brought you a gift last time?"

The girl nodded, this time more quickly, and tucked a strand of hair behind her ear.

I fished into my pocket, pulled out the yellow ribbon, and held it out to her. The smallest corner of her mouth twitched. "It's yours," I said. "Wear it in your hair if you'd like."

The girl took the ribbon and stared at it, fingering the shiny cloth. A bug zapped against the porch light. The child was four-and-a-half years old, born September 1, 1941. I remembered the date, I remembered it well.

"That ribbon's real pretty, Susannah, just like your name. You remember what I called you when you were first born—I told you last time I was here—Sunny Susannah. They ever call you Sunny around here?"

She shook her head.

I paused and eyed her closely. "Well, it's no matter. That's what I'll call you every time I visit. I brought you another present. You like licorice?"

The girl shrugged.

I fished into my pocket again, brought out the licorice whips, and handed one to her.

She took it and stared, her hands unmoving.

"It tastes good. Here—I'll show you." I took one of the whips, bit the end off, chewed, and smiled.

Cautiously she bit the end of hers and chewed. Her eyes brightened.

I hoped she'd sit down next to me. I hoped I could tell her how much I loved her and hug her close, but I didn't want to press my luck. Sometimes when you're just getting to know a person, it's better to eye her from a distance. You watch her out of the corner of your eye, and she watches you. Each time you meet you sit a hair closer. The poor child knew me mainly by my letters; I was pretty sure they'd been read to her, but getting used to a person in real life is different for a child. Last thing I'd ever want to do is scare the little gal.

"Everything's going to be fine, Sunny," I said. "I'm going to make sure of that. I'll come again and visit you real soon, and I'll bring you another present then. If things aren't fine I want you to tell me. Okay?"

"The girl can't talk yet, fool!"

Sunny and I both jumped at Rance's voice. He was standing in the doorway, his hand resting on his .45.

"Time's up, Rowdy. You ain't paying me so you can put fool ideas in her head." He glared at the girl and added sternly, "Get in the house, rat." She scampered inside.

I stood to my full height and glared at the man. "Be warned how you talk to her." I wasn't smiling in the least.

He glared back at me. "The girl ain't yours, Rowdy." He laughed. "I'll do what I want. Now, what's your new plan? I'm all ears."

It had been nowhere near the half hour I paid for, but I wanted to keep on the man's good side, so I unclenched my fists and tried to keep my tone casual. "Got me a job not far from here. Pays room and board and a monthly stipend. I can cut firewood and bring in extra. New plan's for her to come with me right away. I'll pay off what I owe on installments—plus thirty percent interest. That's the new part of the deal. You make more money if you let her go today."

"And who'll guarantee that?!" Rance laughed in my face. "Law's on my side, Rowdy. The day you pay your debt in full is the day I release her. Nothing sooner!"

I stared hard at the man. He stared hard back at me. Neither of us blinked. Neither of us moved. Finally I said, "What if I make it forty percent?"

"Make it fifty." He chuckled. "Make it sixty. Make it a hundred. It don't make no difference—you ain't taking her until your debt's paid in full. We got lots of girls in this house, lots of ways to make money more than trapping. True enough, that don't happen 'til the buds ripen on the vine a bit. But last time you came around I warned you that time's coming quick for the rat. You've still got time before I put her to work, but it ain't much, so you best be quick in your full financial delivery—you hear?"

My eyes blazed. "If you put her to work I'll—"

"You'll do what?" He unsnapped the holster of his .45. "Look Rowdy, we're no stranger around here to shooting fellas who disagree with us, and it's your own fault the child boards with the Chicorys. Let me refresh your memory of how you got yourself into this mess. It's such a prime story."

"Won't be necessary."

"Well, it brings a smile to my face to recount it again, it rightly does. Let's see—you were dating Sally's Jo's sister, I remember—Nancy Clugman. A comely girl, folks considered, but a genuine skunk of a gal, everyone agreed. You knocked Nancy up. She had your baby then fled town leaving you holding the bag. What she say to you again?"

I stayed silent. Rance was doing this to taunt me. I knew the man's ways. His telling of the story dripped with venom in a way my own remembering wouldn't.

"'You're the daddy, Rowdy, so you deal with the problem.'" Rance laughed, swatted a mosquito, then continued. "Like a sap, you did the honorable thing, although Lord wonders how you kept going like you did. Working all those extra shifts at the mill, paying for a wet nurse, keeping the child at your boardinghouse. Must have come as a relief when Pearl Harbor hit and you knew every unmarried man in America would soon get drafted. Remember how you came crying to me then? Do you?"

I hated this man with every yard of being.

"Gal at the boardinghouse said she couldn't look after the baby no more, what with the war starting and real money to be made. So in desperation you brought the child to us, her only kin, and offered twenty dollars a month for us to take care of the child while you were away. You enlisted in the army, started writing all those letters to her—oh, we read some of them, I remember. But twenty dollars doesn't stretch far when raising a child these days, and when I heard you became a paratrooper, well, I had no choice but to double the fee. You paid it heartily all the time you were overseas, but then—" He let loose with a long, lusty cackle. "You got yourself thrown in jail!" He laughed again.

"I'll be going now," I said. "Be back in two weeks for another visit."

He grabbed my arm roughly. "But this is where it gets good, Rowdy. Real good. See, right about the time you go to jail, Nancy Clugman wanders back to town. She doesn't know of your noble arrangement with me and doesn't care. All she wants is whiskey money. For two bottles of Wild Turkey, she signs over the custody papers. The child's all ours now—all shiny and legal. You're still fool enough to have mercy on the brat and keep paying for her keep, so your six months in the clink equals two hundred and forty dollars owed. Seven months later with no job, your bill comes to five hundred and twenty. Oh, I realize it's tough for a man with a black mark on him to find work, but now we was talking real money, weren't we? And then—" He let loose with his longest laugh yet. "Once you finally figured out what we do with our girls around here, you had the frantic notion to come to me one night and bet the high card. 'Double or nothing' you said! Oh you begged me to play. You pulled jack of hearts and thought you'd won. Until I pulled king of spades. Then you owed me a grand total of one thousand and forty dollars." He cackled again and scrunched his face in mockery. "Oh, how will the poor hero ever pay his debt now?"

I was down the porch steps and striding up the long driveway.

"You're a desperate man," Rance called after me. "A desperate man who wants his daughter back! And I like that about you, Rowdy Slater. It's good for business. Save her from a life of working for me, that's fine. We don't want her anyway! Just pay me my money, and I'll sign those papers straight across!"

The farther away I walked, the more the devil's laughter lessened. I hated leaving his house empty-handed, but the man had me over a barrel. I was a desperate man indeed. Sure enough that's why I did what I did. If a choice came to Rance Chicory laying a salacious hand on my child, or me taking a chance in crime with Crazy Ake, well even the fool plan of Crazy Ake's looked to have merit. It did.

I found my way back to the DUKW, dusted off the foliage, started up the engine, and started driving back to Cut Eye. I knew the math already. If I saved my ten dollars salary and cut and sold five loads of firewood each month, then it would take three years for me to get Sunny back. Three years was better than nothing. I didn't like the job in front of me, but it was all I had. That is, if Rance didn't think up some devilish new reason for me to need the money quicker. The DUKW roared down the highway into the night. I kept the pedal flat against the floorboards as I let loose a roar of war.

If Rance touched her before then, I had no problem killing the man.

*No problem*, I thought. No problem indeed.

# TWELVE

It was long past midnight when I got back to Cut Eye. The town was quiet and I topped the tanks of the DUKW at Gummer's station, then drove through town and over to the parsonage.

There were two packages on the doorstep and a lone note tacked to the front door. The first package was from Augusta Wayman. It was filled with more clothes and shoes. *Missed you tonight at dinner—come by real soon for some more peach shortcake,* was carefully written on a note card and set on top. The second package was from Mert Cahoon. In it were sheets for the parsonage bed, an alarm clock, a clothes iron, and a homemade quilt. *Make sure your shirt's always well ironed,* was scrawled on top.

The sole note tacked to the front door was stuffed in an envelope of quality stationery grade and looked feminine, yet all business.

Dear Reverend Slater:
A missionary's coming into town this weekend. He'll take care of the evening service. For this, your first week only, I'll teach Sunday school for the children and lead singing. All you'll need to worry about is the morning service.
*Sincerely,*
*Bobbie Barker*

It felt funny to read a note signed from Bobbie. I don't know why it made a good shiver run up and down my spine. I put it out of my head and focused on the content. It was good—and meant a few less things I needed to concern myself about. I did my overhand pull-ups for the night, added some sit-ups to keep my gut strong, made up the bed, and flopped into a restless sleep. At dawn's first light I was up. It was Saturday, and I drove over to the café for breakfast. Neither of the Waymans were there. It was the cook who was handling business, and the weekend fare wasn't nearly as sumptuous as the weekday fodder. After eating, I headed back over to the church to begin work on my very first sermon.

Oh, I'd heard a few sermons in my life. Never liked none much. There was that going-to-Sunday-school business when I was a kid. Then in the service there was always a chaplain or two who had something to say. I didn't mind when the chaplains spoke. We was usually heading into battle, and the words they said were uplifting to a man. I went into my office, found a pencil, notepad, and the big old Bible that Bobbie had mentioned, and started into work.

I had no notion where to begin. No idea what to do. An hour went by and I scratched down a thought or three. They looked okay on paper, but when I read back my words out loud, nothing sounded like any sermon I'd ever heard. Another hour went by, and then another, and then another. It was lunchtime, and I drove over to the café, downed a quick sandwich and a cup of black coffee, and went back to work. The afternoon heat was stifling. My eyes drooped, even with the coffee floating in me, and I propped up my head with my elbow. At one point I jolted myself awake. Clock on the wall said 2:15 p.m. This would never do. Never do indeed. I've always been the type of fella who thinks better on his feet. I left the office, headed over to the firewood awning beside the parsonage, grabbed the axe, and hiked out into the pine stand.

I walked about a quarter of a mile, found a tall slash pine, and begin to chop. My mind cleared a bit and I found I could think much better as I swung an axe. When it came to the Bible, I figured I just needed to start at the beginning and work my way forward. The folks might have heard sermons from the book of Genesis before, but now they'd need to hear them again from me. The first chapter of the Bible was all about God making the heavens and the earth. He made light and darkness and called the light "day" and the darkness "night." All basic stuff. I reckoned once I stood up in front of the people, I could just read the chapter straight through, then give a few thoughts on being outdoors. I could tell stories about fishing and hunting, being out in God's great creation. Memories would come to me of when I was a boy. How proud I felt the first time I went deer hunting. The folks might get something from that, I guessed. I didn't know what else to do.

Well, I chopped the rest of that afternoon and felled the tree. I headed to the café for dinner, came home, limbed the tree, and started sawing it up for firewood. Late after the sun sunk in the western sky I headed home, did my pull-ups, brushed my teeth, and flopped down for bed, my hands good and blistered, my body calmed and tired.

Funny, but in my dream I thought I heard the sound of a car's engine. Lots of engines, in fact. They was coming into my bedroom, parking right at the foot of my bed. My eyes opened. The alarm clock! Sunday school started at 8:30 a.m. The service at 10. It was already 9:45.

I never overslept. Why today of all days? I was up in a panic, scrambling to find my suit. I splashed cold water from the sink in the tub, shaved my face, washed the tree sap off my body, dried myself with an old work shirt, and jumped into my clothes. No time to iron my shirt—I hoped Mert wouldn't notice. Grabbing my notes and the big Bible, I eyed the full parking lot from the doorway of the parsonage, then sprinted across the lot toward the church. Mert met me at the front door, a dark stare in her eyes.

"You're late!" she hissed. "Real late! Go at once and sit on the platform. Reverend Bobbie's going to start the service in two minutes. Hurry!"

I stumbled forward, trying to eye the crowd as I walked up the aisle. Word musta got around there was a new preacher in town, because I counted thirty-two people in the pews, a higher count than what Bobbie said was normal for Sunday morning. A few folks shook my hand on the way up and offered complimentary greetings such as, "Nice to see you, Reverend," and "Glad you're making your home with us." Bobbie was already standing behind the pulpit, an open hymnbook in her hand. Augusta was on the organ, launching into a prelude. My, but that Bobbie sure cleaned up nice. She wore a pale pink dress with a touch of pale lipstick. I would have liked to see her standing aside from the pulpit so I could view her willowy figure more, but I quickly pushed those troubling thoughts out of my mind, climbed to the stage, and sat down.

The congregation was already standing, already belting out "Shall We Gather at the River?", and I noticed they skipped straight over the third verse for no good reason and sprinted straight on to the fourth. I fumbled around for a hymnbook, looked on the wall chart to note what page number we was on, and found the correct page just as the final verse was sung. The song ended, and all the folks sat down. Bobbie led in a prayer. Every eye closed and every head bowed, and I figured I'd better do the same. We stood in a jiffy and sung another hymn. "Come Thou Fount of Every Blessing." All verses. I liked the feel of the words but didn't understand what they meant, and then we sung a real rouser, "A Mighty Fortress Is Our God." Sounded just like a beer-drinking jig if only the tempo was lilted up a bit.

An offering plate was passed around like a rake, then Halligan Barker took the pulpit and I heard him introducing me. All eyes were on me now. I'd hoped I could look over my sermon notes before it was time for me to talk, but the folks was all clapping my welcome, looking my direction. My face grew hot. The sheriff shook my hand, then slapped me on the back. He was letting everybody know we was in for a real treat today, we was.

Then, all of a sudden, I found myself alone onstage.

A lump slid down my throat. I looked across the congregation. Time for me to start talking. Mostly it was all old blue-haired farming ladies, all pushing eighty. Mert stood at the back, glancing at a clipboard. Deputy Roy sat near the front next to the sheriff, Bobbie, and Emma Hackathorn and her four children. Augusta Wayman sat near the middle and gave me a smile, but her husband must have been back at the restaurant because she sat alone. I recognized old Woburn Jones from the mercantile. I didn't see Gummer there, nor any other men except for one real fat cat slouching in the back row. He was dressed in a fancy white suit and his eyes were half closed. Three young women sat on either side of him. Those women didn't much look like church ladies. Their lips were painted a vivid red, their dresses were cut low, and their bosoms spilled over bountifully. I recognized Luna-Mae, the woman from the car crash. She was painted up like a new barn door though her nose was swollen. She was staring at me with a quizzical look in her eyes.

"Well, uh . . . good morning to y'all," I said to the folks.

"Good morning, Reverend!" they all yelled back.

That upset my stride—them all shouting in unison like that, and I wasn't exactly sure where to go next. I decided more introductions would appeal to their down-home natures.

"Uh . . . name's Rowdy . . . uh, but my real name's Zearl, but everybody calls me Rowdy. Rowdy Slater. Um . . . and I guess I'm your new preacher. Uh . . ."

I was finished. No more was coming out of my mouth on its own accord. I glanced high on the back wall. Staring straight at me was the bold-faced glare of a clock. I had at least thirty minutes to fill and already I was short on material. A bead of sweat formed on my forehead. From the back row I heard an uncomfortable cough. I cleared my throat and looked at Bobbie, hoping maybe a previous preacher would give me some kind of clue as to how to proceed. Her eyes were wide, her Bible in her lap. She pointed emphatically at her Bible and mouthed, "READ IT!"

"Oh, yeah . . ." I said. "We're gonna read the Bible now. I reckoned we'd start with Genesis. So I'm gonna read from this here Bible I got in front of me, and um . . . maybe you'd like to listen."

I flopped open the Bible, paged through to where I was supposed to read, and read the first chapter as clear as could be mustered. Sweat poured off me. Drops ran down my nose and onto the page. There was a strange tingle in the tips of my fingers too, like no blood was reaching my extremities. I felt like hightailing it for the back door, but it was time for me to say some more words. I cleared my throat again.

"Um . . . reckon this chapter's all about God making things outdoors," I said. "Uh . . . you like to do things outdoors, because I like the outdoors real fine." I glanced around at the congregation; they was all giving me blank stares. "Like . . . uh, after you get your first deer . . . or . . . uh . . . after you . . . shoot a squirrel. You . . . uh . . . remove all four paws at the wrist joint. Then . . . uh . . . you make careful cuts around the belly skin." I paused for emphasis and wrinkled my forehead, picturing that dead squirrel in my mind. "When that squirrel's cut open you . . . you don't want to nick into the muscle wall neither. No, and, uh . . . you want to cut down the insides through all four legs and around to the . . . uh . . . rectum . . . the base of the tail. So that's how you skin a squirrel. There's real good eating on a squirrel, and I hope you've tasted it . . . uh . . . before."

I glanced at the sheriff. His mouth hung open.

I glanced at the clock. I had twenty-seven minutes to go, I was completely out of material, and my mind was blank. A long, awkward silence filled the room. I decided to quit while I was ahead. "So . . . um, that's what the first chapter of Genesis teaches us, I reckon. It's that God's creation is a good thing, and . . . uh . . . it's good to be out in the woods as much as a fella can muster. So the next time you're cleaning a squirrel, you think about God and do some praying. Okay? That's the end of my sermon. Um . . ." I glanced at Bobbie. Creases of pain lined her forehead. She stood and walked onstage, led the congregation in a closing hymn, dismissed the service with a benediction, then turned around and hissed at me, "Go to the back of the room as quick as you can. The people will want to shake your hand before they leave."

I hightailed it to the door. Mert was still standing there. She wasn't glaring at me no more. She was looking at the floor, shaking her head. "Stand on the steps outside," she said. "Air's not as thick out there."

First person out the door I didn't recognize. She looked about ninety and mostly dead, although there was fire in her eye. "Worst . . . sermon . . . ever," the woman said, and walked by with a *humph*.

A second elderly lady walked outside the door. She took one look at me then slapped my face. She slapped it again, then kept on walking to her car.

A third elderly woman sized me up and down with eyes of scorn, let out a long disparaging sigh, and said, "Well, at least there's no danger of burning the roast in the oven today."

Fourth person out was Augusta Wayman. She gave me a little hug, and said, "It'll get better, Rowdy," then headed out.

Deputy Roy came outside, shook my hand warily, said nothing, and left in his squad car—the same one he'd shot at me from.

The sheriff shook my hand in the same motion he shook his head. "Deacon meeting. Tuesday morning, seven thirty a.m. sharp. Don't be late." He headed for his car.

Bobbie tried to smile at me, but it was hard for me to look her in the eye. She headed for her jeep and was soon gone.

One by one the rest of them filed out. None were happy. None were smiling. I knew I was the worst preacher they'd ever heard. Maybe the worst in the world. It was my first sermon, and all I knew to talk about was how to field-dress a dead squirrel.

The last person out the door, however, gave me a grin and a little poke in the ribs. It was the fat cat in the white suit. His painted ladies had all walked ahead of him, and all six were wedged into a shiny Cadillac parked near the front of the church. He was a tall fella with a large ruddy face. It was a cruel face, I could see in an instant, and I wondered what a fella with eyes so full of quiet hatred was doing in church. To my surprise, he gave me a hearty slap on the back.

"Young fella—that was exactly the type of message our folks need to hear. It was so down home, so honest, something we could all relate to. And the length of message was exactly correct. If I were you and knew what was best, I'd keep preaching exactly like that—" Here he laughed. It was too long of a laugh, I thought, and it didn't seem kindly. "Yes, my boy, if you keep your quality of preaching on that level, then we've got nothing to worry about as far as this church is concerned. Nothing to worry about indeed."

I didn't rightly know how to answer the man. On one hand, it sounded like he was complimenting me. On the other, it sounded like he was saying to keep my sermons muddled and hopeless.

"Didn't catch your name, sir," I said.

"Oris Floyd. I'm town mayor, as well as a church deacon. We'll all meet again Tuesday morning. I also own the building that rents to the tavern and a good many other real estate ventures throughout the county, so you'll find most folks know me real well, as I'm sure you soon will, too." He'd been holding his Stetson in his hand all throughout church, and now he set it on his head, touched the brim with his fingers as if in dismissal, and headed toward the Cadillac.

After the mayor of Cut Eye left, all was quiet. I had no idea what to do next. I felt like lying down. Or throwing up. Instead, I walked to the parsonage, changed my clothes, grabbed the axe, and headed out to the tree stand.

I was doing this job to stay out of jail, that was true. I was also doing this job for the sake of my daughter. The quicker I paid my debt, the quicker I could get Sunny back and living with me, back to where a child belonged with her father. With the first stroke of the axe against the tree trunk, I vowed I'd learn this preaching job. I'd learn it real good. I'd last out the year and give my daughter a safe home.

The big tree I picked to fell was solid, I soon found. I hacked and sweated, chopped and blustered. I knew that tree wasn't going down without a fight. It was gonna be a long and large fight, I reckoned, and the top of the tree hardly swayed except when I thudded the axe against the base. If I wasn't careful with that big tree, I got to thinking, it might well cost me my life.

# THIRTEEN

onday, my day off, I cut wood all morning at the tree stand. At noon I left a note on Mert's desk, asking her if she knew any folks who wanted to buy firewood. At suppertime I checked back. She'd swung by the church in the meantime and left a note with a hundred names and addresses on it, and also a directive to keep track of which trees I cut so as to replant them with seedlings from the hardware store next spring. I'd have no problem selling all the firewood I could cut, she reckoned. I went back to the stand and cut wood until darkness fell.

Tuesday morning dawned bright and early. The deacons met in a back room off the Pine Oak Café, and I filled a plate with eggs and bacon, grabbed a cup of coffee, and headed inside the back room. The sheriff was already there, plus Deputy Roy, Oris Floyd, and a sickly looking fella who introduced himself as Clay Cahoon, Mert's husband. I counted four men total plus me.

"Ain't there supposed to be five deacons?" I asked. "I thought that's what you said once, Sheriff."

"That's first item of business." The sheriff took a long swig of coffee. "Got word early this morning that Woburn Jones passed away during the night—you met him—the mercantile owner. Old age got him, and we all knew the day was coming soon. He was our fifth deacon. God rest his soul."

A moment of silence went around the room. The fellas all

looked at the floor, although I shot a quick glance at Oris Floyd and saw him stifling a smirk.

"Woburn has kin out east who'll be here later in the week to pay their respects and settle his estate," the sheriff said. "Emma and her children will mind the store in the meantime. His funeral is set for Thursday, Rowdy, so you'll need to handle that. Meet with Bobbie and she can fill you in as to how to conduct a memorial service."

Deputy Roy chewed on the side of a doughnut. "We need to find a fifth deacon," he insisted. "It's right there in the church's constitution. We need five deacons or else we can't continue."

Sheriff Barker scowled at him, but Oris Floyd smiled. "Roy's right," Oris said. "And I got just the fella in mind who can fill the job."

"Bet you do," the sheriff muttered under his breath.

"Deuce Gibbons." The mayor ignored the sheriff and said the name triumphantly, almost like he'd been planning for this moment for a long while back.

"Deuce Gibbons?!" The sheriff's eyes flashed contempt. "The man's a can of gasoline just waiting for a lit match. He's got a problem with the bottle, too. Just last week he fell over drunk and cracked his head in my jail cell."

"Deuce Gibbons listens to me," Oris said. "He's a hard-charger to be sure, but he's been doing some odd jobs around my place lately, and I like the man. Besides, he'll clean up his act soon enough." The mayor chuckled. "That is, under the good Bible teaching of our new reverend."

"I move we table the motion until next week," the sheriff said. "That'll give us some time to think things over. Do I have a second? Rowdy, as church staff you don't vote."

"Second," said Clay Cahoon.

"All in favor?"

"Aye," said the sheriff and Clay Cahoon in unison.

"All opposed?"

"Nay," said Deputy Roy and Oris Floyd.

"Hmm, split board," Roy said, looking bemused. "What's our constitution say about that?"

"It means we table the motion until we can vote in a fifth deacon," the sheriff said. "Let's close this meeting. I've got work to do." The other fellas nodded their heads. It looked like they all reckoned the meeting wasn't going anywhere, and it was too early in the day for a fight. The sheriff turned to me. "Rowdy, you stay behind. I've got a few more things to say to you directly."

One by one the other men finished their last swigs of coffee and bustled out, leaving me sitting alone with the sheriff. My mind had been churning all through the deacon meeting. I decided to ask questions first.

"Why's Oris Floyd on the board, Sheriff? It's plain you don't think much of the man."

"Well, when a man's got as much money as Oris Floyd, there ain't much he can't do in a small town." The sheriff let out a belch. "That's the problem, Rowdy. Whenever we vote, Deputy Roy and Oris Floyd always vote together. Clay Cahoon usually thinks things well through and votes along with me. So did Woburn Jones before he passed. That's why we can't let Deuce Gibbons on the board. He knows nothing about church, that's for sure, and it's a downright certainty he'll be bought by the mayor. That will make three against two, and then Oris Floyd runs the church— along with everything else in this town."

"I reckon that's a problem."

"Rowdy, there's some important things you need to know about Oris Floyd." The sheriff looked like he was going to say more but stopped and added, "All in due time. No sense in alarming you about the job more than you already are. Let's talk about your sermon first. Bottom line is you need help, son, which doesn't surprise me any considering where you been. From here on out until you get the hang of it, I want you to meet weekly with Bobbie and have her teach you about public speaking. The gal's a bit flowery sometimes, that's true, but she can speak with an eye to folks listening, and you'll do best to do as she says."

I forked up the last of my scrambled eggs and took the last sip of my coffee. I wasn't sure how I felt about meeting each week with the sheriff's ornery daughter, but I figured if I could follow the orders of a drill sergeant in boot camp, then I could learn to work with Bobbie Barker. I swallowed my breakfast. "Be glad to, Sheriff. You mentioned a few more things."

"Well . . ." He appeared to be thinking long and hard. "Another item is why I hired you in the first place. It's about the men of this town. There's a heap of them, and they all make trouble, and you need to figure out how to get them in church. That's all."

I shook my head. "I meet a number of them each morning at breakfast before they head out to the plant. They know I'm a reverend and they don't have nothing to do with me."

"That might be true. But you'll never get them to fear Jesus if all you do is say hello at breakfast. You need to go where they like to go. Talk to them in a language they can understand."

"What you saying, Sheriff?"

Halligan sniffed and looked off into the distance. "Your best bet's the tavern come Friday night."

I was silent a moment, contemplating the ramifications of what the sheriff was instructing me to do. "Sheriff, all due respect, but I'm no stranger to what goes on in such a place. Surely there's a better plan."

"No . . . really there ain't. I've given thought to it over the past while, and this plan is exactly why I hired you. You can get started end of this week. In the meantime, I've been thinking about Cisco Wayman as our new fifth deacon. He's the only man in town eligible. Clay'll vote for him in a heartbeat, and I'm pretty sure I can swing Deputy Roy on this one—Roy's awful partial to Augusta's cooking. Oris won't vote for him because the café's one of the only things he don't own in this town, but I don't care. Oris won't get his way as long as Cisco's on the board."

"You think Cisco can handle it, sir?"

"Cisco's grieving in a powerful way right now, that's true, and he's known around town for his anger. But the man's got a base of understanding about God, one of the only fellas in this town who does. Beggars can't be choosers, and when it comes to God-fearing men in Cut Eye we're beggars on this church board more days than not. You talk to Cisco next chance you get, and I'll talk to him, too. See if we can't convince him to get over his grieving enough to come on board."

I nodded. "Anything else, Sheriff?"

Halligan scratched behind his ear. "There's one more thing, Rowdy, and it's a whopper of a project, but you best get started on it as soon as you can. Bottom line is the church building's fit to be condemned. It was built in a jiffy and hasn't hardly seen a lick of repair work since 1900. I went over there the other day along with Chance Farley, fella who runs the lumberyard, and we made an inspection. Foundation's cracked. Walls are warped. Roof's about ready to fall in. Outbuildings are set to topple over. Driveway needs new gravel. Everything needs paint. We really should put in a septic field one of these days, and all the repairs needed are doubled when it comes to the parsonage. Plus all that, we still owe on the deed to the tree stand. Farley added it all up, and all that plus paying off the land deed totals ten thousand bucks."

I let out a low whistle. "How you ever gonna come up with that?"

"Not me, Rowdy. You. That's the question. One of your jobs is to spearhead the vision when it comes to the church building and grounds, so you're in charge. What we need at the Cut Eye Community Church is a building program."

"A building program?" My coffee was empty, and I wished for another cup.

"Call it a fund-raising campaign if you like. Give yourself a stretch of time. Maybe six months. Maybe a year. Lay out the vision to the folks. Ask them to give to a worthy cause. Urge them to volunteer their time. If the building's in top shape, then that's only good for the community. We can help lead this town with an eye to the future. You can gather a crew of men and do some selective tree harvest, that'll help raise funds. Men like to be given a task anyway, something they can see take shape with their eyes. That's your job, Rowdy—raise ten thousand dollars and get the building and grounds in top shape. Start as soon as you can. If you raise more than that you can always give it to Bobbie's missionary fund. Any questions?"

My mouth opened but nothing came out. This job was becoming more impossible with each passing conversation. Ten thousand dollars was a fortune. Why, to raise that kind of capital, it would take a fella robbing a bank.

# FOURTEEN

Well, all the rest of that week went smoother than not. Bobbie met with me Wednesday morning and explained how a lot of the work of being a preacher was relational—there was a whole heap of folks in this community and I needed to learn who they were, what they cared about, and how they could best move forward. She sat outside the parsonage alongside of me on the steps and looked mighty fine in her gray skirt and a blue top. She gave me a carefully scripted-out eulogy to deliver for Woburn's funeral the next day.

When service time came around on Thursday, I read Bobbie's words to a T, then added a few words on my own. I know a few things about men dying and just spoke as plain as I could. Afterward at the reception, I ate cake and sipped fruit punch, and talked to as many people as I could, just asking them questions and listening to their stories. Folks seemed to go away from the church that day thinking the funeral was a fitting tribute to the man. Given that I hadn't said nothing about field-dressing dead animals, it felt like a small success for me too.

Bobbie met with me again Friday morning and we worked from scratch on how to prepare and deliver a sermon. She talked about watching closely the text first—how a preacher needs to read and reread straight through a passage ten or more times to grip it firmly in mind. Then a reverend will study to interpret the passage correctly—he'll want to make sure he knows what he's talking about so he can explain it to folks. Last in the outline, but perhaps most important, he'll make an appropriate application to people's lives. Folks need to know that the Bible tells them something about God's character, or how he relates to them, or how life will be different for them come the next day. She showed me how to settle down and deliver a message calmly and clearly, and yet with passion, how to tell stories and ask questions of the folks from within my preaching, and then she made me go outside and practice giving my next sermon to the woodpile first, promising she'd come by next week and teach me more.

Sure, it made more sense when Bobbie explained the process like that. But all and all she was still standoffish in my direction. She kept quoting her poems and saying how she was going to be leaving for the mission field soon, and that was fine with me. Laced throughout her prattling was talk of some boyfriend out east and how he was coming to visit her soon. *Fine, fine, fine*, I thought. *It's a good life for you, Bobbie Barker, so the sooner you get hitched, the sooner you'll be out of my thoughts once and for all.*

---

Funny what thoughts your head still contains from tenth grade.

It was social studies class, and the teacher ordered us to write a report on anything that interested us. I wrote mine on liquor.

The great state of Texas is divided into 254 counties. Now, folks might think we're all big drinkers in Texas in 1946, given that the war is over and everything else we do in this state is huge. But for the most part, it ain't as easy as you'd think in Texas to buy a shot of whiskey.

I recollected from my tenth grade report that of all our state's counties, there are only 93 in which distilled spirits are legal. Half those regulate the precise location you can buy a drink, and in nineteen of those you can only get a drink with 3.2 percent alcohol. If you want something harder, you need to cross a county line. Throughout Texas, it's almost impossible to buy a drink near a church or a school. You can't buy a drink on Sunday or election day, and although the federal law against prohibition was lifted in 1933, it took Texas a full two years more to legalize the sale of all liquors in the state.

And then, by contrast, there's Cut Eye.

I asked around and soon learned that Cut Eye mostly follows the letter of the law when it comes to liquor. Oh, it's a fact, you can't buy booze anywhere in Cut Eye except in one joint. Every thimbleful of booze for two hundred miles around funnels straight through the Sugar House Tavern. The building is owned by Mayor Oris Floyd, it's named after a mob of bootleggers from Detroit, and it sits right across the street from the Cut Eye School. The tavern came first, and since the school's first principal didn't want to walk too far on his lunch hour to get a drink, the town founders passed a special ordinance that got around state law. The school was built, has sat across the street from the tavern ever since, and nobody's dared to question hide nor hair of the arrangement in a hundred and thirty years.

These days the Sugar House Tavern is open all hours, day and night, seven days a week including Sunday morning, due to special city ordinances passed by the mayor. The booze—and all the cash that flows with it—runs like a river. Since most fellas in town work at the plant with its regular shifts, the tavern does most of its business come day shift's closing time and on through the wee hours of the morning, but a fella can still get a stiff drink when graveyard lets off at 8 a.m. On Friday and Saturday nights, business booms. Friday is busiest, seeing most fellas get their paychecks Friday afternoon.

The signature drink at the Sugar House is a privately distilled brand of whiskey known by the officious name the Sam Bass Black Hill to Round Rock Private Reserve. Rumor has it that Oris Floyd owns majority stock in the company, but it's never been proved. Regular customers order the drink by tossing a fifty-cent piece on the bar and calling out "Sam Bass!" or simply "Sam!" It tastes oily and foul, like a mixture of kerosene and horseradish, and I know this because I tried it while scoping out the bank about a month before the robbery took place. But it's effective at pickling a man quicker than you can say "Here's mud in yer eye," and on weekends it sells like a rainstorm in spring.

The real Sam Bass, for those who care to know, was a famous Texas train robber and outlaw who terrorized the terrain from Rio Grande to the Black Hills in the late 1800s. He held up, robbed, and pillaged at least four trains in the spring of 1878, and Texas Rangers and sheriffs' posses chased him and his outlaw gang around most of the state for the next long stretch of time. They eventually shot him dead in a gun battle, but never found his fortune, leading to a heap of speculating about lost treasure in this state. His grave today is a popular tourist joint, attracting the curious, the condemning, and those who'd sing his praises as a legendary Texas hero, a man who fought the law and the law won.

Which is all to say that when Friday night rolled around, I drove the DUKW into town, parked near the baseball fields (the only spot available near the tavern), walked across the street, swung the tavern doors open wide, and knew a bit about the trouble I was getting myself into.

Inside the Sugar House it looked the same as any other tavern. There was a standing window table closest to the street already filled belly to back with drunks. Six round tables sprawled behind that, each jam-packed with fellas playing cards. Behind that sat the main bar with its mirrors overhead and rows of bottles behind. Three bartenders were working, all busy as jaybirds, each pouring rounds of Sam Bass as fast as he could. Behind that was a kitchen and grill, and to the side was the darts area with three billiards tables in front. Next to that was a staircase leading up top to the brothel. Men smoked and cussed, laughed and hollered. Barmaids called out drink orders. The working girls sat on fellas' laps, laughing and smooching their faces. The jaunty blare of the horn section in "Shoo-Fly Pie and Apple Pan Dowdy" could be heard over the din from a jukebox in the corner. I walked to the bar and nodded in greeting to the closest bartender.

"Shot of Sam's?" he asked.

"I ain't drinking tonight."

"A fella's got to drink in here." He wiped the counter in front of me and set down a small, square paper napkin. "It's rules."

I looked the man square in the eyes. "I said I ain't drinking tonight." My voice was firm, just loud enough so he could hear it.

He leaned closer. "Then it'll cost you a half dollar to stand at my bar."

I fished into my pocket, pulled out a fifty cent piece, and slid it over.

The man eyed me quizzically. He wasn't smiling. "How come you ain't drinking?"

"That's my business."

"You came into my bar. I got a right to know."

"Not necessarily. But if you must, it's on account of my employment."

"What kind of job keeps a man from strong drink?"

"I'm a preacher."

The bar hushed up in an instant. The card games stopped. The working girls stood up from fellas' laps and tried to look presentable. A bottle of beer crashed on the floor and broke. I glanced around the room. Nobody was smiling. I reckoned it would happen like this, and the trouble was brewing, just like I thought.

Across the tavern one man stood up. His face was sneering on the end of a thin brown cigar and stubbled over with five o'clock shadow. He was real tall, a few inches taller than me even, and just as muscular. "What you say, boy?" he called out.

I swung around and faced him direct. "You heard me."

"Sounded like you's a preacher."

"You heard right."

The man pushed his chair out of the way and walked over. He stood five paces in front of me. "Then you need to leave."

I shook my head.

"I ain't repeating myself," the man said. "Either you leave, or the boys and I make you leave. What'll it be?"

I sized him up as either a logger or a railroader. He wasn't wearing a plant uniform, but he was the leader of the pack, I could tell—the sergeant who every other fella followed.

"What's your name?" I asked.

"My name . . ." He clenched his fists. "Is Gibbons. Deuce Gibbons."

I eyed the man closely. "Well, Deuce Gibbons. I reckon I'll leave in a minute, but before I do, I need to say something to the men of this tavern. That okay by you?"

"Nope."

"Well, your response is noted, but I'm going to do it anyway." My eyes didn't move from his and I called out in a loud voice— "I'm here the new preacher in town. All you men need to be in church this next Sunday. That's an order, and I ain't gonna tell you twice."

Deuce Gibbons blinked, like his mind was working mighty hard but couldn't rightly fathom where to land with this information. A snort came out of his nose. Then another. His sneer broke and he busted loose into a long laugh of hilarity. The rest of the bar followed closely behind. For five solid minutes every breathing soul in the tavern laughed his fool head off. Men pointed at me and slapped their knees, held their guts, and rolled on the floor. I was counting Mississippis in my head. Finally Deuce raised his hand and the room shut up. He took a step closer toward me.

"Listen, preacher." This time he was smiling an untrustworthy smile. "I'll make you a deal." He shrugged, grinned, and looked at the fellas on either side of him. "You like fights, Reverend? Every man in here you can whip will show up in church this coming Sunday. That's the deal. If you can beat a man with your fists, then he'll show up in church."

I inhaled sharply. I reckoned it would come to this. "Seems like a reasonable enough bargain." I clenched my fists.

"Ain't finished explaining the deal yet." Deuce's smile faded. "The deal is we all come at you at once."

I was about to say, "Seems a mite harder that way," when the bartender cold-cocked me from my blind side. The wallop caught me off guard and I careened into the closest table, sending cards scattering. All six men sitting around the table stood up while I scrambled to my feet. Closest one hit me with a right cross. I plowed my fist into his jaw and he went down hard. The next fella swung toward my nose with a left hook. I blocked his punch with my forearm and hit him square in the eye. The rest of the joint broke loose in a brawl. Friends swung at each other. Coworkers thudded into each other's guts. It was as much chaos as the fight in the mission.

I slunk to the floor, crawled closer to the pool tables, and stood in a clearing so I could survey the mess. All around me men pounded on each other. A fella barreled into me and I popped him on the side of the face and kept looking through the smoke. Across the tavern was the man I wanted to see. Deuce Gibbons spotted me right back. He was the only man I needed to beat. I lunged forward. He did too. I ducked a flying beer bottle, dodged a thrown chair, and waded back into the frenzy toward Deuce.

First punch to my jaw came from his right cross. Deuce's fists were as rawboned as a mule's kick. He must have served with the tank corps. I shook it off and walloped him back with a one-two combination. He jabbed twice on my chin with his left, then hauled off and punched me low in the gut. His tactics were dirty and I kept my breathing even, fighting to control the pain, then came back quick with a left-right combination. He countered with a crusher of a left hook. I dodged and pushed him hard toward the wall. He struggled to break free, but I knew I had him. I held him in place and pounded with my right. Each punch connected with his face, power and strength of mind flooded out of me. I was winning. This man was coming to church.

*Crack!*

From behind, a bottle smashed over my head. Glass shattered all around me. I remember reaching up and feeling blood pour out of my head. I remember seeing Deuce Gibbon's battered face. He was smiling again, now that my grip on him was broken. I remember my hands feeling heavy, and I couldn't lift them anymore to protect my face. Deuce Gibbons pasted me square on the cheek. I turned to him the other cheek, and he pasted that one as well.

After that I remember no more.

# FIFTEEN

Next Sunday morning I preached on the second chapter of Genesis. It was my second sermon ever, and it was all about how God planted a garden of perfection called Eden and grew trees in it. I liked that. God walked in that garden in the cool of the day, and I wondered if he ever took hold of an axe, same as I liked to do, and poured out his aggravations against the hard trunk of a slash pine. Probably not, considering he was God and all, but it made for interesting speculation.

Genesis chapter 2 was also where God first created a woman. He made that fella Adam nod off into a deep sleep, and while he was dozing, God created this gal he called Eve. Everything else in that garden was good, God said, except one thing. That poor fella Adam was all alone, so God made him the naked woman—they were the first husband and wife, I gathered—and God called that good. Well, I'd never looked at a union before in that holy light.

That Sunday I preached with a black eye and busted-up nose and a bandage on my head, but nobody slapped me this time when my sermon was finished. My message was ten minutes from start to finish, and the sheriff shook my hand on the way out and said, "Keep practicing, son." Deputy Roy still eyed me warily and walked off without a word. Another missionary was passing through town, and he took the evening service that night, which I was sure glad about.

Bobbie said I did better all around when we met again

Wednesday morning. She'd fixed us a snack and brought it over in a picnic basket. Some deviled eggs, two apple turnovers, and a jug of fresh spring water. Said it would help us study, she did. She helped me outline my next sermon, quoted me some poems she'd composed, and ordered me to practice my sermon again in front of the woodpile.

I visited with folks in the congregation all during the week. I met with Mert and discussed how a fella might begin a building campaign, and tried to talk with Cisco Wayman about coming on the board, but he wasn't listening yet. Sheriff was called away on business all week, so the vote for a new deacon didn't come up in the deacon meeting, so all was fine for another spell.

Friday night I went to the tavern again, got into another fight with every man I could find, lost again to Deuce Gibbons when six of his gang jumped me all at once, and drove back to the parsonage in the DUKW to ice my head.

Next Sunday I preached from the next chapter in Genesis, chapter 3. There, the devil deceived Adam and Eve. The folks ate from the tree they wasn't supposed to, and God banished them from the garden of Eden. That made me a mite angry, it did. Maybe if it wasn't for them, we'd all still be back where we belonged, back where things made sense. My sermon was a whopping fifteen minutes long. Sheriff actually gave me a grin when it was over. None of the men showed up still, but I didn't expect them to yet seeing as I hadn't beat any in a fight. Oh sure, if I picked them off one by one, I could take out a whole roomful no problem, but I knew I needed to beat their leader first. If he wasn't won over, then the rest of the fellas might well come once or twice, but they'd still follow their leader back to their old ways. No, it would take me beating Deuce Gibbons man to man. Get the leader, the rest will follow.

That Sunday night, Bobbie took the evening service out of kindness for me, I gathered, which gave me some more time to think. Then on Wednesday I met with Bobbie again. This time she brought a hunk of cheddar cheese along with four biscuits. She ate one and quoted her latest poem. I ate three, and we outlined my next sermon and I practiced it again in front of the woodpile. I wanted to preach again on Genesis chapter 3, since I didn't get too far in the chapter last time, so this sermon was about the curse that was laid out against mankind after the fall. Thorns and thistles grew, making the man need to work hard his whole life. Well, I could understand that. Then the woman would have pains in childbearing, too. I'd never seen a woman give birth, but I'd heard it described as a whale of a cursed time.

The one hopeful note in all that cursing was something Bobbie pointed out to me in the chapter, for I wouldn't have grasped its importance if I'd simply been sailing through the text by myself. The thought sprang from the fifteenth verse: something about a future fight between the devil and the woman's offspring. The devil would strike the child's heel, and okay, so he'd be wounded. But that little tyke would really be a fighter, he would, and he'd end up crushing the head of that snake, the devil. In the end, good would triumph over evil, and I liked the sound of that.

Friday night I returned to the tavern. I never did quite savvy who owned the bar, but the fellas behind the counter didn't seem to mind the fighting much. They may have been hired hands themselves, merely looking for a good show, or perhaps they had such a powerful love of fighting themselves that they considered all the broken chairs and glassware and such to be a small price to pay for all the fun. This time while I was whaling away against Deuce, somebody clocked me with a chair from behind. It's mighty hard to fight a whole room of fellas, I thought, when you've got a bright red bull's-eye painted on your back. I drove back to the parsonage and flopped on the front floor feeling blood-spattered and defeated.

Sunday my sermon lasted a whole twenty minutes. I found

I had more to say now, more of substance anyway. I was getting more comfortable with being up in front of folks, speaking in public like that. Oh, I had no problem telling a squad of soldiers to dig a foxhole, set up their mortars, and establish a machine-gun field of fire, but speaking to church folks was different. More people were coming—and they were listening more intently, too. It was mostly all women in the congregation still, though a few old farmers and oil men started coming along with their wives.

I took the Sunday evening service for the first time and spoke out of the book of John. In the beginning was something called the Word. I gathered that Word was Jesus. Bible said he was with God and was God. Well, that was something to think about.

Tuesday I met with the deacons, Wednesday I met with Bobbie again, Thursday night I met with the youth for the first time. Emma Hackathorn's oldest two children came, as did one other fella who introduced himself only as Mike and said he didn't like me much and was only there because his parents made him come. Also showing up was a highly opinionated red-haired girl by the name of Martie who asked a lot of hard questions I had no idea how to answer.

Friday night I drove down to the tavern again, walked inside, plopped my half dollar on the counter to pay for the drink that never slid down my throat, and turned to square off against Deuce Gibbons.

He was as bruised as I was from a month of fighting. All the fellas were. We all nodded our hellos to each other, caught up on small talk, then clenched our fists and prepared to wallop each other.

"There's one thing I'll say about you, Reverend—" Deuce said. "And I respect this about a fella, no matter what he does for a living." We were shuffling around each other, warming up before we charged. I noticed he looked a little flat-footed tonight.

"What's that?"

"You got grit." He popped me with a left jab, then another. I threw a lunging left and missed. I was running on adrenaline instead of using smart fighting skills. Right away I followed my miss with an uphill combination. Deuce deflected the blows and nailed me across the eyebrows. A scab split and blood spattered. It started running down into my eyes, making it hard to see. Quick, I wiped it away and hammered Deuce with a shot to the chest, then grabbed him and threw him backward. A chair sailed my direction and I ducked it. The other fellas were all fighting now too, not against me just yet, just among themselves for the fun of it. I pushed Deuce away and followed up quick with a hook to the shoulder to knock him off balance, then a right cross to the ribs.

He was glancing around for his gang, I could tell, not wanting to call out to them to appear weak, but breathing heavy, looking for a quick way to finish me off. He threw a left uppercut, but I dodged it along with a bottle that came at me from behind, then smashed him across his nose, hearing the bone snap. The punch drove Deuce to his knees. I pivoted and pummeled another fella who attacked me from the side. He went down like a stack of bricks and I turned and faced Deuce again. He rose, panting, and I walloped him in the cheekbone. He went down again, this time to his knees and from his knees to his back. I spun again in time to duck another broken bottle heading straight for the back of my head. I ran three steps forward and caught the thrower with a crack to the jaw. Then ran back to where Deuce was. The big man was still on the floor.

And this week—glory be—he wasn't getting up.

---

The next Sunday morning Deuce Gibbons sat in the front pew at church. Even though he didn't like preachers, he was true to his word and, sure enough like I'd reckoned would happen, a whole gang of men followed him through the front door.

Oh, I knew most of them by name now. There was Hoss and Cash and Slim and Stitch. There was Tick and Harry and Hank and Boone. At one time or another I'd punched most of them in the face. We breakfasted every morning together at the Pine Oak Café before we all went to work, and they'd all warmed up to me considerably since I started fighting with them. I was speaking a language they knew, I reckoned, meeting them on their home ground. Gummer came along to church too, although he and I had never fought. He was friends with all the fellas, so he figured wherever they went, he'd go along too. In all, about thirty new young men crowded into the sanctuary.

Along with all the men came the barmaids from the tavern, the cleanup crew, and most of the working girls. There was Trixie and Dolly, Opal and Marlis, Zelda and Sal—they'd been watching me fight at the tavern too, and I'd always talk to them if I had a moment or two before each week's fight started.

Ava-Louise ran the show at the brothel. She was a handsome woman, maybe sixty years old, and she came to church to keep track of her gals she said as she walked in. I watched her while we were singing. She was looking to a faraway spot in the corner of the roof, her eyes misting over like she remembered a better place from long ago.

Luna-Mae was in church, of course, and the rest of the gals who came along with Oris Floyd, but he wasn't here for a spell. Word had it that he was in Oklahoma looking over a line of purchase on some new oil wells. He'd be away for at least three months, maybe four, and that suited me fine. With him out of my hair, I could get some real preaching done.

"Today we're talking about two fellas named Cain and Abel," I said, grasping the pulpit with both hands. "Most folks when they read this story picture themselves in the shoes of Abel, the brother of righteousness. But I've been reading this text every day this past week, and I'm seeing things different."

The folks all looked to be listening to me. Deuce Gibbons made sure all the boys kept shut up.

"See, Cain was the ornery brother," I continued. "He was a fighting man, a scrapping man, a man so bent on destruction he hated his own kin. Cain hated Abel so powerful that Cain ended up killing Abel. It's harder to see ourselves in Cain's shoes, I reckon, as a man who's hardened around the edges, but I can tell you from reflection that it ain't as hard to attack a man in anger as you might think."

Deputy Roy was chewing gum, his eyes fixed on my face. The sheriff was staring at me too, not knowing where I was going. Bobbie was taking notes, her brow furrowed intently. Emma Hackathorn was shushing her children.

"That's the funny thing about this passage," I went on. "Frankly, when I read it for the first time, it stopped me cold. It was after all the destruction took place—not before—that God met with Cain. God asked the murderous Cain where his brother was, and Cain didn't have a smart answer for that, claiming he wasn't his brother's keeper. But God knew the truth. As a punishment, God told Cain he'd need to leave the area, and Cain obeyed. The man was fearful of leaving a place of safety. He was scared others would attack him. But God said, 'Not so,' and put a mark on Cain so no one who found him would kill him, and God promised that his presence was still with Cain, even after he'd done all that evil."

I looked around the congregation, at that room full of rough-hewn folks. They was all becoming familiar to me now. I'd been visiting them at their homes and speaking with them on the streets of Cut Eye. I'd met them at a funeral and at the filling station and at the mercantile and at the café. I was getting to know who was related to each other by blood and lineage, what one person thought about another, what one person was struggling with, and what another needed to overcome. For the first time I looked at them not with eyes of duty, but with eyes of heart. I wasn't fighting these folks no more, not pushing my way forward only to keep a job and stay out of jail. I was beginning to care. I plumb was.

"So that was good news for all of us," I added. "If God could care for a ruffian like Cain, even with everywhere he'd been and with all the wrong he'd done, then I reckon God could care for someone like me."

The congregation was nodding their heads, agreeing with what I was saying. I heard someone call out an "amen." I cleared my throat. They was still with me, still on the same page.

"It's no secret I went to Sunday school as a child," I said. "I was taught who Jesus was, and that he was a man worth following. It's also no secret that I've strayed far from the path of right living since then. I believe that same spot of hardship is where a heap of folks are today. Some folks here are finding God for the first time. And some of us are finding our way back to God. I don't know all that I believe yet, nor can I explain all that I hold true. But that's where I'm going. I'm traveling this road with you. I'm discovering something that gives me a hope and a future. And I invite you along with me in this good and noble direction."

That's all I said.

I sat down. Bobbie got up, led a song in closing, and then we were done. I'd preached for a solid half hour, the rightful amount of time. But it didn't seem like the amount of time I preached was all that important anymore. That morning after service was over the folks filed out the door and shook my hand genuinely, not out of pity or consternation. The old lady who'd once slapped me asked me to bend my face over so it was close to hers, and when I did she kissed my cheek. Deuce Gibbons muttered that he'd be back next Sunday, and so did most of the other rough fellas.

Well, and Bobbie Barker plumb gave me a hug.

---

Those next few weeks in Cut Eye, Texas, were some of the happiest of my life. I reckoned they were happy days for all the townsfolk, mostly. Some talked about a new spirit in the air. Others called it "revival," but I didn't know nothing about that. I kept meeting with the deacon board and with Mert, kept learning things from Bobbie and eating her picnic snacks, kept preparing sermons and delivering them, kept visiting folks at their homes and in jail, kept chopping firewood every chance I got.

I got paid in cash and paid off my bill at the mercantile. Emma Hackathorn decided to buy the place from the estate of Woburn Jones. She wasn't bringing in any money since her husband died in the traffic accident, so times were tough for the family, and she reckoned she'd go forward even grieving as she was. Her youngest child was able to play in the store while the three oldest children were at school. Emma looked genuinely happy most days, and even happier once Gummer Lopez from the filling station started courting her. I didn't see them right off as a couple, but he had a gentle way with her. In time, I could see him becoming a husband to her, a father to her fatherless children. The sheriff spoke to me about it once, asked what I thought of the matter, and all I said was, "Well, it's worth a wait and see."

Four times over the next two months I traveled up the highway in the DUKW to visit Sunny at the Chicorys' house of evil. I still hadn't told anyone in Cut Eye about my daughter, nor did I plan to unless necessary. She still wasn't talking yet, which concerned me plenty, but she began to warm to me, to understand I had a substance of history with her, and that I was at least one trusted grown-up in her life. I paid Rance seventy-five dollars I made from cutting wood, and he seemed both surprised and pleased to see that amount of cash. I promised Rance I'd return as soon as I could with more. Sunny looked to be at peace for the time being, although it was still mighty risky every moment of her living with the Chicorys.

With Mert's help, the church began a building program, and the fella from the lumber store drew up plans telling us how to proceed. Each Saturday I gathered a group of fellas—most of the same who'd fought me at the tavern—and we hiked into the tree stand to work. We chopped and sawed all morning, broke off for lunch and a short men's Bible study, then got back to work for the rest of the afternoon. Just like the sheriff said, the fellas seemed to enjoy a sense of purpose to what they was doing. They understood that a church was only a building, but it was a building worth having in a thriving community.

We began to discuss how what we were doing at the church involved more than creating a new building, which sounded funny at first to many folks. Bobbie pointed this out to me first. A man's faith could spring forth at church, but a man's faith wasn't the same thing as the church. The building was related to the faith, but the faith was separate. It could exist outside the church building too.

What mattered most was that a man understood his position before a holy God, Bobbie explained. There was redemption to be had, provided a man asked God for it. This redemption could be gleaned in a manner of receiving, much the same way Cain received from God even after Cain had done all his wrong. Bobbie called this grand idea grace—it was all about giving a man a favor he didn't deserve. That sounded strange to me, although I liked how it sounded too. Grace meant a man could truly change with God's help, no matter what the fella had done. He might need to suffer some consequences for the wrong he'd done as a matter of the natural course of things, but grace meant that his overall debt was paid and the slate was clean. With grace, there was nothing that came between him and God. It didn't matter if the fella had a rough background. It didn't matter, even, if he'd once committed a crime.

It was the first week in September 1946, I reckoned, because Sunny just turned five and her birthday's on the first. It was stifling hot on a Friday morning, and I showed up as always for breakfast at the Pine Oak Café. Cisco had agreed to come on the deacon board, I forgot to mention, although he still had a lot of grieving to do, he insisted. He wasn't there this morning, but Augusta was. She served me up a grilled T-bone steak with a side of scrambled eggs, a platter of flapjacks with salted butter and hot maple syrup, and I sat back with a big smile on my face and ate until I was stuffed. For the first time I was feeling hopeful about surviving my year as the preacher of the Cut Eye Community Church. I rightly was. In seven more months, after that year was over, well, no saying what I might do then. It wouldn't be preaching, but with some solid job history behind me, there's no saying what I couldn't do.

That's when a memory flashed at me. It was a returning voice, one I'd heard before. I swear I did. It sounded like the voice was coming from outside the Pine Oak Café, and I couldn't rightly say the voice was speaking to me out loud, but the voice was clear in my ears.

"Hey fella!" said the voice. "You want to live?"

How that man's voice was reaching me so far through those walls, I couldn't rightly fathom. But there, eating until my stomach was bursting with Augusta Wayman's good breakfast cooking, I nodded my head.

"Then find the good meal and eat your fill," it said. "Swear you'll do that?"

I nodded again, and that's when I understood what that voice was getting at.

Once I was so hungry, so scared, and so desperate, and a tree broke loose like a strong hand moved it. A tangle of branches passed over my head, and I shot to the surface from the river of destruction. A moment later my knees scraped gravel on a shallow section of riverbed, and I stumbled forward out of the river, that river that seemed so far away now.

Well, I walked three steps onto dry ground, and started searching for that good meal. After much searching I found that meal. Or perhaps it found me.

'Twas what I was eating today.

I wish that feeling of near pure bliss would've lasted longer than it did. But if there's one thing I've ever found in this life, it's that the ups and downs have a way of evening things out. As soon as something powerfully good happens, something's prone to be right around the corner, something mighty wicked. And sure enough, my hunch wasn't wrong, although time would show it would happen in stages. A twinge of sorrow would arrive first. And then a bit of dread. And then would come an avalanche of pure terror.

But all that would come only after I finished eating.

# SIXTEEN

It was a still a glad day that late September Sunday when we took a special offering for our building campaign, and Mert, who'd been keeping track of the cash, informed me that folks dug deep.

We'd gathered money for weeks before. The fellas and I had chopped a heap of wood and raised a pile of loot on our own. Plus, some of those single fellas had money tucked away in their mattresses and were hot to the idea of giving to a worthy cause, so that added to the mix. Plus, with attendance at an all-time high of nearly a hundred and ten folks on Sunday mornings, the special offering had been powerful generous.

That glorious total was written carefully in a lined ledger. Mert held out the page to me that showed the amount: well over ten thousand dollars, plus change. The church folks had all gone home by the time the offering was counted, and Mert wore a mysterious smile as she showed me the books, the strangest smile I ever saw in that woman. Maybe it was strange only because she wasn't prone to smiling, but she looked to be reaching a decision in her own mind. I didn't know what the decision might be, so I opted not to press the matter further and chose to be happy in the moment. We'd reached our goal, and that was worth much.

In fact—Mert pointed to another line underneath the sub-total—we'd actually raised close to twelve thousand dollars, enough to send Bobbie out to the mission field, thus fulfilling the girl's dream of helping folks live well in other countries. We raised all that cash three months ahead of schedule, and right away from the church telephone I called the sheriff at his house and told him the good news. He said, "All right then." And just like that we were set to begin work repairing and making new the building and grounds the following Saturday.

I drove to the café and ate lunch—it was braised beef shanks in butter sauce—then drove back to the church in the DUKW. Later that same Sunday afternoon, Bobbie Barker drove her jeep over to the parsonage where I was studying for the evening service and knocked on my front door.

I'd mentioned to the sheriff that we had some good news for her. I was thinking of the extra two thousand dollars, of course. But after I opened the door and before I could get a word in edgewise she said her daddy already told her about the cash and she had something else to tell me. She looked happy about the news. Mostly, anyway. The girl was wearing a T-shirt with a men's oxford shirt layered over it, its tail hanging baggy and the arms rolled at the sleeves, a pair of tan shorts, and sneakers. She'd been shooting baskets outside her house when I'd phoned her daddy about the building campaign and extra money. She sat down on the parsonage steps and patted the seat next to her, the way we often sat together outside when she helped me study for my sermons.

"Rowdy—" she rolled one of her sleeves down to her wrist then rolled it back up to her elbow, as if she was killing time. "Before I say what I need to tell you, can I ask you a personal question?"

I sat on the steps and stared across the roadway at her jeep, at its black seats, green army paint, and familiar grill with the bars running up and down. "Sure," I said.

"It's . . . um . . . do you have a philosophy of love?"

"Hmm." I pondered the girl's question. "Not sure what you're getting at."

She looked at the field across the road. It was blooming with mescal bean, least that's what I've always called it—the shrub that flowers blue every autumn, and the field was filled with color.

"Well," she said, "the great classic poet Percy Bysshe Shelley talked about fountains mingling with rivers, rivers with oceans, and winds of heaven mixing forever with a divine law. You know what a 'law divine' is, Reverend Slater?"

Now, that was strange. She seldom called me "Reverend" anymore and hadn't used the title in weeks. I'd reckoned it sounded too formal for her to address me anymore.

"Well, I'm getting to understand an idea of divine law, if that's what you mean," I said.

"No." The girl wrinkled her nose. "It's not about you learning how to preach. When I talk about a 'law divine' it's . . . oh . . . hard to describe. It's from a poem. *Nothing in the world is single, All things by a law divine, In one spirit meet and mingle—Why not I with thine?* See what I mean now? That last line of the poem is key. It's important to me that you understand what I'm asking you here. Do you?"

I nodded like I understood. But I didn't. Not really.

She snapped her gaze away from the field like someone had given her a pinch, exhaled through her nose, and said—almost like she was annoyed—"Let me see if I can ask this another way. You got any PT gear in that parsonage of yours?"

"Sure."

She stood. "Let's go for a run then."

"A run?"

"Don't question my ways, Rowdy. Just see if you can keep up."

There she was being ornery again. I decided not to rile up her aggravations further, went into the house, changed into some old PT gear of Danny Wayman's that Augusta had given me, and came back outside. Bobbie untied the oxford shirt and tossed it on the steps, stretched once and touched her toes, and I noticed for the first time she was wearing a small pistol strapped tight against her T-shirt at the small of her back. It was a Stevens Old Model Pocket .22, a nice little handful for a lady's purse, single shot and easy to reload. I've always admired a gal who packs a concealed weapon, although this wasn't much of a gun. It was further wrapped in plastic, which made me curious. Bobbie noticed me looking at it.

"Snake gun," she said matter-of-factly.

"Snake gun?"

"Yeah, back when I was thirteen, Daddy and I were out hiking one day. I jumped over a pile of brush and scared up a rattlesnake inside. It caught the tip of my heel as I passed. Daddy threw me over his shoulder and rushed me to the doc. Fortunately I lived, but I was mighty sick for a spell. I think we all were. Sick with worry. Sick with death. Ever since then, Daddy made me carry this."

"Ever fired it?"

"Only during training. Daddy taught us all how to hit a bull's-eye—me and Mama and Emma, although the gun always made me tremble. I haven't encountered a snake up close since that day on the trail, but I got no problem shooting a snake in the head. There's enmity between me and a snake anyhow—know what I'm saying, Rowdy? An enmity that longs for the evil that turned the snake against me to be crushed. It's just my mind doesn't naturally prompt me to draw a weapon and fire."

"You hate snakes. I get that."

She repeated carefully, "No. I hate the evil that turned the snake against me. That's what I long to be done away with completely."

I grinned her direction. She was a spritely one, that Bobbie Barker, despite her innocent ways—I'll give her that much. Yet I had one more question before I dropped the matter. "What's the plastic for?"

"To keep it dry, of course," she said pertly, as if everyone carried a pistol that way.

We struck off running at a good clip. It was nearing four o'clock, the sun was beginning to lower in the hot sky, the dust rising off the roadway. Evening service didn't start until six, and I was almost prepared.

We headed west up the Lost Truck Road for about fifteen minutes, then Bobbie veered off onto a trail to the south and cut her way through the slash tree stand. I knew my way around these woods pretty well by now, so I passed by her on the trail and picked up the pace to see how much fire was still left in her legs.

Back in Georgia during basic training, every man in our company wouldn't think twice of running seven miles before breakfast. They called the run Currahee: it was up a high stack of mountain three miles up, three miles down, a half a mile away from camp. The name *Currahee* came from a Cherokee word that meant "We stand alone together," and the trail was formed in rutted ugliness when a bulldozer crashed its way up and down the side of that hill. When we new recruits first started running Currahee we all hated it and grumbled at our misfortune, but after a while the trail began to stand for something. At night the fellas would be standing around and somebody would say, "Let's go run Currahee." So we'd run that cussed trail for the fun of it. Just for pride's sake. Just to show we could.

Through the pines, I could hear Bobbie running behind me. She was keeping pace, panting on my heels, so I sped up even more. We were flying now, weaving in and out of the timber. We hurdled roots and fallen trees. We leapt stumps. We splashed across a stream and blazed up the side of a hill. At the top, another rise lay before us and we charged up that one too. Again came a rise, and another, and another. Up and up we sprinted. The trail bombed and swooped, sometimes visible through the bracken, sometimes not, and soon we reached a plateau at the summit of the hill.

For a quarter mile on the plateau the trail cleared and widened so two could run side by side. Bobbie lengthened her strides and ran next to me now. She was breathing easier than I was and spitting every so often the way runners do. "Hey Rowdy! Do paratroopers . . . believe in faith?" she yelled between breaths.

"This one's . . . starting to—why?"

"Up a hundred yards ahead . . . comes a cliff." Bobbie's face was flushed. "We're going to fly right off it . . . just like you fellas jumped out of your airplanes. You don't know . . . if it's twenty feet to the bottom . . . or a hundred. But I do. The only way to find out . . . is to jump with me."

"You're crazy!" I yelled back.

The girl sped ahead. We neared the cliff's edge now, both of us sprinting full out. The edge of the cliff was less than ten feet away. There weren't no time to think or ask questions. Bobbie was running straight over a sheer drop, and I was running right behind her. Five steps. Four. Three. The edge was upon her first. Bobbie shouted: "*See the mountains kiss high Heaven . . . No sister-flower would be forgiven if it disdained its brother!*" And she vanished. Two steps later the ground gave way beneath me. I was falling, falling, counting as I fell. *One Mississippi. Two Mississippi. Three Mississippi. Four*—I looked down and sucked in a lungful of air.

The river smashed into me. Down, down, deep beneath its inkiness I plunged. Water swirled far over my head. I clawed and fought my way to the surface, kept my wits, burst up out of the blackness, sucked in a fresh lungful of air, and stroked my way back to the shore.

Bobbie was already standing in the shallows of the river, looking at me strangely. The girl seemed full of mysterious muscle, hidden strengths she kept reserved and showed to no one except by her choosing, and I found myself staring back at her with new admiration.

"You know how that poem ends?" Her clothes clung to her sides. "It's 'Love's Philosophy' by Shelley."

I shook my head and waded closer. I was nearer to her than I'd ever been before.

"These are its last lines—" Bobbie closed her eyes, reached forward, and grabbed my hand in hers. But it wasn't same hands, right on right, like we were going to shake. It was opposite hands, her right with my left, and I didn't know what to do with that. *"The sunlight clasps the earth,"* she said, *"And the moonbeams kiss the sea—What are all these kissings worth, If thou kiss not me?"*

Now, I'd grown accustomed to meeting with Bobbie Barker every week, to hearing her poems that didn't make sense, and to having her explain to me things about preaching. Of course, I'd never told her of my growing accustomedness to her—I hadn't. Sure, her hair was honey colored and wispy in the right places around her ears, and, sure, her orneriness had settled down a mite and I wasn't afraid of her poisoning me anymore with arsenic in my coffee. But the idea of a ruffian like me courting a girl as pure as Bobbie Barker didn't make sense in the big scheme of things. It wasn't fear that kept me from speaking my mind. It was respect for her. I'd been too many places. I'd done too much evil in the world. She'd said as much—that she'd never date a ruffian—although not with her words, so I'd never brought up the subject. Meeting with this girl every week and having her tell me to preach to the woodpile—that was my contentedness in this arrangement. That was all I reckoned a friendship with this girl would ever bring.

"Oh, for heaven's sake," she said. She pulled me closer, and my thinking stopped in its tracks. Her eyes were still closed, and her pulling caught me off guard. To my surprise—as quick as you could say Percy Bysshe Shelley—she opened her eyes and kissed me. Her lips were warm and wet, her mouth still hot from our run, and if I'd been a thinking man I would have drawn her close and kissed her right back. But instead she pulled away, looked me over from head to toe, slapped my face, then closed her eyes and kissed me a second time, this time much longer. When she released me, one corner of her mouth was upturned, as if in bemused satisfaction.

"Don't you ever speak of this," she said, backing away once more. "Don't you ever . . . ever . . . mention a single word . . ." Her voice trailed off.

I grinned. "I take it you've done this before." I glanced upstream at the cliff we'd just jumped off.

She slapped me again for good measure, then realized what I'd meant and gazed at the cliff gratefully, like she was gazing at an old friend who'd helped her over a rough patch. The rushing river had chiseled away at the rock for hundreds of years until a high bluff formed. The bluff lay flat against the river, and the gorge underneath flowed clear and deep. She kept looking at the cliff and spoke with her voice far away, as if in reverie— "All that time when I was preaching every Sunday while the men were at war, I'd preach in the morning and visit with folks in the church all afternoon, then get ready to preach in the evening. There was always an hour in late afternoon when I'd drive back to church and have so many burdens within me. Burdens I didn't know how to unload. For a long while I didn't know where to put those feelings. I didn't." The girl snapped back to attention, waded to the riverbank, sat on a flat rock, and stretched back so the last rays of the sun could begin to dry her. I followed and sat a short distance away on the sand.

"That's when I started running," Bobbie added. "Each Sunday afternoon I ran and ran until all the problems of the world faded." The girl squeezed water out of her hair, running her fingers along its length. "After my run, I'd come back to the old parsonage, heat water on the stove and take a bath in the wash basin, change my clothes and fix my hair, then go preach again. That was the only way I made it through."

I'd never thought about how it might have been difficult for her, having all the weight of a congregation on her shoulders. What a fool I'd been. "I'm sorry," I said.

"Well, don't be. Running like that was the only way I could sort out the weight of my mind. That's all. Today was another day I needed to run, so that's the reason I asked you to come. I thought you might like to know my secret of surviving in the pulpit. I'm just passing it along to a fellow minister. That's all."

She was a genuine introvert, this girl of guarded solitude, a person who needed time alone to recharge like she needed her next breath. I decided to press the matter and asked, "What was weighing so heavy on you today that you needed to run? Was it your money coming in? You worried about going overseas now that it's finally happening?"

"No." Her word was clipped and she looked at the river with that same, strange, faraway look in her eyes, the one she had when she looked at the field of blue wildflowers.

"What then?"

"Because I got a phone call." She cleared her throat. "Right after church."

"From who?"

"The fella I told you about. My boyfriend."

"What did he want?" My voice was flat.

"He asked me to marry him."

"Oh."

She didn't say anything for a spell, and I didn't know what to say next neither, but now it was me looking at her, looking at this girl like I'd never looked at her before. Finally I found my tongue and asked, "What was your answer?"

"I told him yes."

I didn't like the sound of that. Didn't like it one bit. Bobbie's

eyes turned forlorn, like she wasn't happy about her answer neither, and I reckoned the fella who asked her was a smart man. A
smart single gal such as Bobbie wouldn't be around forever. Some
quick fella was bound to snag her like a beautiful trout on the
end of a fishing line. I wanted to say something more, but I didn't
know what. Foolishly, the only thing that came out of my mouth
was, "So what are you doing here with me then?"

Bobbie sniffed. "I'm trying to ask you important questions
about poetry. Questions I'd hoped you'd understand."

I stared at her, confused.

She shook her head like she was changing course then added,
"I guess you could say congratulations."

I swallowed. "Congratulations then."

"This is what folks do after a war, Rowdy. They get married.
I've always dreamed of being married someday, and my fiancé is a
good man—as upright and dependable as the color brown. He is
highly determined and sits at the front of the classroom and filled
with every intention to save the world, same as me. Why, he's
as good a husband as any woman could ever find in these parts,
and I should be grateful to have him. I wanted to tell you about
the engagement right away, because I know we've been getting
along as friends lately. All this time we've spent together these
past weeks—I liked it, I truly did. I don't have many friends my
age in these parts. The girlfriends I went to school with are all
married now and living on ranches or farms. Next to my sister,
you're about the best friend I have anymore. In fact, if I can make
a request of you, from one friend to another . . . I'd be obliged if
you'd perform the wedding ceremony, seeing as how you're the
only minister beside me I know around these parts."

I coughed. "When is it?"

"Six months. Maybe a year. Maybe two. There's a heap of details we haven't worked out yet. He's studying to be a missionary

in China, and God's calling me to Haiti, so we haven't worked that out yet."

"Well, I'd like to meet him. Shake his hand. When's he going to see you next?"

"It'll be a while. He's in Dallas all this year, finishing up his seminary training."

"You love him?" The question blurted its way out of my mouth. She paused.

"No," she said.

The girl stood up quickly, took a few steps forward, found the trailhead, and began to run. She was thirty feet ahead of me before I realized our conversation was over. I stood in a jiffy and began to run after her.

Bobbie blazed a different trail back to the parsonage. This one meandered alongside the river for a mile, then cut sharp to the north. It merged with another trail, then dumped us out back behind the outhouses at the back of the church building. I let her lead the run the whole way home. She ran independently, not alongside of me this time, and Bobbie slowed to a walk only when she reached the church property. Her hands were on her hips and she was breathing hard.

"It'll be good when this old place . . . is fixed up again," she said, looking at the back of the church.

I wanted to ask her more questions, to peer under the surface of what had just transpired between us, but all that came out of my mouth was, "It'll be good indeed."

"Daddy said everyone will start work . . . this Saturday, now that the money's all in."

I nodded, started to say something, then changed course and began to walk back to the parsonage. I reckoned a girl such as her had already made up her mind when it came to who to marry and for what reasons. I certainly wasn't one to change it. "You need anything?" I called over my shoulder. "A towel?"

"No," Bobbie Barker said.

That one, solitary word left her lips. It was the only word she spoke to me, and she shook her head and headed toward her jeep. That one word told me all I needed to know about Bobbie Barker as far as our futures together were ever concerned. She slid herself up and over on the seat, started the jeep's engine, and put the transmission in gear with the clutch held in. She wasn't moving anywhere, and out of the corner of my eye I saw she gave one long last look my direction.

By now I was a few feet away from the parsonage steps, so I stopped and held her gaze. She was framed in the distance by that field of blue wildflowers, as if caught in one of those new photographs that was bathed in color.

I nodded respectfully to her. And she nodded respectfully to me.

After that she let out the clutch and drove away. She shifted gears quickly as she drove down the road, and I could hear the familiar rumble of the jeep's engine in my ears for a long time to come, even though it gradually grew quieter the farther away she went.

———

Well, I cleaned myself up, dressed myself in church duds, and when it was time to preach for evening service I headed back over to the church. My mind wasn't tied tightly to what I would be preaching on, and no, even as the words were leaving my mouth from behind the pulpit I knew it wasn't one of my finer sermons. Bobbie wasn't in service that evening, and I kept glancing at the empty space between her daddy and her sister where she always sat.

When the service was all but over, the sheriff motioned to me like he had something to announce. I called him up and he stood at the pulpit. I thought he'd be wearing a smile at the thought of announcing to the congregation that our building program was set to begin next week, but he wasn't smiling. Come to think of it, he'd worn a peculiar frown all the way through service.

"Got some good news and some bad news," the sheriff began. "It's one of those occurrences that's plumb difficult to explain to y'all, but I'll lay it out there and we can talk more as time progresses."

I sat on the platform on one of the chairs reserved for staff. From behind him, I could see a red hue creeping up the back of his neck. The sheriff was working on something powerful, perhaps even more powerful than he was letting on. He cleared his throat.

"The good news is that we took in a heap of cash today for our church's building program. The money was set in an envelope and put in its usual hiding spot for safekeeping before it could be brought to the bank on Monday." He cleared his throat again. "But the bad news is that when Mert went to count it again, the money wasn't there."

A ripple of talk buzzed around the congregation.

"Only six folks know about this hiding spot—the five on the deacon board and our church secretary. All those folks, the ones who are in town anyway, I've questioned. And all don't know where the money is. So . . . for the time being we're treating this as a theft."

Another swell of murmur rose.

The sheriff held up his hand for silence. "I know we're all disappointed and even angry, but until the money's located, there ain't anything more that can be done. If anybody knows anything, come talk to me or Deputy Roy. That's all for now. Church is dismissed."

Well, it was a strange evening after that, it rightly was. I shook hands near the door, but there was a strange odor in the room, like the church stunk of death. All Mert could do was look at the floor. Poor, righteous woman. I bet she felt responsible. Wasn't her fault the money was gone.

Folks stayed longer than usual that evening, talking, arguing, laying down theories as to where the money went, vowing that justice would be levied against the thief. By the time everybody was finished and I swept up and closed the building, the outside night was darker than an inkwell. A cloud had formed in the sky and joined with others. No stars were out, and the moonrise was showing only a tiny sliver far in the eastern sky.

All was dark toward the parsonage. Deadly quiet too. I never left lights on, and the gravel of the church parking lot crunched under my feet as I walked toward my home. My shoes clattered as I walked up the steps and I moved to open the front door. It was already swinging on its hinges. Maybe I left it open. I stopped and stood on the steps, listening close for sounds.

"Anyone there?" I called.

Crickets chirped in the night air. A breeze blew from across the field. The breeze was colder than I expected, and far in the distance a coyote howled.

I reached around the edge of the doorframe, keeping myself as close out of shooting distance as I dared, found the light switch, and turned on the porch light. It provided enough illumination for me to walk forward another two steps, locate the chain dangling from the lightbulb in the middle of the living room ceiling, and give it a quick tug. Streams of white light burst into all corners of the room.

"Watch out. I bite," said a voice. My pupils dilated in a wink and I looked upon the figure. I didn't need to. I'd recognize that voice of shadows anywhere. He was leaning back on one of my hard-backed chairs and had his boots on my dining room table. A rifle rested across his lap. I stared at the man hard, swallowed, then found my voice. I could only choke out four words. They were enough to start a conversation, one I knew was a long time coming.

"What do you want?" I said.

There came a pause while the man raised his rifle to eye level and pointed it my direction. He was taking his time, taunting me with the power he held from assuming I was unarmed. He was right. I held no weapon. He laughed and said, "I believe you owe me some money, Rowdy Slater."

It was Crazy Ake.

— **Part 2** —

# SEVENTEEN

W hen a man levels a rifle at your face, it complicates matters greatly if you're honor-bound to that man, like I was
to Crazy Ake.

See, on my first day of prison, so many months ago now, the
fella behind me in the chow line shoved me to one side. Although
I had not yet learned all the unspoken codes of prison life, I had
the good sense to see I was among roughs—men who valued in-
stinct and aggression—and if I didn't shove this fella back, then
I would be branded a coward. All manner of aggravations would
befall me the rest of the time I was locked up, and that would
never do.

The fella and I got straight into it, hammer and tongs, but
what I didn't know was that he was only a scout—the soldier
walking ahead of the company to test the action and see what's
what. In two hits he was already on the floor, crawling away from
me as fast as he could, which is when the rest of the gang took
their cue and piled on me. A dozen fellas started beating me, all
hard-fisted prison thugs, and I walloped the first five before the
rest of the squad pinned me to the floor and their leader pulled
a knife.

Their leader was a huge alligator of a man, the one they called
Big Red. He was the toughest, most belligerent brute in prison,
and he was making a preemptive strike, I learned later. See, when
another big-framed fella walks into prison, a man such as myself,

then it's natural that Big Red would feel threatened. Right away the convict in charge needs to exert his supremacy. If he doesn't, then he's equally branded a coward. Plus, he's forever walking around on pins and needles, waiting for an up-and-comer such as me to make my move and take control.

So there was Big Red with his knife held to my throat below my left earlobe. He was aiming to slice straight across to the right and take my head off. The guards weren't looking. They didn't care. And I reckoned I was as good as dead when along came Sergeant Akan Fordmire, a man about twenty-six years old, who broke a chair over the back of Big Red's skull.

Crazy Ake, for that was the sergeant's nickname, served as a mortar man during the war. He was a thick-necked Kansas native with bushy sideburns and tattoos on his arms who was sent to prison for stealing supplies from battalion headquarters. Later, when I asked Crazy Ake about why he saved my throat from Big Red's knife, he put one of his green-painted arms over his face and giggled an eerie laugh. It took nearly a week to pry forth the fuller story.

His saving my life boiled down to cash. Big Red owed Crazy Ake money, or at least that's the way Crazy Ake saw it. Around prison, if Big Red wanted a new toothbrush, a nail clipper, or a dirty magazine, he wasn't in the habit of paying straight out for it. He got one of his minions to trade around for him. But the minion flaked and didn't pay this time, so Crazy Ake was stuck still being owed. When Big Red's back was turned with the knife at my throat, Crazy Ake spotted a prime opportunity to announce to the whole prison that nobody better not mess with a man's money, particularly if that man was Crazy Ake.

Big Red was sent to the prison hospital with the back of his head gushing blood and then—fortunate for everyone—was transferred to another lockup out of state. Crazy Ake was slapped with a week in solitary and then, much to my astonishment, he traded around so he could become my cellmate.

He was starting to collect on the debt I owed him, I gathered soon enough. He was shorter than me and not as muscular, but more wily, I'll say that much. More shrewd. With Big Red out of the way, Crazy Ake became the new man in charge. As an ex-mortar man he knew how to organize a team, and within a week he had the first tier of brutes under his control. Those brutes controlled the next ranks, and they the next, and all of them put together soon controlled the prison population. Within another two weeks, Crazy Ake bought the guards, at least some of them. And within one short month, a rumor went around that he even bought the warden. There was no way to confirm this. But one afternoon a warm apple pie showed up in our jail cell. No note. No explanation. Just all the sticky goodness Crazy Ake could eat.

Now, in prison a fella's locked away in his cell for twenty-three hours each day. Sure, you get your meals in the mess hall and you're allowed to mill about in the yard for an hour, but nothing ever tastes of freedom. There's always the guard towers to remind you where you are, the razor wire to hold you in, the shouts of profanity that echo off the concrete walls. Surrounding your soul is a depth of deception and trickery you ain't used to on the out-side—it's always another man doing another man in. The walls talk to you after a while, and simply put: you hate your life.

Well, Crazy Ake told jokes to ease our misery—long, non-sensical stories that sometimes had a point but usually didn't. He frothed at the mouth and paced wild-eyed in our cell, but he could get a fella to laughing, he could. And he was a charmer in a decep-tive sort of way. I confess that with all that time on our hands I was drawn to his high-jinks stories, if only for the entertainment.

I never actually worked for Crazy Ake myself, and I'm not exactly sure why. He never asked me outright for favors and I never offered. In retrospect, I think, he was biding his time until he could collect on the debt I owed him once and for all. My cellmate had not a bit of a heart for goodness, he was rotten to the core, and over the next months together I watched him operate around prison and saw him stop at nothing to get what he wanted most: a fat fistful of dollars earned the easy way.

That's what he proposed we take for ourselves after we both got out of the joint. He'd been in longer than me and was released two months before I was. On the day I got out, I was given a change of clothes and a twenty dollar bill, was driven to the bus station by a guard and told to get lost. Crazy Ake was already waiting for me in the shadows. He told me to forget the bus ticket; he had an old truck he was driving. Then he took me to lunch and picked up the check and afterward when we were lumbering down the highway he said he had a plan for getting rich, although he couldn't pull it off alone.

Debt or no debt, I said no to his proposition at first. I wasn't a criminal, not really. Much to my relief, he simply gave me his address at a boardinghouse in Memphis and told me to think about it. But as soon as he let me off at the next town I threw the address away. I didn't want nothing to do with the man.

That's when I started drifting. I hitchhiked from one town to the next, always looking for work, always mindful of my responsibility to my daughter. But one month turned into another and my belly got emptier and emptier. By the time I finally reached my home state of Texas, dropped in on the Chicorys, and discovered the full extent of danger I'd placed Sunny in, then I knew I had a real crisis on my hands. In my desperation I bet the high card to Rance Chicory, lost, and knew I was sunk.

That's when Crazy Ake caught up with me again—when I was at my lowest. I reckon that's the way evil often works. The morning after losing to Rance Chicory, I was eating from a garbage can at the back of the Cool Hand Tavern in Rancho Springs. Crazy Ake rumbled up in his truck, opened the door with a smile on his face, and said, "Get in, Rowdy. Your luck is about to change."

I couldn't tell you how he tracked me down. Maybe he followed me around the whole time. Sure, his was a foolish plan, even though it sounded rational to a man as deep in his misery as I. Crazy Ake never outright said it, but he hinted around at my being honor-bound to him for saving my life, particularly when I started to waver.

"Old Rowdy boy, well, if it wasn't for me, then that knife of Big Red's sure had your name on it—didn't it?" he said, just before we reached the bank in Cut Eye.

"Yeah," was all I'd said.

Crazy Ake handed me a rifle. It wasn't even loaded. We set the old truck's hand brake and jigged out the side while the motor was still running, shrugged off the rain while throwing sacks over our heads, and bustled straight up the middle with our rifles aimed forward.

Shoot, I never would have hurt nobody innocent. Never in a million years. I just needed money real bad.

Real, real bad.

Like every man does if he's spent time in the clink and nobody will give him a job once he gets out.

Like every man does if his four-year-old daughter boards with a devil who's only biding time before he makes her start working in the worst way for him.

---

"So where's my cash?" Crazy Ake's rifle was still aimed at my head.

"Nearby," I said.

"Get it then."

"Well, it ain't in the parsonage, if that's what you mean." I tried to laugh but my words came out choppy and nervous. All I could think to do was keep him talking. "If you put down that M1, we'll catch up. I'll get the cash for you soon."

"Get it for me now." His trigger finger twitched.

"That'll take some doing. Law was hot on me after we jumped off that bridge. It's stashed a bit aways from here."

Crazy Ake grinned. He set his rifle on his lap and ran one hand up and around his sideburns, scratching. "Rowdy, I tell ya, a man of your devilment is an object of wonder. What a team we make! What a team! The idea of posing as a preacher." He cackled heartily. "That's something only a man of great cunning could pull off, I tell you what."

I took a step closer toward him. He set his other hand back on the rifle and shot me a cold stare.

"Relax," I said. "I'm only going to make some coffee. Thought you might want some."

"Coffee? Since when you drink coffee?"

"No whiskey in a parsonage." I raised an eyebrow.

He laughed again. I glanced at the rifle. It was still solid in his hands.

"Rowdy, here's what I propose." Crazy Ake slid his boots off my table and let the front legs of the chair clump to the floor. "It doesn't surprise me that our cash is well hid. That was a smart thing for a fella to do, and I would've done the same myself. So let's do this. Now that you know I'm back in town, I'll leave for a day or so. When I'm gone, you dig up the money. I'll come back and we'll square up. How's that sound?"

I stared him in the eyes. He was being smart, not kind, and I knew it, but what could I do—tell him I'd decided to follow Jesus then taken the money back to the sheriff's office? There'd be a bullet between my eyes faster than I could say skedaddle. I took another step toward the kitchen and asked, "Out of curiosity, how'd you track me down?"

He shrugged. "Wasn't hard. Came back into Cut Eye last week, stopped by the Sugar House, shut my mouth, and listened." Crazy Ake shifted in the chair. "The place was real quiet. Hardly no men around, but some yahoo was talking about sawing timber with a reverend every Saturday. 'Mighty big fella, too,' the yahoo said. 'He could saw timber all day.' So that got me to thinking. I hung around town awhile more, then saw you driving up the highway one afternoon in that DUKW." He laughed loud. "You own that outright, or did you steal that too?" The rifle was ever near both of his hands. He was telling stories now, but he wasn't off guard. Not in the least.

"It came with the job," I said.

"Well, I see that's not all the job came with." Crazy Ake's eyebrows flew up to his forehead. "Who's that pretty young gal I saw you jogging with earlier today down Lost Truck Road? I bet she came hard to bargain for." He cackled a full thirty seconds.

"That's the sheriff's daughter." I wanted to include some truth in what I was telling him, lest he'd done more homework, so I eyed him closely then added, "She worked as the minister before me. She's been showing me the ropes."

"I bet she has."

"Nah, it's not like that. I'm not with her."

"That's not how I saw it." He wiped froth from his mouth with the back of one hand. "But what does it matter. Look—here's how this is going to go down. I'll give you a full forty-eight hours to get the money. Tuesday night we'll meet again and get squared. Seventy-thirty split, like we agreed. And don't think you're gonna run anywhere in the meantime. I know you wouldn't do that to a friend anyway, but if I can track you here, then there ain't no place safe for you to hide."

Crazy Ake stood to leave, still loosely aiming the rifle toward me. He circled around me and walked backward toward the door, ever keeping me in his line of sight.

"Time's ticking, Rowdy." He winked. "And I want mine in small bills."

# EIGHTEEN

I was in a jam. A real hamstrung jam.

I contemplated sleeping in the DUKW that night, but it was all open air, so that would never do. Instead, I stayed inside and locked the front door of the parsonage, and I never locked my doors. Not sure why that would do me any good even. A bullet could come straight through those walls if Crazy Ake wanted it to. I contemplated digging a foxhole and sleeping out in that, but without a weapon, even a foxhole wouldn't do me much good. There was nowhere safe from that man.

All night long I paced and figured, paced and figured. Sleep fled from my eyes. There was nothing I could do to get out of this mess, no matter how I saw it. I sure couldn't come up with the cash, that was for certain. Crazy Ake didn't know the exact amount of what we'd snagged, but by the size of the sack I carried out the door, he knew his take was going to be in the thousands. Where would I ever borrow that kind of cash?

I couldn't go to the sheriff and tell him the story to get justice on my side. If I did, then that was the same as admitting my guilt to robbing the bank. Halligan would be obliged to throw me in jail for a long time to come. Sunny would never get free from the Chicorys. The state would pounce on the sheriff for costing the taxpayers money. He'd lose votes come next election, and Oris Floyd would run the town. Lots of folks would be in a mess then.

I couldn't run nor hide, not that I even wanted to. Just like

Crazy Ake said, he'd find me no matter wherever I went.

It was a heap of trouble even to buy a rifle and defend myself. All my money went to pay off Rance Chicory. Maybe I could get a cash advance from Emma at the mercantile, but even then, what was I supposed to say when I bought the rifle? That I was taking up hunting? With me eating at the café, there was no need for extra food. That I'd been a sharpshooter during the war and wanted to practice my skills lest they wither? Nobody wanted to hear about war exploits these days. Maybe I could buy a gun in the next town, but even if I could pull that off, I wasn't sure how much good it would do anyway with the cards stacked in Crazy Ake's favor, especially the element of surprise. If I came out on the good side of a shootout with Crazy Ake, it'd likely land me back in the slammer, or worse—the law would see it as murder unless I could explain the fuller story behind why I was shooting at him. I was sunk. A man without a plan.

On Monday morning I got up, tossed on some clothes, and headed into the pine slash with my axe. Didn't even get breakfast. I just chopped and chopped, trying to get my head around my predicament. I kept chopping all through lunch and on past dinner until it was dark. About 9 p.m. I headed back to the parsonage, still without a plan.

A note was tacked to my front door. It had come out of the blue while I was away, and the note flapped in the evening breeze.

*Dear Reverend Slater:*
This past Sunday when we sang the hymn "Shall We Gather at the River," you failed to omit the third verse. In this church we always omit the third verse of that hymn. That is the way we have always done things around here, and did you know you offended a great number of people by doing things differently? If you truly love God and care for this community, then you will never again change

the music at this church. I am highly upset with you, and I am certainly not the only one.

*Prayerfully yours,*
*A parishioner*

When it came to leaving a name, the note was unsigned. The coward. It struck me so strange, such a contrast—here I was with my mind so full of life-and-death matters, some spiritual, some physical, and then one of my congregants jabs at me over something as petty as a skipped verse of a hymn.

I didn't rightly know how to respond to this criticism. Or even if I should. I felt like shouting at this person to stop being so easily irritated, but a shout didn't seem reflective of my ministerial office. Without me knowing who signed the note, I couldn't speak to the note writer in person to address the matter head-on. Maybe when it came to music, I could make a mental note of different folks' individual preferences within the congregation. Maybe that was the solution. But music being what it is, and folks being folks, there were bound to be plenty of conflicting preferences—so I had no idea what to do. Maybe there was a different solution, one I didn't savvy yet. I was still getting used to this strange life as a reverend. I hoped I'd have a good number of years left to do so.

The note, I crumpled, and used it to light a fire in the stove to take the chill out of the air. I hadn't eaten all day, not since lunchtime the day before, but I wasn't feeling the pain in my stomach. I was feeling it deep in my bones. I went back outside and did overhand pull-ups on the awning until I thought I'd about pass out. Then I came back inside and paced around the parsonage some more.

Long after midnight, I fell into a shallow and restless sleep.

---

Early Tuesday morning I was startled awake at quarter after five when a horn blasted in rapid bleeping outside my window. I was still dressed in my chopping clothes and flew out the front door to check the commotion.

Halligan Barker's patrol car was parked outside the parsonage. Dust still billowed around the tires where he'd slid to a stop. Deputy Roy was in the passenger's seat leaning over and honking the horn. The sheriff was jogging up my steps, a worried look on his face.

"Good—you're already up," Halligan said. "We got a heap of trouble, Rowdy. Real bad state of affairs. C'mon, get in the car."

Roy jumped outside the patrol car and sprinted around to open the rear passenger door for me. He acted like he was doing me a favor, but he looked a mite too gleeful as I hopped in the backseat.

It didn't matter. I was still rubbing the sleep out of my eyes, straining to understand the trouble at hand. Halligan threw the car in gear, stomped on the accelerator, and cranked the steering wheel around. We flew down the road back toward Cut Eye. I wondered who knew what.

"Deputy Roy's car is over at Gummer's getting a head gasket fixed," Halligan explained, the speedometer inching to 100 m.p.h. "He had me pick him up at his place south of town when a call came over the radio. We figured we'd pick you up on the way over."

"Where we headed?" I asked.

"To the café. It's Cisco Wayman. The man's mind took a turn for the worse."

We rocketed up Highway 2 and on into town. Past the tavern, we pulled to the right near the mercantile, screeched to a stop, and jumped out. Already a crowd was forming in the dawn's early light.

Augusta Wayman hurried straight over to us, her face white as salt. "Cisco's got a gun to his head." She pointed to the café. "It's bad, Sheriff, real bad. He keeps calling out for Danny." Her voice broke, but she found it and added, "The only person he wants to see is Rowdy."

The sheriff snapped into action. He ordered Roy to clear the street, shouted at me and Augusta to get behind iron, and buckled on an old military flak jacket—it would stop artillery fragments but not bullets—in preparation to get closer to the café to check things out for himself.

Augusta and I ducked behind the patrol car while Deputy Roy dispersed the crowd. A jeep pulled up and Bobbie jumped out and ran over to us. She shot me a fearful glance, bent down and gathered Augusta in a ball in her arms, and held the woman in a close crouch.

From behind the patrol car I watched as the sheriff snuck to the side of the café. He peeked his head around and glanced in the window, then sprinted back to us behind the car.

"Cisco's in there with a gun all right," Halligan said. "Rowdy, can you still handle a rifle? There's an old Springfield in the front of the car. I want some extra cover. I'm going in. Get set for the worst."

"No, wait—" Augusta caught the hem of his pant leg. "Please try talking to him first, Sheriff. He won't turn his gun on the crowd, I promise. He's not angry with anyone. He asked to see Rowdy. Please. Let Rowdy go."

The sheriff furrowed his brow as if thinking things over, then spoke all business. "The man's not in his right mind, Augusta. You know I like Cisco same as any neighbor around here, but it isn't safe. I'm going in."

"It's okay," I said. "I'll go."

The sheriff glanced my way with a look that said he was still pondering possible plans of action. Deputy Roy was positioned around the corner now, one arm and his rifle in view. His Remington was fixed on the café's windows. The sheriff began to unbuckle his flak jacket. "Okay, Rowdy," he said. "The only neck you lose is your own. At least put this on." He held the jacket out to me.

I shook my head and said, "It'll spook him. I'd rather keep things friendly," then turned to Bobbie and asked, "You got a makeup mirror and a stick of gum in your handbag?"

She nodded, ran to the jeep without quizzing me on why I needed those things, and ran back with the two items in hand. I grabbed them and headed out from behind the patrol car toward the café.

The street was deathly quiet as I walked across it. Sun was breaking in the eastern sky, and a chill blew in the autumn air. The door to the café swung on its hinges and I crouched down to one side. I put the gum in my mouth and began to chew, opened the door a crack, then called out, "Cisco—it's Rowdy. You want to talk with me?"

All was quiet for ten seconds. Then a voice called back, "Yeah. Come on in."

I took off my boot, stuck the makeup mirror to the end of it with the chewing gum, and peered around the doorway by looking into the reflection of the mirror. Sure enough, Cisco sat in the middle of the café, his elbow pointed my direction, a revolver aimed at his ear. His back was toward me, so I brought my boot back, plopped it on my foot, stuck my head around the door frame, and called out, "I'm coming in now, Cisco. We can have a talk, just like you want."

It was only fifteen steps distance to where he was, and along the way I eyed out places where I could duck and cover in case he started to fire. I stayed low and kept my eyes on his trigger hand to gauge the slightest flicker of movement.

"Cisco—" I asked as I was getting nearer. "What's going on?"

The big man's face was blank. Underneath his eyes lay dark circles. His trigger hand trembled.

"I ain't slept much lately. That's all."

I paused in my tracks. A silence went around the room. I decided I'd walked close enough. "Well, I can understand that," I said. "Maybe you want to take the gun away from your head and set it on the floor. We'll talk some more then."

"Can't do that, Rowdy."

"Why not, Cisco?"

"Because there's no hope in me living anymore. That's why."

I swallowed. "How come you say that?"

Another long pause pitched around the room. "Because he's gone, that's why. And nobody cares that my boy's dead."

"Of course we care. We care a heap. This whole town cares. Everybody loved Danny. He was just doing his duty—that's all. Plenty of fellas met the same fate. I've seen them with my own eyes."

"Were you there when Danny died?"

"No sir. But I was alongside plenty of other fellas just like Danny. I saw it firsthand. They were brave. I know Danny was brave too. Nobody's ever gonna forget what those fellas did for us over there."

Another long pause. I kept my eye on his trigger finger. Finally Cisco asked, "You know why I wanted to talk with you, Reverend Rowdy?"

I shook my head. "How come?"

"A spiritual reason. It's because you're a reverend, and a reverend speaks for God."

A drop of sweat ran down my forehead. I wasn't sure where he was going with this and said, "I don't know about that, sir."

"Well, that God of yours could have stopped Danny from dying." Cisco's hands were trembling something fierce now. "But he didn't. So you know what that makes God?"

"No sir, I don't."

"Makes him responsible."

"Maybe so, maybe not," I said. "Why don't you put the gun

down and kick it over to me. We can get Bobbie in here. She studies lots and knows about these matters far better than I do. We'll look up some passages. See what the Bible says."

"No need to involve her."

"Why's that?"

Cisco stood to his feet, swung my direction suddenly, and pointed the revolver at me. "Because killing you will even the score." In a flash, he pulled the trigger.

*Bang!*

His bullet whizzed across the top of my ear. Few men are good shots with a revolver, but I wasn't waiting around for him to aim straight. I was already running, hightailing it out the door, zigging and zagging in a crisscross pattern back across the street. I dived behind the patrol car. All the while Halligan was shouting at Deputy Roy, "Hold your fire! Don't shoot! It's Rowdy! Don't shoot!"

I peeked around the car's fender in time to see Cisco stumble out of the café after me. He held his revolver to his ear again. His trigger hand was shaking something fierce, and if his gun went off again either due to his decision or due to accident then this new bullet would find its mark no problem. He stopped walking and stood still. His eyes bore a crazed look. His finger flickered against the trigger, then paused. He scrunched his eyes tight in preparation for the blast. The man was a split second away from death.

On reflex, I jumped to the open side door of the patrol car, grabbed the Springfield, wished it was a Garand, and aimed at the man who'd just tried to kill me.

One shot rang out.

The Springfield fired true. Cisco's revolver flew high in the air with a zing.

"Go!" Halligan yelled. "Go now!"

I was already running across the street, already tackling Cisco in the gut before he could find his bearings and scramble to pick up his revolver. He went down hard and Halligan piled on right after me.

"Hold him, Rowdy! Hold him 'til I get cuffs on." Halligan wrestled the big man's arms behind his back and snapped the handcuffs around his wrists. Deputy Roy had caught the vision by now and followed up with his cuffs around the man's ankles.

Cisco was sobbing. Stunned. Broken. Hurting.

Halligan held him, cradling the big man as he lay on the ground. "It's all okay," the sheriff said with a hush. "You're gonna be fine, Cisco. Just fine."

---

They took Cisco away, the sheriff and Deputy Roy. Augusta sat in the backseat of the patrol car alongside her husband to give him comfort. His face was blank again and his eyes stared straight ahead like nothing had ever transpired.

"Where will they take him?" I asked Bobbie.

"There's a mental hospital northwest of Rancho Springs. I've visited a few patients there before. He'll get good care until he's better again." She looked me over and sniffed. "You okay?"

I nodded.

"Welcome to the real work of being a minister," she said. "Your calling is to mix and mingle with a world of pain. When folks are hurting, they're prone to take a shot at you—sometimes with a gun, sometimes with just their words—and it's your job to get up inside people's hurt, or else you'll never understand where they're coming from. They don't mean to lash out at you, not really, because it's not you they're actually angry at." She shivered, then asked, "You get bloody anywhere? I can take you over to the doc's if you'd like."

"No, I'm fine thanks. I've seen worse." I tried to smile her direction.

"Where was that exactly—the place you saw worse?"

The girl's question was unexpected and serious, like an honest answer was anticipated from me. She was fulfilling her calling as a minister, entering the world of my pain. I could see the sincerity in her eyes, but still I asked, "You truly care to know?"

Bobbie nodded.

"I guess a year ago from last December, fighting in Bastogne. You heard about Bastogne?"

She nodded again. "Read about it in the papers."

"One of our replacement officers had seen too much blood too quickly, I reckon, because one morning his mouth froze open and he just stopped talking. Rest of the boys didn't think much about it at first. When you're in a foxhole, there ain't much to say anyway. By mid-afternoon the medic took a look at him, and the officer still wasn't saying a word. Then, when the medic left to go tend on another man, the officer just walked away, out into the snow. We were stretched real thin on the line, positioned a hundred yards away from each other, and nobody noticed he was gone until they saw his tracks heading across the road."

"What's that mean?" Bobbie asked.

"Well, it means no one got to him in time."

Bobbie shrugged, searching for the rest of the story.

I sighed deeply. "The Nazis were dug in across the road. A couple shots rang out, and our officer was gone. Just like that. That's how he chose to end his pain—by walking straight toward the enemy—as if that would do him any good. It took two more days of fighting before we could retrieve the officer's body. His corpse was frozen solid by then, and they'd dragged it over a fox-hole to use as insulation against the cold."

A faraway look came to Bobbie's eyes and she stayed silent a long while. Finally she said, "I've got a story for you, okay? You need to hear it."

I shrugged. "Okay."

"I went to school with Danny Wayman," Bobbie said. "He ran

with a different crowd—the boys on the baseball team. I didn't know him well, but in tenth grade I sat ahead of him in English class. When the teacher wasn't looking I used to turn around and doodle these funny pictures on his notebook cover. Smiley faces. Flowers that waved hello. Those pictures always made him smile. When Danny went to war I wrote him every week, telling him hello. Saying that we were all thinking of him. I wrote letters to every boy from this county. Each week I read the casualty lists published in the newspaper. Thirty-two of those boys didn't come home."

I was silent for a while myself with that news. Then I said, "I'm sorry I told you the story I did in so much detail. All it did was make us think of difficulties."

She wiped away the wetness in her eyes with the back of her sleeve, then said, "No, don't ever apologize for talking about hurt—particularly when it comes to the war. I asked you because I wanted to know. It's difficult to hear, but that's the only way I can get my mind around these recent matters of horror: by listening to the stories of those who fought for our freedom, and then by telling those stories in their honor to all who'll listen in return."

---

Bobbie drove me back to the parsonage in her jeep. She didn't even ask if I wanted a ride. She just climbed behind the wheel, and I climbed in next to her on the passenger's seat, and we didn't say another word all the way home.

A million thoughts coursed through my mind after she dropped me off. Of chief concern, of course, was still my meeting with Crazy Ake come that evening. I still didn't see a way out of the plan, but one thing I did have to my advantage now was the Springfield. The sheriff and Deputy Roy had been bustling about caring for Cisco, and I'd plumb held on to that old rifle, I had. I kept the weapon in my hands all the time Bobbie and I talked, and the rifle felt unnatural but necessary. When I'd climbed into the jeep, I kept it across one knee and pointed down toward the road. I took it inside the parsonage and hid it underneath my bed.

I milled about the parsonage by myself for ten minutes or so until it dawned on me that I had another meeting I needed to make this day. It was nearing lunchtime already and I hadn't eaten yet this morning, but I reckoned I'd better get to this meeting as quick as possible. It was with the one person who wouldn't be friendly with a missed meeting. I jogged over to the main church building.

"You're late!" Mert Cahoon said when I walked into her office. "Mighty late! Don't you know I needed to run through the entire attendance chart by myself?!"

"Well, we had some trouble in town, ma'am—" I started to say, but she was having none of my lip.

"You sit right down, Reverend Rowdy. We got work to do, and I'm already late for my mail route. Today of all days is when I needed you here the most, and you failed me, boy. You failed me good."

I sat in the chair opposite the church secretary and set one boot on my knee. I was in no mood for her feisty ways today and I probed for the real reason behind her hurt. "What're you talking about, Mert?"

She shut her mouth tight, and that same mysterious expression appeared on her face, the same I'd seen the day she counted the money from the building campaign. Only this time it wasn't near to a smile like it was then. Again, she looked to have reached a decision in her own mind, but I didn't know what that decision might be. This time I chose to press the matter.

"Mert." I looked her straight in the eyes. "Come clean. What aren't you telling me?"

A long lump went down her throat. "I couldn't believe you'd be late this morning, that's all."

I leaned forward. "I know I'm late. But what's really eating you, Mert?"

She swallowed again. "I wanted to tell you something today—just as soon as I could. I'd made my mind up to tell you, and then you weren't there, so I couldn't."

"I'm here now."

Mert sniffed. "You know my husband, Clay?"

"Of course."

"He's been ailing real bad, you know."

"I know."

"He went for his medical treatments yesterday. I drove him up to Rancho Springs, and he had an operation yesterday afternoon. They needed to fly in a specialist and everything. I couldn't stay with him in the clinic on account of the mail route, but the doctor telephoned Martha at the switchboard early this morning and relayed a message to me. Clay came through the operation fine." She nodded for emphasis but still wasn't smiling.

"That's good news, then, yeah?"

"Of course it's good news!" she snapped. "But this is why I needed you here this morning, Reverend."

I gave her a quizzical look.

She sighed in annoyance. "It's because of the building campaign money." She shuffled in her chair, not finishing her thought.

"Mert?"

"I stole that money," she said. "I stole it all! I stole it to pay for his dang-nabbed hospital bill!"

# NINETEEN

My mouth hung open.

I stared at this morally upright woman, my church secretary who'd selflessly worked to serve the church for the past eighteen years. "It was you who stole the twelve thousand dollars?" I said.

"I'm not proud of it, Reverend, but it needed to be done. I lied to Clay—told him the money came from an encyclopedia sweepstakes I'd won. I know what I did was wrong, but I can't go to jail. Clay's going to need a heap of nursing when he comes home, and there's nobody around here who can do that except me. I'm sorry for stealing, and that's why I'm confessing my sin before you and God. I don't know what else to tell, so that's all I got to say about the matter." Mert shut up entirely.

I exhaled sharply and leaned back in my chair. I could feel my body sagging. The weight of what the woman was telling me was almost too much to wrap my mind around. "I honestly don't know what to do right now, Mert."

"You going to tell the sheriff on me?"

"No."

"That's good. How come not?"

"Because you're correct—Clay will need a heap of nursing. And if you go to jail, that won't help anybody right now."

"That's what I reckoned you'd say."

"Still, you can't go around stealing money." I sat forward in

165

my chair and stared at the woman. The irony of my words did not escape me, but all I could think to add was, "Let's give it a week. A few days more maybe. We'll both set ourselves to studying the situation. Maybe we can come up with a better plan forward—a plan that satisfies both justice and mercy."

Mert nodded. "I best be off, Reverend. Mail's waiting." She patted me on the shoulder, not unkindly, and walked out of the office.

I knew the real reason I wasn't going to tell on her. I'd been in the exact same position as her once—in fact, my secret crime still burned within me. Oh, I was fairly certain Halligan Barker knew the truth, or at least he had a solid hunch it was me who robbed the bank. But I'd never paid in jail time for that crime—not specifically, not in how Lady Justice was bound to see the matter. All I'd done was grown remorseful, confessed the crime to myself and God, and then escaped punishment because of Halligan's bargain. How could I, in good conscience, turn Mert in to the law for doing much the same thing?

My mind whirled—this crazy preaching job was getting harder by the minute. Undoubtedly I had a legal responsibility as a reverend to report an actual crime—which this was, but . . . somehow I couldn't bring myself to report this one. It was too much like my own. Besides, I figured, the church money was gone now anyway, spent on Clay's operation. The church wouldn't get the money back neither way.

I walked outside Mert's office and around to mine. The door was unlocked, same as always, and I sat behind the desk I seldom sat at and took out the big old Bible I kept there. Bobbie had lent me a smaller one to use for study that I kept in the parsonage. But this one held a warm place in my heart. It was the first I'd preached out of, so many months ago now. I flipped to any old random page. My finger landed at the beginning of Jonah. The entire book of Jonah was only two pages long, and right then and there I read it straight through in ten minutes. All seemed like a big fish story to me.

Sure, I got the point of Jonah's story—it wasn't hard to get—but I didn't quite know what to do with that information. Jonah was a prophet of old who was told by God to go preach against a wicked city named Nineveh. Jonah didn't want to do it—fulfill his calling, I mean. He wasn't an eager preacher; he was a reluctant reverend, same as me. So he sprinted the other direction, got tangled up with some sailors, launched himself into a storm, and got tossed overboard from the deck of a ship. A big fish swallowed him whole, and there the man sat and stewed in its juices. I liked how the second chapter began in my King James. "Jonah prayed unto the Lord his God out of the fish's belly." Well, in all the history of literature, that was undoubtedly its crowning understatement.

But then good things began to happen. God heard the prayer and ordered the fish to puke Jonah onto dry land where Jonah got his marching orders again. This time Jonah obeyed. He hiked to Nineveh, told all the folks they was about to be destroyed, and then—this is where Jonah the man turned peculiar in his ways—all Jonah did was sit back with a big grin on his face.

Peculiar indeed. There sat Jonah condemning folks right and left, waiting on God's justice to strike them all dead. But those same folks got busy with their confessions. They turned real humble, dressed in sackcloth to mourn their failings, and dumped ashes on their heads to show sorrow. God saw the city turn from its evil ways, and instead of throwing justice at them, God showed mercy. In the end, those city folks didn't get a lick of what they deserved.

Maybe that's what I was doing now with Mert Cahoon—trying to hold forth mercy to her. She was genuinely sorry for what she'd done. At least I think she was. She was sorry like I was sorry, and the sheriff having mercy on me was similar to me having mercy on Mert.

But, oh that Jonah. That wasn't all there was to his story, for he continued his fussed-up ways. He was like Deputy Roy, wanting nothing except law. A crime was committed, Jonah reckoned, and even now, in spite of the city folks' repenting, God needed to call down wrath on the Ninevites. Jonah got plain mad and worked up a big head of steam. He went outside the city and sat near a wall to sulk. It must have been hotter than a Texas summer afternoon because a vine grew over his head, one that provided a relief of shade, but right away that vine withered and died. Jonah grew so irate he declared a desire to die.

"Well, look at you in all your huff and puff," God said, or words to that effect. "You're so fired up about a dead vine, Jonah. If that's how you feel about something so small as a vine withering, then why aren't you concerned about all the folks in the city? There's a hundred and twenty thousand people living in Nineveh, and you and your outrage want to bury them all."

Jonah didn't have a smart answer to that, I guess, because that's where the book ends—with God's thoughts and not Jonah's. God's question is left hanging, jagged and without a conclusion, a question raised without an answer received. I closed up the Bible, and right then I got a small idea what to do about Crazy Ake.

The vine provided a clue. Not in any mystical way. It was just that the wood of the vine made me think of the wood of the tree stand. One of the jobs I applied for months ago was with the Angelina County Lumber Company out of Keltys, Texas. For years they was known for their selective cutting of high quality Southern yellow pine. *It's the forest behind the mill that counts most,* was their motto.

Well, we could log the tree stand and pay our debts. Replant trees and keep the forest growing. We could pay back whatever Mert took to keep her husband alive, and somehow I could get the church folks to pay back what I owed Crazy Ake too.

Hoo boy. I sat back in instant deflation and rubbed my face

with my hands. It was a foolish idea, and I knew it already. There were a trillion holes with the plan and Crazy Ake would never go for it. Shoot—the church folks wouldn't neither. How would I ever explain to them why I needed to pay Crazy Ake. *He robbed your bank, see, and now I still owe him.*

I put that foolish plan far out of my mind, then ran back over to the parsonage and clattered up the front steps. It was only 1 p.m., and Crazy Ake wasn't set to come around until dark. I wanted to get my rifle ready, to put it in a position where I could reach it easy. If it came to a showdown, then I wasn't going down without a fight.

Now, if I was truly watching over my shoulder for the evil that was following me, I would have noticed that the handle to the parsonage doorknob was warm. Too warm. But I was in too much hurry to reach the rifle. Straightaway through the front door I heard a voice that wasn't mine and knew I'd made a deadly mistake.

"Wasn't expecting you so soon." The voice came from out of the front bedroom, the one with the crib and cots.

I whirled to face the man.

"Take it easy, boy," Crazy Ake said. "I ain't gonna shoot you without my money in hand first." He laughed and emerged from the shadows. "Maybe we could cook up a little grub first. You hungry?"

My heart pounded in my chest. "I . . . I don't keep any food in the parsonage."

"Well, that's a shame. A crying shame. No food except coffee? How about brewing me a cup?"

I nodded and turned toward the kitchen. Another mistake. Such a tiny mistake it was—turning my back on Crazy Ake. Did I really think he wanted a cup of coffee?

A sudden thud sounded on the side of my head. It was one of those star-seeing whacks you hear about in books but can't quite describe until it happens to you. My knees grew soggy but I kept standing. Crazy Ake walloped me again with his rifle's butt. My mind reeled. My head wasn't thinking straight but I spun around anyway and moved to get my guard up. The next blow flew toward my chin. The rifle came at me too fast for me to stop.

He set the rifle down on the floor so as not to damage it, I reckoned. I recoiled, and another blow came to my cheekbone with his fist. I was staggering now, wobbling on my feet. He slugged me in the gut and I was finished. I coughed and hacked and went to my knees, struggling for my next breath. Last thing I remember seeing was his boot fly toward my jaw.

After that I knew no more.

---

"Ain't no cash at all, ain't that right?" came an angry voice.

I struggled to open my eyes.

*Crack!* Crazy Ake hit me bare-knuckled on my face. I struggled to sort out my surroundings. We were still in the parsonage, I could see by the familiar floor, though I was tied now with ropes to one of my hard-backed chairs. A gag was stuffed in my mouth. I tried to glare at him. My mind blurred.

*Crack!* Crazy Ake busted his fist against my jaw again. My head felt on fire. He drug over another chair, turned it around backward, and sat down in front of me. He picked up his rifle in his left hand. He was about three feet away, and I could smell the sweet-ugly scent of whiskey on his breath.

"You think I'm stupid, Rowdy? You haven't gone anywhere since we last spoke. No digging. No tracking. No traveling to old barns. All you did since our last talk was cut trees!" Crazy Ake's voice rose and he yanked the gag free of my mouth. "What have you done with my money? Answer me when I speak to you!"

I spat blood and managed a frown. "How much you wanna know?"

"Just tell me where it went!" He slapped the side of my head.

For a moment I saw stars, then my head cleared and I said, "It's all back in the bank."

"Back in the bank?!" the man spluttered. He was frothing at the mouth again and he stood up, paced from one side of the parsonage to the other, then sat back down and tried to breathe so it wasn't uneven. "Now . . . why in the name of all that's hallowed would our money go back to the bank?"

I tried to steady my breathing. The man was as loony as he was wily, and I knew he didn't want to hear the full truth. All he wanted was a solution to getting rich—and I didn't have one, same as him. What was I gonna say—*Take a seat, Crazy Ake, and lemme tell you a fun story about a war hero turning into a preacher, about a fella overcoming his less-than-stellar past.* I spat again. Well, my past was catching up to me now. The key for me was to be as truthful as possible without revealing more than he wanted to know. I found my voice: "I encountered the sheriff, and the sheriff struck a bargain with me. I need to fulfill my role as preacher for one year, or else he'll come down on me with the full weight of the law. That's what I've been doing this whole time."

Crazy Ake shook, like he didn't have any place to land with this information. "What kind of idiot follows a plan like that?"

"The plan kept me out of jail." I tried to shrug nonchalantly and not reveal to him my changed ways. That was too much information for him to handle in his escalated state. "The sheriff is head of the deacon board. It's a rough town. He reckoned I could do the job."

Crazy Ake slapped my head once more for good measure, then snorted in disgust—"So you're a real reverend. Well, I doubt that." I could see his eyes were working in his head. Working hard. He was already on to the next thing. He didn't want to kill me so much as he wanted his loot, and it takes at least two fellas to rob any place of substance. He wanted me alive more than he wanted me dead.

"I agree that staying out of jail is respectable," he added. "But lost cash is lost cash, so here's what we're going to do. We're gonna finish this job and we're gonna do it right this time. Up in Rancho Springs, I know folks there—and one got his hands on a Kraut 88. Know what that is, boy?"

I nodded.

"His gun's on wheels. He assembled it for me once just to brag. Only took two and a half minutes. It could shoot down a plane if needed. But we don't need to shoot down no plane. All we need is a vehicle big enough to haul it, and that's where you and the DUKW come in." He grinned. He'd already worked out a new plan.

I tried to swallow and spat again.

"The job won't be at Cut Eye this time," Crazy Ake continued. "The bank in Rancho Springs holds ten times as much. We'll wait until nightfall, haul the gun to the side wall, and blow a hole clear through. We'll use my truck as a getaway vehicle, same as last time, but we'll have a third man stay in my truck to keep it running. I reckon we've got a solid five minutes from the time the blast hits to when the law shows up. You and I will sprint into the vault, fill as many sacks as we can carry in three minutes, and shuttle out the loot to the truck in a jiffy. You savvy all that? Answer me, boy. Yes or no."

I paused and knew in the predicament I was in there was only one option I could choose and stay alive. Slowly I answered, "Yes."

He busted me on the jaw with his fist again. "You were a military man, Rowdy!"

I nodded.

He smiled wide. "When you address me, you say 'yes sir.'"

# TWENTY

C razy Ake's truck was parked in the bushes a quarter mile down the road. He left his rifle on my kitchen table so as not to be seen, pulled a .38 special out of an ankle holster around his lower leg, and kept the revolver aimed at my back as we walked down Lost Truck Road to retrieve his vehicle.

"Why you carry a tow bar?" I asked, nodding with my chin toward a mess of tools he kept in back of his pickup.

"For stealing police cars. Now shut up and get a move on. You drive."

Crazy Ake slid into the passenger's seat, and when we got back to the parsonage he had me hitch up his truck to the rear of my DUKW with the tow bar, then come inside while he retrieved his rifle. We headed back outside and he stored his rifle in the cab of his truck for safekeeping and kept his revolver pointed at me.

We climbed in the DUKW and I started the engine, then backtracked down Lost Truck Road, turned left on Highway 2, and headed through Cut Eye with him sitting in the seat beside me, his revolver pointed low and out of sight toward my stomach. His truck rattled along nicely behind us, and to anyone who saw it, it looked like their preacher was giving a neighborly pull to a fella whose truck broke down and needed a tow. Gummer wasn't at his filling station when I pulled up, and I felt a bit of panic brush over me, although I didn't have a plan for tipping him off anyway. I topped up both of the DUKW's tanks as well as the gas

173

tank in Crazy Ake's truck, and we headed northward up Highway 2 for the four-hour drive to Rancho Springs.

The DUKW roared along easily at an even 45 m.p.h. My face must have looked a mess, but Crazy Ake had the good sense to scrunch a ball cap tight on my head while we were still back at the parsonage and throw aviator sunglasses over my eyes. He'd been planning on beating my face for a while, I gathered. We didn't talk none as we drove. There wasn't nothing more to say. I knew I was being commandeered into doing another bank job with him, and for the time being the only plan I could think of was to shut up and keep driving.

By eight p.m. the outskirts of Rancho Springs were in sight, and when we came to a regrettably familiar dirt road, Crazy Ake ordered me to pull off the highway near a thicket of trees. I started sweating something mighty fierce. A man with his connections both in and out of prison was a man with eyes throughout the country, but I confess I hadn't given much thought to who our third party would be until a possum scuttled across the start of a long driveway. We drove the remaining fifty yards up the dirt tracks to our destination and when we came to the front of the ramshackle old pigsty, we screeched to a stop. Crazy Ake stayed where he was sitting and fired a single shot into the air. Sally Jo Chicory ambled out the front door and scratched underneath her armpit.

"Rance!" she yelled, turning into the house. "This one's for you."

Two minutes passed before Rance walked out. He was dressed in army fatigues and carrying a carbine, which he aimed directly at us. He squinted, broke into a long laugh, and called, "So this is your crew!"

Crazy Ake called nothing back but turned to me and hissed, "Get out. Keep your hands where I can see them."

I climbed out of the DUKW and Crazy Ake climbed out behind me. We walked over to where Rance stood near the porch.

He lowered the rifle. Crazy Ake nodded in Rance's direction then cast a glance toward me.

"Rance Chicory, I believe you already know this sorry excuse for a man. We're here to do what I talked to you about last time I came around."

Rance nodded. "When you want to go?"

"Tonight."

"Fine by me, but you trust this scum to do the job right?"

A corner of Crazy Ake's mouth turned up in a smile. "When it comes to Rowdy Slater we've got security. How's the rat doing?"

Rance laughed. "His little cutie-pie is just about ready for work, I'd say." He eyed me closely. "What happened to your face, boy?"

I hated this man with every ounce of my being but kept silent.

Rance shrugged. "No matter. Gun's in the barn. Let's hook up the gear and go to town."

Crazy Ake slapped Rance on the shoulder like an old friend and motioned to me to walk ahead. My stomach was growling something fierce. I glanced toward the house but didn't see no sign of Sunny. Just as well. I didn't want for her to see any of this.

The barn doors felt cold in my hands as I creaked them open. The 88 antiaircraft gun squatted behind the doors. It stood taller than a man, was about the size of an automobile, although wider, and its huge muzzle of a gun stuck out from on top of the mount. Neither of the two men lifted a finger and I surmised they wanted me to do the heavy work, which was no problem. I swung the muzzle rest up to vertical and secured the gun to it, disengaged the gear clutch, released the hand brake, and connected the prime mover to the drawbar. The 88 was a marvel of a killing machine, one that could easily take out a tank.

"All right," Crazy Ake said, surveying my handiwork. "Go get the DUKW and hitch 'er up."

We strode back over to the vehicles and I disconnected Crazy

Ake's truck and let it roll free. Rance let Crazy Ake take a breather and kept his rifle aimed at me while Crazy Ake lit a cigarette and relaxed. I fired up the DUKW and backed it over to the open barn doors. The two greasy apes ambled behind me, smoking and jawing, and I climbed out, checked the gun to see if the recoil, recuperator, and rammer cylinders were filled with the proper oil levels, then hooked up the 88 to the back of the DUKW.

"Okay then." Rance was all smiles. "What time you got?"

Crazy Ake studied his watch. "Time to rob a bank." He grinned. "While we're waiting, your woman got any more of that beef brisket on the stove?"

Rance rubbed his belly. "Might as well fill up while we wait. What about him?" He glared at me.

"Rope or chain. It don't matter to me."

Rance bustled off to a sidewall of the barn where an old horse rope was coiled and hanging, then brought the rope back, knotted my hands behind my back and my feet together with the rope, then tied the other end fast to the German gun. He stuck a rag in my mouth as a gag, then they walked off toward the house together leaving me alone and tied.

Silence fell, except the scurrying around of a mouse somewhere high over my head in the hay. An hour passed and darkness closed in around me as I stood tied against the gun. I tried to think of a plan, even something to take my mind off the job at hand. Maybe there was a poem that Bobbie had quoted to me once that I could remember, a song we'd sung in church, a verse I'd read that would give me some cheer. But nothing came to mind. All I could think was all was lost. Another hour went by and then another. From the open doors of the barn I could glimpse the night sky. The moon rose and another hour went by, and then another. I reckoned it was close to midnight when I heard a screen door burst open then slam shut, and two shadows walked toward me.

"Time to go," Crazy Ake said. He leveled a rifle at my face

while Rance untied me and took out the gag. I spit a few times, rubbed my wrists and ankles to restore circulation, then climbed in the driver's seat of the DUKW. Crazy Ake slid up into the passenger seat beside me. Rance hiked over to Crazy Ake's truck and started it up.

"You know exactly where to go," Crazy Ake said. It was an order, not a question.

The town of Rancho Springs and I were no strangers. I drove down and out the Chicorys' long driveway and kept to back roads until the city's lights came into view. I skirted the highway, then circled around town until I got to the general location of the downtown district, drove across a field, and cut across a back lot. We hit pavement and rumbled along for two blocks, made another right and a left and stopped. We were directly behind the bank. This being a Tuesday night, every soul for blocks around would be home and in bed already, snoring soundly until sunrise the next morning.

Crazy Ake climbed out and motioned to me with his gun. Rance pulled up behind us in the truck, got out, and left the motor running. He brought sacks for our faces, all three of us, and we quick threw them on over our heads. I secured the mount in position by driving the stakes through the bottom carriage. We didn't need to be overly accurate. Rance went to the far corner of the bank then heel-toed his way along the back wall to an area he'd evidently marked out earlier when casing the joint. He fumbled in his pocket, pulled out a piece of chalk, and scratched a broad X on the wall. My target would be no problem to hit.

"Gun's ready," I said to Crazy Ake.

He grunted. "What you waiting for? You wanna take a nap first?"

I placed a shell on the loading tray, swung the tray in line with the axis of the bore of the gun, and pulled the auxiliary trigger on the right side of the cradle.

*Kaboom!*

The gun blew a hole in the side of the bank's outside wall and straight into the inner chamber of the vault. Concrete groaned and shuddered. I could see jagged spikes of rebar sticking up, down, and to the side. Dust and smoke billowed out of the hole.

"Three minutes—go!" Crazy Ake yelled, and handed me a stack of gunnysacks.

I started counting Mississippis in my mind, took a deep breath, and crawled through the hole ahead of Crazy Ake. The hole was big enough for a big man to fit through, but the broken rebar meant a fella needed to duck and shimmy his way around so as to not get cut up. He followed me inside, a flashlight in his hand, and we both got busy. It took a full seventy-five seconds for us to each fill a sack and tie it off. I shimmied through the hole to the outside. Crazy Ake stuffed the sacks through to me to take to the truck while he turned to another sack and kept stuffing.

Rance didn't even look my way when I ran up. The driver's side window was rolled down. He'd taken off his army jacket as he waited and was smoking a cigarette, drumming his fingers on the steering wheel. I threw the sacks in the bed of the truck and ran back to the bank, crawled through the hole, and emerged again inside the vault. Crazy Ake was almost finished with another two sacks, still stuffing in wads of money as intent as a hungry man gobbling up a meal. We were coming up on three minutes. He threw the first sack to me, turned his back, and tied off the second sack.

That's when I spotted my moment of opportunity.

Now, when a fella is fighting another fella in a bar, he doesn't use his deadliest moves. Not the one's he's learned in the service anyway. If a man pastes your jaw in a bar fight, you turn in the most gentlemanly of fashions and paste him back. But if an enemy soldier has his hands around your throat and aims to crush your windpipe, then all the judo and self-defense moves they teach you in boot camp comes flooding back. You strike to hurt then. You disable or kill.

With Crazy Ake's back turned, I reached forward in an instant and chopped above his collarbone at the back of his neck. Immediately he collapsed to the ground. He wasn't dead—I didn't want to kill the man in cold blood. Not yet anyway. But I sent him unconscious. He was down for the count. I grabbed the revolver from his ankle holster, shimmied back through the hole, and sprinted to the truck. We were coming up on three minutes, fifteen seconds. Rance was still smoking, still drumming his fingers, still looking the other way. I pasted him in the side of the neck with the butt of the revolver. He broke like a beer mug and I opened the truck's door, yanked him out, and dumped him to the cement. Three minutes, thirty-five seconds. I jumped inside the cab, threw the truck in gear, and barreled down the road.

Rance wouldn't be out for long, I knew. Maybe thirty seconds at the most. Crazy Ake would be out a little longer, but I strongly doubted if Rance would leave Crazy Ake behind. As slimy as Rance was, he still valued his life, and if Rance left Crazy Ake behind, then Rance would be a hunted man the rest of his days.

I started doing the math. If Rance came to at minute four, then it would take him another forty-five seconds to drag Crazy Ake out of the bank. That meant I had a minute-and-a half head start, tops. The law might have arrived by then, but the boys in Rancho Springs were undoubtedly slow at this late hour. If the law wasn't at the bank, then both Crazy Ake and Rance would jump in the DUKW and chase me down. They would want to kill me at very least, but they'd also be chasing the sacks of money in the back of the truck. That might provide a bargaining chip for me—the money or my life—if it came to a showdown. The truck could outrun the DUKW on the highway, offering me a bit more of a window of time once I reached smooth sailing, but it would take me at least five minutes to reach the highway. Fortunately, Rance and Crazy Ake didn't know I had some things I needed to do first. And their inevitable confusion would offer me yet another short window of opportunity, I was betting.

The truck roared out of town. I hit the familiar dirt road near the thicket of trees and roared up the long dirt driveway to the old ramshackle house. All was still dark, and I parked the truck with the motor running directly in front of the pigsty and left the headlights on so I could see if I needed to. A heap of confusion rolled around inside me, but this one thing was crystal clear: I would do this. I clattered up the front steps and across the porch, pushed open the front door, and flipped on the first light switch I came to.

"What's all this about . . ." came Sally Jo Chicory's sleepy voice from out of a bedroom. I kicked open the door and stuck the revolver in her face.

"Where's Sunny?" I hissed.

"What about Rance and Crazy Ake?" Her words mumbled out of her mouth.

I grabbed the woman by the front of her nightgown and hefted her out of bed. "Where's my daughter! Take me to her now!"

Sally Jo pointed toward the back hall. Her voice grew instantly clearer. "Second door on your right."

I dropped her on the bed, sprinted down the hallway, stopped in my tracks, composed myself, and gently opened the bedroom door.

Walls of bunks lined two of the walls. Sleeping girls were piled two to a bed. The room was filthy. Trash was piled everywhere, and I went to the first bunk and checked the bottom, middle, and top berths. No luck. I moved to the second bunk. There was my daughter, sleeping wall-side in on the middle bunk.

She hardly stirred when I picked her up. A dirty stuffed monkey was clutched in her arms. An old towel lay on the floor, and I scooped that up with her. I made sure the stuffed monkey was still secure in her arms, then carried her out of the room, down the hall, and outside the house. Sally Jo watched me from the window, and I made sure she could still see my revolver. I kept an eye on her in case she went for her shotgun, but I wasn't worried much with Rance not being around for her backup. I opened the passenger's side door, made a little bed with the towel, lay Sunny on the bed, and covered her with Rance's army jacket. The door I closed gently. I sprinted around to the other side, hopped in, circled the truck around, and floored it down the dirt road.

We were on the pavement in thirty seconds. On Highway 2 heading south in another wink. The wind whistled through the open window and I rolled it shut to provide quiet for the sleeping child. I didn't know where Rance and Crazy Ake were at that moment, but I didn't care. I was heading back to Cut Eye, and Sunny was coming with me. As far as I was concerned, my debt to Rance Chicory was long since paid.

Highway 2 is mostly flat and straight. But near sixty miles out of Rancho Springs you hit a few low hills and curves. If I was gonna make a move, that's where I needed to make it. The truck maxed out at 60 m.p.h. That was fine by me. The DUKW would only do 45—and maybe not even that, seeing how they were still dragging the trailer with the gun on it. I didn't know whether Rance and Crazy Ake were in front of me or behind, but I wasn't taking any chances. I kept the pedal floored until I knew for certain otherwise.

Sure enough, about mile fifty-eight I saw red taillights glowing in the distance. I switched off my headlights and slowed to fifty so I could inch up closer. When the vehicle ahead hit the hills I floored my truck again while they couldn't see me through the curves. Before the highway straightened out I roared up behind the DUKW, veered into the other lane and around them, and switched my headlights on as I passed by. Ahead was all flat road south.

Rance was driving the DUKW, undoubtedly still the more alert of the two. I could see his figure shake his fist out the window in my rearview mirror. A moment later the fist clutched a revolver. One flash showed behind me. The shot went wide. Another flash showed. It, too, came nowhere close to its target.

By then Sunny and I were too far out of range. I kept the accelerator pressed against the floorboards and hurtled down the highway as fast as the truck could fly.

# TWENTY-ONE

The hour neared 4:30 a.m., I guessed without a watch, by the time I spotted the lights of Cut Eye in the distance. A streak of pink showed in the eastern sky, and the dark prickly shapes of cacti and tumbleweeds showed as shadows in the desert around us. We flew straight past the sign for the Murray Plant and kept heading south. In another two minutes we were on the front end of town. Sunny was still fast asleep on the floor of the truck.

I slowed to 40 m.p.h., careened past the laundry mat, the livery and feed supply on one side, and the hardware and lumberyard on the other. The needle on the dashboard mentioned the truck's gas tank was nearly empty, but that didn't matter no more—I downshifted and roared right past Gummer's filling station. When we hit Main Street, I took a hard right, shifted into second, and drove past the sheriff's office and jail. Another hard right and we pulled up into Halligan Barker's driveway where I turned off the engine, jumped out, and ran around to the passenger side.

Gently I opened the door. Carefully I scooped up Sunny. She stirred and nestled her head into my shoulder, and I kept Rance's jacket over her for warmth as I headed toward the back door of Halligan's house and knocked. A minute passed and no one came. I knocked louder. This time a light flipped on. Ten seconds later a voice came from inside. "Who's there?"

"Halligan, it's me, Rowdy. Open up."

The door opened a crack and an eye looked me up and down. Halligan opened the door all the way. "Your face is a mess," he said.

"I got no time to explain things fully, Sheriff. Is Bobbie here?"

Halligan nodded. "Who's the kid?"

"My niece. Her name's Sunny. She needs a safe house for a while. Have Bobbie take her to Emma's. I'll pay Emma back for the aggravation as soon as I can."

"No need for payment." Halligan was already walking toward the back hallway.

"Sheriff—wait. There's more. In less than an hour by my reckoning, my DUKW's gonna roar into town. It's pulling a German 88 antiaircraft gun, and the two fellas driving my DUKW are looking for trouble."

Halligan stopped and stared cold. Bobbie appeared in the hallway. She belted a bathrobe around her and rubbed her eyes. "Rowdy—is that you at this hour? What's wrong?" She came closer. "Oh . . . your poor face."

Halligan was piecing things together and snapped into action. "Bobbie, take the child from Rowdy. Use the jeep and take her over to Emma's. Go inside and lock the door. Make sure Emma's shotgun is within reach. Nobody comes out until you hear word. Understand?"

Bobbie nodded. She ran into her room and emerged a minute later wearing jeans and a sweater. She carried a quilt with her, bundled Sunny in her arms, and was out the back door in a flash.

Halligan turned to me. "How many total?"

"Just two."

"You sure about that?"

I nodded.

He ran to the telephone on the side wall. "Martha—you awake?" He grimaced. "I know, I'm sorry about the hour. Look, we got some police business that can't wait until morning. Call Deputy Roy and have him come to the sheriff's station as quick as he can. Tell him it's urgent." He frowned as if in remembrance. "Wait—Roy's patrol car is still at Gummer's. Call Deuce Gibbons first. He's south of Deputy Roy. Tell Deuce to pick up Roy and get them both here on the double. Got it? Good."

He hung up the phone and stared at me again. "Is why they're chasing you have anything to do with the child?" he asked.

I nodded.

"I bet there's more to the story—right? Is it money?"

I nodded again.

He exhaled sharply. "Will these fellas talk to reason?"

"They're beyond that, I'd say, Sheriff. I'm real sorry about all this."

He looked at my face again and shook his head. "Did I make a mistake about you, boy?"

"Probably."

"Well," he said. "We'll sort this all out when it's all over."

He grabbed me by the arm and hustled down the back steps toward the jailhouse. His keys were already in the jailhouse's front door. Once inside, he walked around the desk and headed straight to his office. He unlocked and opened the door and went to the back cabinet where he kept rifles. I stayed right behind him. He wasn't being clear about his plans, and I thought for a moment he was going to lock me in a cell, but to my surprise he handed me a container of clips and a Garand and took three more rifles off the wall along with two more boxes of bullets.

"Consider yourself deputized," he said. "I only got one flak jacket. I'd offer it to you, but it won't do much against an 88."

I said nothing. Already I was examining the M1. I sighted down the barrel and took off the sling. The standard clip for the Garand holds eight rounds. I inserted the clip, released pressure from the top round so the first bullet chambered, and snapped off the safety catch. I was ready.

Halligan's mind was already far ahead of my action. He

scratched a note with a pencil and tacked it to the front door of the jailhouse so Deuce and Roy knew where to find us. We jumped in the sheriff's patrol car, headed east on Main for a block, turned left, and drove a half mile north out of town. He pulled off the blacktop onto the shoulder, circled around, and parked the car across the road.

"Won't stop a DUKW," he said, patting the hood of the patrol car. "But at least it'll give us something to shoot behind."

I nodded.

Ten minutes later Deuce and Roy pulled up in Deuce's car and jumped out.

"Deuce, you're deputized," Halligan said. He handed the big man one of the rifles. Roy took the other.

"What's this all about, Sheriff?" Roy asked.

"Trouble's coming down the road," Halligan said. "We need to stop it."

Roy nodded, jumped in Deuce's car, and drove it south down the highway two hundred yards. He stopped, got out, scrawled a note on a piece of paper and affixed it to the side with a wad of gum, and ran back to us. The sign, we hoped, would alert any drivers from the south to stop.

We all had a lick of time to think just then. The four of us lined up on the south side of the patrol car and pointed our rifles north. There was nothing to do but wait. The first rays of the sun broke over the horizon, and all around us the desert lit up. The cacti in Texas have a wide range of size and color. Blooms can last until late fall. A stretch of medium-sized prickly pears spread out to our left. A plain of Golden Wave to our right. I stared at the swath of yellow and brown flowers that grow all over the roadside in these parts. My mind snapped back to the matter at hand.

Half an hour ticked by. The sun steadily rose. In another forty-five minutes or so, the plant workers who lived north of town would start trickling in, looking for breakfast at the café. Fortunately most of them lived in the apartments and plant housing east of city hall and wouldn't be coming toward us. Time passed on the roadway, and we didn't see so much as a semitrailer come our way.

Deputy Roy exhaled and shifted in his boots. "You sure someone's coming?" He was eying me warily. "Reverend Rowdy, might I ask what happened to your face?"

I looked at the man without knowing how to answer. I was finished keeping secrets, but it wasn't the place or time to start spilling my whole story.

Deuce Gibbons gave me a head nod. "I got a jug of water in the back of my car," he said. "I should have thought of it before now. Help yourself to as much as you'd like."

I gave a slight smile of thanks his direction and glanced at the sheriff.

"Go ahead," Halligan shrugged. "We'll keep an eye out in the meantime."

I didn't want to leave my post, but my right eye was hurting something fierce. Deuce's car lay two hundred yards down the road, the length of two football fields. I set off toward the car at slow jog, the M1 still under my arm.

Sure enough, his trunk was open. A jug of water lay inside. The cork snapped off in a jiffy with a *thunk*, and I started pouring water on my face, down my throat, and then on my face again. A rag lay in his trunk. It looked to be clean enough. So I soaked it with water to keep with me, set the cork back in the jug with the heel of my hand, and closed the trunk.

"Rowdy! Hey—Rowdy! Come quick!" A yell from the sheriff flew toward me.

The DUKW appeared on the horizon, and I started to run up the highway back toward the patrol car. A cloud of dust formed behind the DUKW, and as the vehicle came better into view I saw the DUKW wasn't alone. Following Crazy Ake and Rance was a whole host of patrol cars—Rancho Springs' finest, I wouldn't doubt—some driving on the road, some driving closer to the shoulders of the road. They were keeping their distance, same as we were trying to keep ours. The law had caught up to Crazy Ake and Rance. We were on one side. The lawmen from Rancho Springs was on the other. The DUKW was smack-dab in the middle.

What happened next happened so fast, I could scarcely see it to believe it. Rance and Crazy Ake must have had a lot of time during the slow car chase to plan their next move.

The DUKW pulled within fifty yards of us, screeched on its brakes, and jackknifed with the trailer across the highway. The lawmen from Rancho Springs screeched to a stop behind them, piled out of their cars, and lined up, their rifles pointed at the DUKW.

Rance came out of the cab in a jiffy shooting his rifle both directions. Lawmen on either side opened up. Smoke erupted. I reached Halligan's patrol car, ducked low, and aimed the M1, trying to get a bead on the action ahead. Crazy Ake was outside the DUKW, working on the 88's jacks. I spotted him toss a shell in the chamber. The gun was pointed straight toward us. I realized the grave danger we were in.

"Run!" Deputy Roy yelled. He had his eyes on the big gun the whole time and found his voice first.

We all sprinted south.

*Kaboom!*

None of us were more than twenty yards away from Halligan's patrol car when the artillery hit. The patrol car rolled up in a giant ball of fire and exploded. Deuce Gibbons was ten steps ahead of me, already facedown in the ditch by the side of the highway. I dived in the ditch behind his feet like a baseball player for home plate. Halligan and Deputy Roy were on the other side of the highway.

The bullets flew now. *Rat-a-tat-tat.* Some eager beaver from

Rancho Springs had brought a surplus machine gun with him. Smoke and dust flew all around. The boys from the north were throwing everything they had toward the DUKW. There was nothing our side could do with all that lead spewing our way except bury our heads in the weeds.

In six or seven minutes the fire died down. One loan jasper fired off a last single shot, and silence covered the desert.

"We're coming out!" Halligan yelled. "Hold your fire." I hoped the lawmen from the north could hear him.

Gingerly, the four of us inched out of our respective ditches. The boys from Rancho Springs were already at the DUKW. We lowered our rifles and headed up the road. Halligan's squad car was flipped over on its roof, still blazing, a hole the size of a city's septic field pipe blown through the side door.

The noble DUKW was likewise shot to smithereens. All tires were flattened. The steering wheel was shot clean away. The side plates and armor were pierced like a sieve.

Rance Chicory lay in front of the DUKW. The back of his head was blown away. I wasn't sorry to see that man dead, although I did mourn for what he might have been. Sally Jo would get along fine without him. Undoubtedly she'd keep running the pigsty on her own.

"Sheriff Barker," called out a voice. It was the sheriff from the north. They shook hands and surveyed the scene.

"Where's the other fellow?" Halligan asked. "You got him in the back of your car already?"

"We thought you had him," said the other lawman.

The two looked at each other with blank stares.

It was true.

Dead or alive, Crazy Ake was nowhere to be seen.

# TWENTY-TWO

The boys from the north wanted to take me to their jail right away. Deputy Roy was all too eager to see me go with them, but Halligan said no. He told everybody to back off—he was taking me to the Cut Eye jail, and he was doing it personally to make sure I got there safely. The DUKW was registered in my name and messed up in the thick of the crime, there was no question of that, and some early riser in Rancho Springs was an eyewitness to seeing a third man flee from the scene of the bank robbery who matched my description, so that further cast suspicion my way.

It was no matter. I wasn't holding on to my secrets this time. The bulk of the stolen money was still sitting in the back of Crazy Ake's truck, which was still sitting in Halligan's driveway, and I wanted to tell the truth, the whole truth, and nothing but the truth. But I also wanted Halligan's help in telling it so as best not to hurt him, the church, or the town.

The sheriff drove me back to the jailhouse in Deuce's car and put me in cell number three, the one nearest the window. The door to the cell he left open while he telephoned Martha at the switchboard to tell the doctor to come over and attend to my wounds. I sat on a lower bunk and stared at the wall. When the phone call was over, Halligan brought me a blanket, then walked across the street to the café to bring me a meal. Augusta was still out of commission, tending to Cisco at the state hospital, but their

190

cooks were on duty at the café, and Halligan brought me a bowl of oatmeal, a grilled cheese sandwich, a thermos of coffee, and a slice of apple pie. Only then did he close the door to my cell and lock it, pull up a chair outside it with a pad of paper in his hand, and say, "Okay Rowdy, let's hear it from the beginning."

I told the sheriff my entire story from start to finish. Not a detail I held back. He took notes most of the time. Sometimes he scratched his head. A few times he chuckled under his chin. A few times he growled. A few times he said, "That's real tough circumstances, Rowdy, real tough indeed."

Funny, but I was the only man in that jailhouse this time, I couldn't help but notice. Sure, it was a Wednesday morning, but it cheered my heart a mite to see a stark contrast to when I'd first viewed the jail cells of Cut Eye, so full and overcrowded.

At 8 a.m. sharp, the middle-aged gal with the thick glasses took her place at the front desk, and the jailhouse officially opened for the day. By then, Halligan had heard my story to the end. He patted me on the arm through the cell bars, said we'd work something out, and shuffled back to his office to begin paperwork. The stolen money in the back of the truck was easy to return to Rancho Springs. Not a dollar was missing, so that was a plus. The hole in their bank wall and its vault would take some doing to repair. There was a heap of overtime needed to pay all their lawmen, as well as all the aggravation our gang had put them through. There was the matter of a dead man and the trouble it took to notify his next of kin. Then there was the frightening matter of having one armed robber still on the loose. Rancho Springs organized a manhunt right away, but by mid-afternoon when I woke up from the nap I took in my cell, the gal at the front desk said the fugitive Akan Fordmire still hadn't been found.

Gummer Lopez was the first to visit. He came in the front door, insisted to anyone within earshot that I had nothing to do with the crime, wept over the lost DUKW, and promised he'd find me another vehicle as soon as he could.

Several of the elderly ladies from the church came in after him. They spit in my eye, insisted I'd been preaching heresy all along, and left in a huff.

Luna-Mae visited before her shift started at the tavern, along with Ava-Louise, who brought me a basket of cornbread. Both said they hoped I'd be back preaching real soon. Their particular business was way down since I'd started my job at the church, but they was actually quite happy to see that, yes sir, they was.

In early afternoon, Deuce Gibbons hobbled in on a crutch. He'd taken a small piece of shrapnel in the back of his right leg. The doc had fixed up the big man in no time, and Deuce shook my hand and for at least half an hour we talked about sharpshooting and the right types of bullets. He'd been in the crowd when I shot the revolver out of Cisco Wayman's hand at thirty yards, and he insisted he winged Rance Chicory just below the shoulder blade right before one of the lawmen from the south blew the man's head away. I was getting to like Deuce Gibbons real fine as a friend, particularly seeing as how he and I weren't pasting each other in the jaw anymore.

Deputy Roy filed in and out of the jailhouse most of the day. His patrol car was now fixed, thanks to Gummer's understanding of the insides of an engine, and Roy and Deuce were heading south to go pick up another patrol car for Halligan before the day's end. Insurance would pick up the tab for the new car, Roy grinned the news to me. But the deputy's grin was about far more than insurance money, he said so as much. "I'm happy any time I see a wild-at-heart man such as yourself behind bars, Rowdy Slater. I've never trusted your kind, and you've never been a minister I looked up to, that's for sure."

At the end of day shift at the plant, the fellas in my tree-cutting Bible study all came in to visit as a bunch. Hoss and Cash and Slim and Stitch; Tick and Harry and Hank and Boone.

Breakfast at the Pine Oak Café would be lonesome without me if I didn't get out of there real soon, they all said. We talked about the rising prices of beef cattle and about a piece of new machinery they was putting in at the Murray, and Slim said somebody should pray for me seeing how I was in the slammer and all, and Tick said to Slim, "Well why don't you pray for him yourself, ya knucklehead?" So they started a fistfight right there in the jailhouse, until Hoss jumped in the middle and knocked their heads together. Then they prayed for me as a group, all except Slim, who was out cold on the floor.

After the fellas left, the barmaids from the tavern, the cleanup crew, and most of the working girls filed in little by little. There was Trixie and Dolly, Opal and Marlis, Zelda and Sal. Marlis was excited to tell me about a new correspondence course in bookkeeping she was taking. Trixie was leaving the business too, starting a new housecleaning service that she hoped to market throughout the town. Zelda was reading Deuteronomy and having trouble with all those long lists of this and that. I didn't know what to do there, but maybe Bobbie had an answer.

Mert stayed away all that day. She was at home caring for her husband, explained the gal at the front desk just before she clocked out. Clay Cahoon was still ailing something fierce, although news had flown all around town at his miraculous operation and the lucky break Mert had by winning that encyclopedia sweepstakes. True, I'd told the sheriff all about my story, but I'd kept that bit of information under wraps still. It was Mert and Clay's story to tell, when the time was right, not mine.

Around 6:30 p.m. Halligan brought me dinner. Beef stew and biscuits. Coffee. Another piece of apple pie. The doc came and checked in on me about 8 p.m., and then I lay back down again and stared at the ceiling and sorted out my mind.

I was feeling good about seeing the folks who'd come and visited me, most of them anyway, particularly how so many had stopped in to wish me well. It felt like I was becoming a part of this backwoods town, it did, and a twinge of new and unusual forlornness bounced its way up and down my spine. No, the Cut Eye Community Church wasn't perfect. Far from so. But I came to see that this church and its strange town with its many peculiar ways was reaching into my heart in ways I'd never imagined. Funny but how a man starts wishing he had a job, some stability, some respect maybe, if he's lucky. In my case, the want of a job was only so I could get my daughter out of a bad spot. Then time goes on and the same man starts realizing the job and stability and respect are all part of something larger he wishes for but never knew how to articulate before then. What he longs for is a community of folks he calls his friends and neighbors. That's what Cut Eye was becoming to me.

Still, by day's end I was feeling sad. That's what it was. Here I was in jail again, and the option of me settling in at Cut Eye for the long run wasn't looking like much of any possibility at the moment. I needed to think about that a spell, I did. Because when the sheriff first dealt me into my job as reverend I couldn't imagine myself in the role for long. Being a reverend was so foreign to me. Yet now maybe I could. Or maybe that new thought was in my mind so strongly because all day there was one person I kept wishing hard would turn up to visit. One person I wanted to see most of all, and yet she hadn't come. No, I didn't want Sunny to see her father while I was in jail, so banged up and locked up as I was. I loved my daughter deep and strong, but it wasn't her. Not just here. It was someone else I wanted to see. Yes sir, it was.

I fell asleep about 10 p.m. and slept all night. My sleep was peaceful for the most part. I didn't know the future, although I was fairly certain it wasn't good. I knew I hadn't killed anyone, and that my crimes could be explained away, which sometimes yields leniency when standing before a judge. But I was still an accessory to two armed bank robberies, that was for certain, and this was

Texas. I'd probably get thirty years to life.

Halligan brought me breakfast again the next morning. A court-appointed lawyer was coming into town that day and the sheriff wanted me to walk him through the whole story too—at least the bit about Rancho Springs. The sheriff let me out of the cell so I could go next door to his house and shower and shave, which I could barely do on account of my face being so broken up. A fresh set of clothes was laid out for me and I put them on and headed back over to my cell. All the rest of that morning I stared at the ceiling.

Lunch consisted of a cold ham-and-cheese sandwich and another thermos of coffee. Then the lawyer came. He was a ruddy-faced fellow and was hard to understand on account of him talking with a thick lisp, but he seemed to know his law and told me not to worry—he was reasonably certain he could get my sentence reduced to ten years in prison. Twenty years at the most.

After he left I did some push-ups on the concrete floor of the jailhouse and chewed on the thought of a long stretch of time behind bars. The gal at the front desk brought me over a Bible and I read through the first letter to the Corinthians, finished it, and started in on the second. By then it was dinnertime, chicken tortillas with a side of peas. I was glad to be eating, but it was nothing like when Augusta was at the helm.

At 10 p.m. I did another few sets of push-ups, then went to bed. Thursday was over, and still the person I wanted to see most hadn't come.

---

At 6 a.m. the next morning Bobbie came into the jailhouse.

It was Friday, and a clear, bright sky already showed through the windows. The gal at the front desk wasn't in yet. Neither was the sheriff or Deputy Roy, so it was just Bobbie and me alone together, although I reckoned a few other rough men would be thrown in the clink by day's end, this being the start of the weekend and all.

Bobbie stood in front of the bars for a long while without saying anything. I kept my eyes to the floor. She wasn't sitting and she wasn't pacing. She just stood there looking at me, and I feared she was eyeing me with wariness, like a human eyes a leopard in a cage at the zoo.

Finally she spoke.

"*He that shall live this day, and see old age, Will yearly on the vigil feast his neighbors, And say 'Tomorrow is Saint Crispian.' Then will he strip his sleeve and show his scars, And say 'These wounds I had on Crispian's day.' Old men forget; yet all shall be forgot, But he'll remember, with advantages, What feats he did that day.*"

She looked to be finished, so I raised my head and asked, "Shakespeare?"

She nodded. "Do you know what that poem is about, Rowdy?"

I shook my head.

"It's St. Crispin's Day speech, from *Henry V*. The poem is talking about the glory of noble actions, about remembering deeds past when men fought for what mattered. I think you know something about doing that, Rowdy. *If we are marked to die, we are enough to do our country loss; and if to live, the fewer men, the greater share of honor.* Do you get what it means yet?"

I shook my head but tried to smile. "If I live a thousand years, I'll never understand why you persist in talking in such riddles, Bobbie. You're right full of sassafras, aren't you?"

The girl grinned.

"How's Sunny?" I asked.

"She's beautiful." Bobbie reached into her pocket, pulled out a folded piece of paper, and held it out to me between the bars. "She drew pictures and colored a get-well card for you." Bobbie coughed. "It's for her uncle."

I nodded then looked away.

"My sister's taking good care of her. You don't need to worry about a thing. Emma does really well with children, and already the child's learned a few words. How old is she now, about five?"

I nodded.

Bobbie coughed again. The girl went to the side wall, pulled over a chair in front of the cell, and sat down. "She's not your niece, is she?"

A hard lump went down my throat and I whispered, "How can you tell?"

"It's her colorings," Bobbie said. "Her cheekbones. The way her eyes are set. She looks exactly like you." The girl chuckled. "That is—when your face isn't so messed up." There was kindness in her voice, not sass.

"Sunny's my doing," I said. "She's my blood and kin. I hardly know her, but I love her with all my heart."

Bobbie pointed to the card. "She drew you a sunflower. There's a packet of red licorice whips next to it in the picture and a yellow ribbon. Do you know what it all means?"

Dang it all.

A tear slid out of my eye and down my cheek. I never cry. Not ever. I jumped out of a C-47 into a hail of gunfire in Normandy. I took a bullet in Holland. I spent time in the hospital ward, looking around at all the spent men. One with his leg blown off. One with no jaw. Another burned so badly he hardly looked human. All that time I never cried. But when I thought of my daughter growing up without her daddy, a hard swallow went down my throat. It wasn't me I was crying for. It was for her. Every daughter needs her father. Maybe she could come see me in the state pen sometimes. Maybe Halligan would bring her by. Maybe even Bobbie would, if she thought to visit.

"Thank you, Bobbie," I said. "Thank you for being so kind."

The girl smiled. "You just said my name. You don't say my name enough. I like to hear you say it."

"I'm sorry I'm such a disappointment," I said. "I truly am."

She was gone after that. There was nothing more to say between us, I reckoned. Nothing more that could be spoken by words. I was who I was and I did what I did. A fella could never truly change, could he?

# TWENTY-THREE

Well, in two weeks' time I appeared before a judge. It was only a preliminary hearing and he established a date far in the future for a full trial for my misdeeds in the Rancho Springs transgression—Thursday, March 6, 1947, which would be one week exactly before the end of my year as preacher in Cut Eye.

My bail was set at ten thousand dollars. Halligan spoke up for me and promised I was no flight risk and that he was personally vouching for my character, so the judge lowered the bail to five hundred bucks, which Halligan wrote a check for right then and there.

Halligan drove me back to Cut Eye, and I found that free air blowing in the window mighty easy to breathe. We stopped first at Gummer's filling station. Clay Cahoon drove an old 1932 Chevy pickup truck, which Mert said he wouldn't need for a while. It was mine to use in the meantime. The Chevy ran okay and had those fine swooped fenders coming off the front, and Gummer already had it filled up with gasoline. The windshield was cleaned so it shined spotless, and the level of air in the tires was just plump.

The sheriff took me over to the jailhouse after that. We went inside his office, he closed the door, and we had a long talk. "A bargain's a bargain," he said, and the original deal between him and I still stood. He understood how life had spiraled downward for me and how it made sense that I got tangled up in blowing up the bank in Rancho Springs. Nevertheless, a good excuse didn't forgive my actions none, and for my part in the Rancho Springs transgression, the law would indeed need to sort out what to do with me come March 6.

In regards to my first crime—robbing the bank in Cut Eye— Halligan admitted he wavered on how best to proceed there. On one hand, he was obliged to uphold the law, and now since I'd told him the truth, the whole story, and nothing but the truth, the duty of his badge mandated him turning me in. He scratched his head and explained how it was his duty as a peace-loving community member of Cut Eye, however, that kept him from pulling the trigger on me.

Many of the men in the town of Cut Eye were seeing better days thanks to my work as preacher, Halligan said, and he still had hopes that I might fulfill my year and help turn the town around once and for good. I'd returned all the money for the Cut Eye bank robbery besides, so there was no harm–no foul, and no one except him was wise to my unlawful behavior. He looked me steady in the eye when he said this, adding that he was fixing to keep his mouth shut, at least until my year was up. In the meantime, "Keep proving your worth around here," he said. "You're not doing as bad as you think," and he shook my hand.

I breathed a big sigh of relief at those words and shook his hand right back. Then he pointed to the door and said "git." It was near lunchtime, Halligan had other business to attend to, so I stopped in for eating at the café just by myself, then drove back to the parsonage in the Chevy. Halligan insisted I continue using the parsonage as my residence until my trial was over and the sentencing finished.

I chewed on one more thing. After he'd shaken my hand, he'd mentioned how the night previous the deacon board had held a special meeting to determine my status as church employee. Deputy Roy was all for firing me outright. A few church members had talked to the sheriff earlier in the day and recommended me be placed on "administrative leave," whatever that meant. The three old ladies who hated me wanted me strung up and lynched. But Sheriff Barker had put his fist on the table at the deacon meeting and said this was America—where a man was innocent until proven guilty. That meant I still had my job as reverend until the trial—and to spread the word.

The parsonage was exactly as I'd left it. The loaded Springfield was still under my bed, and blood was still on my floor from where Crazy Ake walloped me. It was Monday afternoon, so I wandered around the place, then went outside to the awning and cranked out a few sets of overhang pull-ups. I hiked out to the pine stand and cut firewood for the rest of the afternoon, drove into town for dinner, then went back to the parsonage and slept heavy.

The next morning, the regular deacon meeting was canceled, seeing how the board had just met, so I drove to the café for breakfast, then came back to the church. Parked sideways in the gravel was a dusty 1934 Plymouth, the world's lowest priced car, so I knew Mert was inside the church office, undoubtedly wondering if I'd show. I strode inside to say hello for our meeting. She was doing the attendance charts, same as always, and she looked up as I walked in.

"You're late," she said.

I gave her a half smile and sat down. "Maybe you were wondering if I still worked here at all."

"I heard. Although I ain't sure you ever worked much around here even before this last commotion of yours." She stifled a smirk, went back to the charts as if I wasn't there, then added under her breath, "I'm doing the attendance by myself today. You best get straightaway to your other duties while your job is still paying for your meals."

"Well, that's not a bad idea," I said, then leaned back in a chair and looked at the church secretary. "How's the charts look anyway?"

I surmised the answer already. Attendance was down a mite. I'd been in church last Sunday and sat in the back row. Bobbie had preached a real barn burner in my absence, and most folks were there except a few of the fellas I'd worked so hard to bring in, which I'd need to follow up on as soon as possible. I reckoned it might take a few more fights down at the tavern.

Emma Hackathorn and her children weren't there neither. Folks was saying Emma was sick, but I knew better. The sheriff had moved them all over to his house until Crazy Ake was found. He didn't want her children talking in public about Sunny yet, for fear of her safety. So it was better for them to all stay at his home for a spell. Gummer was coming by every morning and escorting Emma and the little ones to her day's work at the mercantile. The sheriff himself walked the older children to and from school.

Mert stayed intent on her work and kept her head down. She paused mid-chart only to say, "You best start today by visiting my husband. Clay told me this morning he wants you to come around as soon as possible. He wonders how his truck is doing."

"Is that so?"

"He thinks it needs a new engine. He wants to make sure you've got enough cash to keep it running until it dies."

That was a curious thing for Mert to say. Gummer was charged with keeping all vehicles associated with the church running, and Mert knew that.

"When did you say he wants me to come over?" I asked.

Mert looked up. "Right away. He ain't feeling well this morning, so you best be quick." She wore that curious expression again, and I knew something else was churning in the woman's mind.

---

I climbed in Clay Cahoon's old Chevy and drove east on the Lost Truck road, passing over Highway 2, and kept heading east. Mert and Clay's place was a hundred-acre dirt farm about two miles out of town. A hundred acres was tiny for Texas standards, but it kept them eating when Clay felt well enough to work the fields.

When I drove up the gravel road heading into the place, all looked quiet. The house looked snug enough, although it needed a new coat of paint. A loose shutter swung in the breeze.

I knocked on the door. Clay didn't show, so I walked around to the barn and found it empty as well. No horses or cows. No sheep or goats or pigs. Not even a chicken. I'd never inquired of Mert exactly what she and Clay farmed, but their place looked downright deserted. The barn was bare of machinery and even low on tools and garden implements. I went back to the front door again and knocked.

This time Clay opened. He was stooped and hobbling with the help of two canes. "Come inside, Reverend. Sit," he said with a grunt. "I heard you the first time you knocked but couldn't get to the door in time." He shuffled back to the davenport, sat heavily, and hooked a tube from an oxygen tank underneath his nose.

"How you feeling today, Clay?"

"Had better." He motioned with his head to the kitchen. "Mert made a fresh pot this morning. Care for a cup?"

"Nah, I drank myself wet at the café this morning, but thanks. How'd your operation take?"

"That doctor was a horse's behind." Clay coughed and wiped his mouth with a handkerchief. He coughed again, and this time I noticed a streak of blood when he pulled away the cloth.

"Sorry to hear that."

He held up his hand for me to shut up. He was breathing heavy. "Lemme cut to the chase, Rowdy. Got a question for you, and I need a straight answer. Promise you'll level with me." He looked my direction with expectancy in his eyes.

I looked at him closely. "Sir?"

"Before you were a reverend you spent time in the crowbar hotel, right? Not the Cut Eye jail, but an out-of-state jail? I ain't judging you. I just needs to know."

"Yes sir, six months," and I nodded without being sure where he was going with his questioning.

"Those prisons, the big ones, they got privies in the cells?"

"Sir?"

"A place for a man to turn over his wheelbarrow when he needs to go in a hurry." Clay coughed again. "Bathrooms. I needs to know."

I nodded. "There's usually a commode in each cell, sir, yes."

"And how much moon-floss do they give you in jail? As much as a man needs?"

I checked myself to make sure I understand his terminology then nodded. "Sir, I never ran short of toilet paper, if that's what you're asking."

Clay's chest shook with a long rattle of coughing. His ribs rose and fell and a pained furrow rose on his forehead. "Okay—that's all good to know. Here's why I called you here. My wife told you she stole the church scratch, didn't she? Be truthful with me, Reverend. Did she?"

I nodded and kept my mouth shut to see where he was going with this.

Clay pursed his lips and said, "Well, I got some news to add to that."

"Sir?"

"What my wife told you is wrong."

"Sir?"

"I'll spell it out for you—my wife is a liar."

I squinted my eyes as a question.

"You heard me right, Reverend. My wife, Mert Cahoon, is the biggest liar in Cut Eye." He looked me straight in the eye. "The full truth is that even though Mert Cahoon is a liar, Mert Cahoon is no thief." He coughed so hard I thought he was nearly dead.

"You need a glass of water?" I asked. "I can get—"

"It was me who took that church money, Reverend! I stole it all! Not Mert. She didn't steal a thing." Another long string of coughing followed. "Mert only said what she said to protect me. The wife figured folks would go easier if they heard the money was stole by a gal." He let loose with another long string of coughs.

I stood anyway and walked toward the kitchen, not sure where to land except to listen. He was speaking in those bare-bones sentences, letting loose all his secrets, and a deeper liberty was beginning to spill forth. I called over my shoulder, "I'm going to have that cup of coffee now, Clay. I'll get you a glass of water while I'm at it." I rummaged around in the cabinets and found a cup.

"No water. Get me coffee—" Clay yelled from the sitting room. "Two sugars and a cream."

I found an extra cup, poured his and poured mine, then opened the cupboards. There wasn't any sugar. I opened the refrigerator. Wasn't any cream. Wasn't much of anything—no butter or eggs, lettuce or jam. I stood staring at the empty refrigerator. My mind swirled around what Clay had just said—around that as well as the empty fridge, then I took both cups of black coffee back to the sitting room and handed one cup to Clay. There was no side table to set the cup on, and I looked harder around the room. There was Clay's chair and one other chair. That was it. No rug on the floor. No pictures on the wall. No wood near the fireplace. It's funny what you don't notice when you first walk in a place.

"Mr. Cahoon." I looked him straight in the eyes. "How come you didn't sell your truck too?"

"What you asking, boy?"

"You sold everything else, didn't you?"

He nodded. "Well, I didn't sell the truck because you needed it. Mert needed her car. You're the minister at my church and you needed something to drive. Everything else we could live without. Reckoned it was the least I could do for the church."

"But you got no food. Why didn't you tell someone?"

He looked at me a long time, then cleared his throat and said, "Because we manage."

"Do you?" My comeback was quick. "What's going on with you two, anyway?"

He coughed, looked at the side wall, and sighed. "How old are you, Reverend? I know that's a personal question to ask a man, but I'm curious."

"I was born in 1921. This coming January I'll turn twenty-six."

"You seem much older than your years. You sure you ain't older?"

I scratched my nose, thinking. "I reckon every man who's been to war comes home an old soul. That's what."

He coughed again. "I figured as much. Me, I'll be sixty-eight next month. And to answer your last question, my head feels these days all mixed up, Reverend, if you really must know. I guess it was ten years ago now when I first got sick. No, make that eleven. The first season we paid the doctor's bills out of that year's harvest. That year we got by. The second year Mert started driving the school bus in addition to her duties at the church. That year we got by, too. The third year we began to sell her canning. The fourth year she added the mail route. The fifth year we sold the sheep. The sixth year we sold the cow and the goat." He looked me back in the eyes and coughed again. "We kept getting by."

"And bills kept coming in."

"That they did." He coughed again. "A man stays hopeful for a lot of years. But it was Mert I worried about most. Those bills wouldn't stop. I kept going to the doctor, and those bills kept piling up, and this year we looked around and saw we didn't have no more to sell. Then Martha called Mert at the church and said the doctor had called about a prospect for this operation. That sounded so good to both of us. Mert said we'd afford it somehow but there was only one way, and I didn't want to sell what she was proposing we sell. So I rolled the dice, thinking that would solve all our problems if it worked. I could keep my land. Begin to farm again. Make some money. Pay back what I owed." He coughed. "But it don't matter now."

"What exactly did Mert propose you sell?"

He coughed. "In the back room is a valise. Go get it."

I rose from the chair, walked to the back room, spotted the valise, and brought it back to Mr. Cahoon. I set down the valise in front of Mr. Cahoon but he didn't touch it.

"It's all yours," he said. "For the church, I mean. It's all there— everything I stole plus interest. Count it and make sure."

I opened the valise. Inside were bound bundles of hundred dollar bills.

"Fourteen thousand dollars," he said. "Twelve thousand for what I stole. Plus two thousand extra for the trouble I put the church through."

"I don't understand, sir."

He coughed. "Mert will stay in an apartment in town. I got enough extra to provide a bit for her, and she'll do okay with all her jobs. Maybe she can drop the mail route. She'll be okay."

I stared at him, suddenly putting two and two together.

He saw the surprise on my face and he laughed, a long, sorrowful laugh. Then he coughed and wiped away the blood with the handkerchief. "Here I was all these years sitting on the very thing that would set us free from our troubles. A man such as me loves my land, but here I was holding on to my land and being hopeful at the expenditure of everything else. Even my integrity." He coughed again.

"You sold your farm, Mr. Cahoon."

"I don't need any dirt where I'm going."

"Where's that exactly?"

He removed the oxygen tube from his nose, grabbed both canes, and struggled to his feet. "Drive me over to the sheriff's, Rowdy."

"To the sheriff's?"

"You heard me right. I'm going to jail."

---

It seemed a shame to me.

Here was all the folks in our church raising a heap of money for a building when one of our own families was in desperate need. I said as much to the sheriff later, and he shook his head and exhaled noisily. He called Mert at the church and brought her and Clay into his office at the jailhouse where he talked to them for a long time. I stood outside the door and they talked in hushed voices for more than two hours. When they came out, the matter was settled. The money from the Cahoon's land was going to go back to the church. Mert and Clay both insisted on that, the sheriff told me later. She and Clay were proud people. They hadn't let their needs be known, and that was their undoing, Mert and Clay both admitted, but that was no reason the money shouldn't go toward what it was originally intended for. The sheriff tried to talk them out of it, saying they could find another way, but Mert and Clay both put their feet down.

Clay insisted on going straight to jail. The sheriff wouldn't hear of it, but the Cahoons were insistent folks, so Clay spent two nights in the Cut Eye jail, then returned to his sickbed in Mert's new apartment east of the city hall and barbershop.

Halligan held a special congregational meeting the next Sunday after the service. A few folks wanted to throw the book at the Cahoons. A few others wanted Mert to resign from her job as church secretary, but Halligan said nothing doing.

Mert and Clay came to the meeting. They hadn't missed a Sunday in more than twenty-five years, and they weren't about to start now. Halligan read a letter the Cahoons had written in advance, one where they both apologized for their transgressions. The apology was sincere, I didn't doubt it. And afterward there were a lot of tears and handshaking. Folks hugged the Cahoons and apologized for not helping carry their burdens better.

There was a new sense of resolve that the congregation undertook, a promise to look in better on folks to make sure they were okay. The next week a new visitation committee formed. The folks on the committee vowed they'd raise special funds to help folks throughout the community, and an offering was held right then and there. More than a thousand dollars was raised, with promise of more offerings to come, and the committee set about disbursing the funds right away in a way that could help the folks that needed it most.

The following Friday, Clay Cahoon died. He passed away sitting in his chair in their new apartment in the city, and Mert asked me to take his funeral, so I did. Halligan secured permission from the new owner, and we buried Clay Cahoon on a quiet corner of the land that used to be their property. The burial plot was situated on a low rise overlooking a stream of fresh flowing water that started underground elsewhere on the land and bubbled to the surface and became a brook.

Everyone in town turned out for the funeral. Clay Cahoon was well-known around these parts, and folks paid tribute to a man who loved to work outdoors, a man who loved his wife, and a man who hoped so hard for a better way of living that he grasped for that which he thought would make things right, even though it didn't.

No one excused his crime. There was a ripple of talk that theft was theft, and folks agreed with that, they did. But there was also widespread talk of forgiveness, of understanding that crimes often carry with them a great deal of complexity, and of renewed resolve to care for the needs of Mert Cahoon, the newest widow in church.

---

The day after the funeral, Halligan Barker drove over to the parsonage and knocked on my door. His brow was furrowed and he shook in anger.

"I just checked the county records," he said. "The contract's already notarized, and it can't be undone. But I'm kicking myself for not checking this sooner. You'll never guess who bought the Cahoons' farm."

I shook my head.

"It's an unnamed developer—some big company from out east—but that ain't the half of it." The sheriff balled up his fists tight.

I shrugged. "What's the whole of it?"

"Mert and Clay didn't know anything about what was going to happen to their land. Nobody did, that I can plainly see. The plans have been on file with the planning commission for more than two years, but they were all kept hush-hush at the courthouse. They're gonna build a new tavern. Oh, it ain't just a tavern. It's a monstrosity. This one's gonna be five times the size of the Sugar House. They want to attract folks from other states. It's gonna have a gambling casino and a hotel, and an expanded brothel with girly shows each night. It's even gonna have a full-course buffet restaurant—shoot, it'll put the Pine Oak Café out of business. They're even gonna build an airstrip out back so rich men can fly their planes in and out for a weekend's amusement. The town's going to be ruined, Rowdy. Plumb ruined."

"Can anything stop it?"

"Not a blamed thing. I drove by the property early this morning. A construction crew's already on the location. They came from Oklahoma and they've got three shifts working around the clock. Foundation for the hotel's already dug, and they're already pouring concrete to build the airstrip. They want to get the strip built as soon as possible so they can fly in more investors as they build."

My eyebrows raised to the roof of my forehead in disbelief. "I can't believe nobody knew about this."

The sheriff snarled. "Well, there's been one man who's known about it all along. It wouldn't surprise me if he's majority owner of the unnamed company that's developing it. When it came to the legalities for Cut Eye, this man railroaded the whole thing straight through."

"Who'd do such a thing?" I asked, feeling the tingles of foreboding that I was getting used to when it came to discussing town business.

Halligan spat in the dirt next to my front steps. "None other than Mayor Oris Floyd."

# TWENTY-FOUR

W ell, I waited for my trial, and October passed and November flew by in a jiffy, and then it was December 1946, and the weather turned cold even for Texas. A skiff of snow fell one morning, but by afternoon it was gone. Mostly the ground packed up cold and the wind blew hard from the northeast. Rain fell a few days but it dried up and more wind blew, and at night the wind snuck in through the walls of the parsonage with enough of a groan to make me check and see if the Springfield was still under my bed and loaded.

Right around then we started work on our church building project. Cold ground notwithstanding, the fellas dug the septic field, and the inside walls of the church building were taken down to the bare studs in preparation for insulation and drywall. New gravel was poured and light fixtures and paint was ordered, and we started fixing up the parsonage at the same time. But I confess there was little excitement for the work all around.

With the thought of this new development monstrosity looming right outside our town, folks talked mostly about how Cut Eye would be dying soon. The old Cut Eye, at least. A new Cut Eye was being built, a modern Cut Eye, and big money would soon be flowing up and down Highway 2 with all the greed and corruption that came along with it. There wasn't anything one small community church could do to change things, folks admitted with a kick in the dust.

Across town, the developers worked night and day on the casino and hotel. The airfield was built in a jiffy and airplanes started flying more investors in and out. I hated the development, but I did sneak a peek or two at those planes. There were Beech and Cessna, Aero and Luscombe. Small, single-prop fliers flown by wealthy ranchers and oilmen, businessmen from the city and their attorneys. My favorite private airplane was the Ryan Navion. A brand-new one flew in one morning and I saw the fella and his copilot climb out of the sliding canopy. Although I'd made more than a dozen jumps out of an airplane, I'd never actually landed in one. Maybe in thirty years when they let me out of jail I'd get to fly in one of those shiny new planes and even get to land. I pushed the thought far from my mind.

Oh, all over town, it seemed development sprung up from the backside of nowhere. Roads were plowed through where cows had once grazed. A new apartment complex began. A field was leveled and graveled over for a new parking lot. The framing began in earnest for the main casino building—the one that would hold the new tavern and restaurant. Permits for the business of bringing in dancing girls were still being held up at a state level, but the mayor promised investors that was but a technicality that would soon be remedied.

Right about then Oris Floyd stepped off the church deacon board. He was too busy with the new development project, and besides, the church wasn't doing much advancement by comparison, he said with a laugh. That left just the sheriff and Deputy Roy on the deacon board, so Deuce Gibbons came on, and that meant three, and Deputy Roy allowed for a revision in the church constitution to make it legal.

Church work became more difficult all around. Sunday after Sunday, attendance was down in the services. I gripped the pulpit with both hands and my messages were clear and bold. I kept up the visitation rounds and the men's Bible study, the jail ministry, and the work projects on Saturdays. But it seemed the spark had left. The excitement of changing a community for the better was over. Our church was a fossil of an institution, folks muttered under their breath. An old-time establishment that didn't matter for nothing in a dangerously modern town.

There were a few bright spots along the way. One was that a bunch of the new folks started a new prayer meeting. The old meeting on Wednesday nights continued, but this one happened Saturday mornings, real early. At first only a handful came. Word trickled out and more and more began to join along. There was no great agenda at all. Just prayer. Prayer and more prayer and then more prayer still. That's all we did. Pray.

Of no small wonderment to me, my ministry of counseling folks began to boom, just like Bobbie had predicted it would back when she first showed me the ropes. A middle-aged father stopped by and wondered how he could help his teenage son. The teen was being ornery, making hard choices, stuffing cotton in his ears to all wisdom. I didn't know much about parenting, but I listened to the fella for a long time, just like Bobbie said to do. I listened, and listened, and listened. And then I prayed with the fella. That was it.

A married couple knocked on my door one evening and said they needed to talk. They was fighting all the time, they said, not listening to each other, and I didn't know nothing about marriage neither, but Bobbie had shown me some straightforward verses earlier to prepare for such a knock on my door. *Husbands, love your wives*, I read to them, and when they left, well, they didn't look quite as ornery toward each other anymore, although I figured they'd still have a long ways to go.

Folks came out of the woodworks with all sorts of problems. One man hated his supervisor at the plant. Another fella cheated Uncle Sam on his taxes and now felt remorse. A woman wanted to stop gossiping but didn't know how. Another was just mad all the time, yelling at her kids, saying she felt ready to explode.

Other problems emerged, problems difficult even to talk about. Person after person came to me to unload, and I found it surprising, even startling to learn some of the things that went on behind closed doors within a community. I reckon it's like that anywhere. I asked Bobbie about this—about why the counseling load had suddenly spiked. She said that when folks know the truth of your situation, or at least know you're not perfect as a minister, then they start to open up more about the difficulties they're going through. That, and it was nearing Christmas. Counseling loads always climbed around the holidays, she added.

Gummer Lopez swung by the pine stand one Monday morning when I was out cutting firewood and asked to talk. His need for counsel proved far more pleasant than most. He'd been courting Emma Hackathorn for a few months now and boldly wondered aloud if a fella such as him would ever stand a chance asking Emma to marry him.

"You love her with all your heart?" I asked, setting down my axe.

He nodded.

"She love you the same way?" I asked.

He nodded again.

"What's the problem?"

Oh, there were a heap of problems, Gummer said. She had the children, for one. And they liked him just fine, and he cared for them a great deal, but he wasn't sure if he'd be any good as a stepfather to them. Then there was limited time between Emma's husband passing and now. Gummer wasn't sure if long enough had passed and worried what folks around town might say. Then there was the whole notion of marriage, Gummer admitted. He couldn't rightly sort it through in his mind—being attached to one person for the rest of his life. He loved Emma, but he wasn't sure if he was man enough to go the distance.

"Gummer," I said, looking at my axe blade, "I don't know a hill of beans about marriage counseling, but the way I see it, marriage is kinda like baseball. Last month when Boston beat St. Louis in the World Series, every man in town's got his ear glued to the radio—right?"

He nodded.

"I reckon the problem is you're closing your eyes whenever you see the ball fly toward you—that's what. But when it comes to playing in the series, Providence ordains it. Your body demands it. You yourself want to play ball. So step to the plate, man, put your fears to bat, and swing for the fences."

Gummer left with a smile. I didn't ask him further what he intended to do, but I reckon he'd tell me when he figured it out for himself.

Another bright spot was that Christmas 1946 came and went with no small amount of joyful fuss. Sunny and I spent every breakfast together now over at the café. She was talking up a storm and even reading a few words, and she drew and colored pictures for me every evening and brought them to me each morning at the café. She loved living with the Hackathorn children, and Emma was enjoying having another little girl around, she told me. Emma and Gummer were spending every wakeful hour together ever since the talk I had with Gummer, and I secretly hoped that if they'd get married one day, and if I ended up in the slammer for a long spell, that Gummer would end up raising my daughter for me. There were far worse plans for my daughter's future, I reckoned. Far worse indeed. But those were all in our rearview mirror now.

For Christmas I built Sunny a dollhouse and painted it up pink and yellow and leafy green. Bobbie made for her enormous families of rag dolls and stuffed animals—oh, it seemed like every week a new present went to the child. I borrowed a scroll saw and built Sunny a menagerie of birds to play with too. All the birds of

Texas—bobwhite quail and Inca doves and band-tailed pigeons and eagles and Cooper's hawks, roadrunners and mockingbirds and even a great blue heron.

Sunny's dollhouse was clean and bright, and Bobbie helped me cut out scraps of flowered wallpaper from some she had left over. Together we built Sunny a home she could delight in. We did.

---

The first week of January 1947, Bobbie drove over to the parsonage early one morning and asked me to drive up to Rancho Springs with her to visit Cisco at the mental hospital. I was a mite worried about this, seeing as how Cisco had shot at me last time we met. But Bobbie stayed in constant contact with Augusta, and Augusta said Cisco was making real progress and wanted to see folks, even me. This time there'd be no guns.

Bobbie didn't want to use her jeep for the four-hour drive. The highway was too windy in a jeep, she insisted, even with the soft top put up. There was too much flapping and fussing, and it was hard to carry on talk. I checked the oil in Clay Cahoon's old Chevy truck, filled up at Gummer's filling station, and Bobbie and I headed out of town and up the highway. All was quiet for some time on the road. I kept glancing over at the girl, but she kept silent and looked out the window at the passing terrain. Finally about mile sixty she turned to me and asked a question.

"You know anything about Creole?"

"The language?" I checked the speedometer. The pickup rattled along at a cool 45.

"I need to learn it before I can become a missionary in Haiti. Daddy and me talked it over, and the original plan was for me to head over to Dallas this spring to get situated before the language program begins at the university early in the summer. I need to take a full year of language study before heading to Haiti for the rest of my life. They call it a 'compressed' program due to its starting early. But there's a big question in the mix now—everybody waiting until your trial is over to see what's what. If you go to jail for any length of time, then the church will need to call a new minister, and that can take up to a year. Sometimes two. So I'll fill in wherever needed until the new fella arrives. That may delay my studies some."

I needed to say something, so I offered, "It makes sense for the sake of the town," and checked the rearview mirror. "But I didn't know your daddy had thought this through already."

"My daddy didn't. I did. I know the money's here now for me to go right now, but I volunteered to stay on in Cut Eye as long as I'm needed. What I'm saying is I'm not going to Dallas just yet."

"Well, I guess they could call any ole fella over from the seminary for a spell. If I'm put in jail, then he could work as an interim if you still wanted to go right away." I downshifted as a semitrailer passed us, and the wind from the truck's wash shook our Chevy.

"I guess they could."

"So why you want to stay here?"

"Oh . ." Bobbie fiddled with the door handle. "There's someone I want to get to know better before I leave Cut Eye for good. Just out of curiosity. Just in case." The girl tossed her hair and looked out the window again.

"Who's that—Sunny? I appreciate all those toys you've made for her. I truly do."

The girl didn't answer right away. She looked back out the window for a while in quietness. Then she said, "You're fairly stupid, aren't you."

A snort came out of my nose. "I don't think so. And, no, I don't appreciate you implying that I am. Not everybody can go to university like you."

"This has nothing to do with university, Rowdy."

"What then?"

Bobbie started fiddling with her door handle again. "I got a call from my fiancé last week. He stayed with his folks in Houston over break, so we didn't see each other at Christmastime. He'll be finished with seminary at the end of May and said that would be a good time for us to hold the wedding."

"Oh. So you're asking about the service, then. I'd do it, sure, but I'll probably be in jail by then—remember."

"No, it's not about that," Bobbie said. "It's about me asking my fiancé about what we would do after we got married. He said we'd go to China, of course, same as he has always been planning our futures. He didn't ask my opinion of the matter, so do you know what I said to that?" She was looking at me now. Glancing at my hand on the gearshift.

I shook my head.

"I told him no."

"No?"

"God's calling me to Haiti, not China. I don't want to go to China, and I'm not going to go, even if my fiancé does."

"So you're prolonging the wedding plans then—is that what you mean by no?" I glanced over Bobbie's direction. Her face was set like flint.

"No. That's not all. It means I don't appreciate any man making plans for my life. Any man except God, that is."

The faintest twitch of a smile appeared on my lip. "So what's this have to do with you calling me stupid?"

"It means—" Bobbie grinned and glanced up from my hand to my face and back down. "I broke off the engagement."

---

The tile in the entryway of the hospital was colored green and beige, and I found myself staring at my feet while Bobbie talked to the receptionist. A buzz sounded from behind the glass partition, and a locked door opened to our left as if on command.

Bobbie and I walked through the door and down the long hallway, heading for the room that the receptionist said was Cisco's.

For a state mental ward everything looked sane to me—no bars on the windows or nothing. It just looked like the inside of a hospital building with rooms and nurses. Off to our right lay a commons area with a sign that read, "Activity Room." As we walked by I glanced through the windows. Most folks were in their bathrobes. A few were muttering to themselves and a few others were pacing up and down. Two fellas in the corner played ping-pong. Everybody had real messy hair.

We kept walking. Cisco's room lay at the end of the hallway on the right. Bobbie knocked on the door and Augusta opened it for us. She gave us both long hugs and thanked us for coming. Cisco was doing real well, she said, and invited us into the room.

It looked like a regular hospital room, similar to where I'd stayed when I'd been shot in Holland. There was a bed and some machines with red lights, and on the wall was a painting of a sailing ship.

Cisco was dressed in everyday clothes and sat in a chair by the window. The big man was reading and he looked up when we approached.

"Hey y'all," he said.

"Hey yourself," we said. Bobbie gave him a hug, and I shook his hand.

Augusta pulled over a chair and offered it to one of us, but it was clear by the knitted afghan on it that it was her chair and she'd spent a lot of time in it these past months while caring for her husband, so we declined and both sat on the edge of the bed.

"I'll get right to it," Cisco said. "They're letting me out next week. I'm coming home to Cut Eye and the café. But before I come home I wanted to apologize for taking a shot at you, Rowdy."

"Don't give it another thought," I said. "You were hurting in a powerful way."

"I was out of my mind, that's what," Cisco said. "I've got some pills now, and the folks here have been awful good about talking to me about things. Helping me to see things in new ways, I mean."

Augusta beamed. "He's doing real well, real well indeed." She looked at me. "How's the food at the café been while I been gone?"

"Nothing's the same." I rubbed my belly. "We can't wait 'til you both get back."

They both smiled. We was all being polite, we was.

"Mr. Wayman?" Bobbie said. "I wonder if I could ask you a question?"

"Sure," he said.

"Looks like you've been doing a lot of reading since you've been here. Did you come to any answers?"

"Answers?"

"About God being responsible for Danny's death."

I glanced at Cisco but his face showed no expression. Boy, that Bobbie could sure drive straight to the heart of the matter when she wanted. There was a long pause. Augusta squirmed in her chair.

"No," Cisco said.

"Nothing at all?" Bobbie asked.

"I've been doing a heap of reading, that's for sure," Cisco said. "And I can give you a lot of answers that come out of books, that's probably right. God's not the author of sin; he didn't dream it up, I know that. He allows things to happen for reasons we don't understand, I get that. We need to have faith—of that I'm sure. But the answer is still no."

"I think that's an okay answer to arrive at," Bobbie said.

Cisco sighed. "You know, me asking the question I asked of Rowdy just before I shot at him—the inquiry into why didn't God do something to stop my son dying—there was nothing crazy about me asking that question. The only crazy thing was me shooting at Rowdy after I asked it."

We all chuckled at that, but Cisco stopped chuckling quickly, so we all stopped too.

"I spent a lot of time reading the book of Job," Cisco said. "There's a fella who starts with everything and ends with nothing, and in the end God doesn't give him an answer why it happened. So that's the only sensible answer I came up with. I don't know why God allowed my son to die, and I may never know the answer, and I'm not okay with that. I'm truly not. When I think of Danny, my gut aches deep within me, and I believe it always will. But God is God and I'm not God, and that's the only answer a man is given."

We all stayed silent for a long time after that, even Bobbie. I was okay with Cisco's answer—that in the end he didn't have an answer.

Augusta asked us to pray with him, and Bobbie asked Cisco if that would be okay, and Cisco said yeah, he never minded anybody praying for him. So we did. We joined hands, and Bobbie prayed for strength and peace for Cisco and Augusta Wayman. She thanked God for the blessing they were to our community. And she prayed that God would restore in some way everything that was ever taken from them, perhaps one day far in the future when God would set all things right again. I prayed too, but not nearly as long, and not nearly with so many poetic words.

After we said amen we hugged again, all of us. Augusta promised she'd be back at the café soon. She patted my stomach and said she was worried I was getting thin.

So, that was our trip.

Bobbie and I walked out of the hospital room and down the long corridor and stopped only to thank the receptionist on the way out. When we came to the old Chevy truck I opened the passenger side door for Bobbie to climb up and into, then I walked around the back of the truck and got inside the driver's seat. We sat in the parking lot of the state mental hospital, and I didn't start the engine right away. I stared straight ahead for a while, and then I reached over and took Bobbie's hand. Her hand felt small and soft and yet powerful and determined—all those things all at the same time, and I wished I could tell her more things about what I was thinking. Oh, I did. But I couldn't right then, I couldn't at all.

She didn't take her hand away, and we sat like that in silence for at least half an hour. Then, only because it was getting dark soon and we had a long way to go, I removed my hand from hers, started the truck, and drove out of the parking lot, headed back for Cut Eye.

When we reached Highway 2, dusk fell and I switched the headlights on. The Texas sky was cloudy and darkened, and a twinge of apprehension ran down my spine. Sure, I wanted something I could never get. But the fear was more pronounced than the possibility of what might be transpiring between Bobbie and me, which I knew was an impossibility. Call it a premonition, perhaps, a feeling of dread. If I had any sense in me, we would never have started down that road at all.

For the first stretch of highway heading south, Highway 2 is flat and straight, and you can see for miles in either direction. Our Chevy was the lone vehicle out. Once or twice a trucker passed, but that was it.

Around mile sixty out of Rancho Springs we hit those hills and curves and the road grew darker. The Chevy hummed along at a steady 45. We came out of the hills just fine. The highway straightened out again and we were sailing back to town.

But about a mile out of the hills, I noticed far in my rearview mirror the tiny yellow gleams of a set of headlights. The headlights flickered off for a moment. Or maybe I had just imagined them. No, those strange lights were there all right.

There came that premonition again. That tingle down my spine. I felt the same way before we jumped into Holland for

Operation Market Garden, a series of battles that didn't go as well as we hoped they would. Back then I had every available weapon at my disposal—an M1 and enough ammunition clips to last for weeks. A sidearm and a trench knife and a musette bag full of supplies. But this dark night I was weaponless.

I shifted the truck into high gear and pushed the pedal as far into the floorboards as it would go.

# TWENTY-FIVE

hat's wrong?" Bobbie asked. "Doesn't that driver behind us realize his high beams are on?"

"He knows." I kept my voice low, not wanting to alarm the girl.

"How long 'til we get back to Cut Eye anyway?"

"About three hours."

"Pull over and let him pass then." Bobbie fidgeted in her seat. "He seems in an awful hurry."

"He'd pass us if he wanted to." I kept my speed even.

Bobbie craned her head around and looked again. "He's about an inch from our bumper now. That fool could kill us. Please stop, Rowdy. Pull over and see what he wants. Maybe he's in trouble."

"No, he's not in trouble." My voice stayed low.

The first high-speed bump from behind felt like a little tap. Our Chevy twisted slightly, like it was pushed on the pavement. The second bump came harder. Like momentum was building and the car behind us planned to ram us if he hit us again.

"Rowdy!" Bobbie yelled. "I'm scared. Real scared."

The car in back zoomed up behind us again, looked to come close enough to crash into us, then at the last minute veered over into the left-hand lane. The car switched off its lights and accelerated ahead. I tried to make out the type of car it was as it passed by. The night was too dark to tell, although I caught a flash of the paint job. The sides and doors of the coupe were white. The trunk

225

and hood were a darker color. It looked like a brand-new 1946 Ford Super Deluxe Tudor sedan, although I wasn't certain. I'd seen one of those back when I was drifting through Oakland. The police in that city used them as squad cars.

Ahead of us, the car's headlights came on again, and with it, the driver applied the brakes. We swerved to the side trying to get around him, but he swerved too and wouldn't let us through, then he slowed to a stop right in the middle of the highway. We slowed and stopped behind him. I decided to see what the matter was, once and for all. He sat directly in front of us with the motor running. We sat directly behind him. Neither of us moved. I switched the headlights on bright to get a better look.

A bullhorn showed at the driver's window. The horn was pointed back at us. It crackled, and a loud voice boomed through the night air, though the voice sounded a bit garbled.

"Driver and passenger, step out of the truck!"

"That's a police car, Rowdy," Bobbie said. "I think it's the sheriff from Rancho Springs. That's okay, he knows my daddy real well."

"Stay in the car," I said. "We'll know soon enough."

"Driver and passenger," came the bullhorn again. "Step out of the truck!"

"Show yourself!" I yelled out the driver's side window.

The door opened and a figure stepped out. He wore a sheriff's uniform and had his pistol drawn and pointed our direction, although his hat was pulled low over his face. He stood at his car and didn't advance further. "Rancho Springs Sheriff's Department," the figure called out. "Both of you—get out of the vehicle."

"Were we speeding, Rowdy?" Bobbie said. "I didn't think we were going that fast."

"No, this ain't about speeding," I said.

The bullhorn crackled again. "On the count of three, driver and passenger step out of the vehicle. This is your final warning. If you don't come out, martial action will be taken. One . . . two . . ."

"He sounds serious, Rowdy. Let's get out."

"Three!"

I opened my door. Bobbie did the same with hers.

"Driver, get down on the pavement with your hands behind your back," the bullhorn said. The voice was distorted through the horn. "Passenger, step to the rear of the vehicle and place your hands on the bed of the truck."

Slowly I crouched to my knees.

"Driver lay flat," came the voice over the bullhorn.

I could see by the light of my headlights that the man held a Smith & Wesson square-butt military and police revolver. That meant he had six shots to my none. I lay flat on the pavement and tried to keep an eye his direction. Bobbie went behind the pickup truck. The man walked over and snapped handcuffs on my wrists—that much I expected. But when he snapped them on my ankles too, I grew more than a mite alarmed. In a flash I rolled over, trying to sit up. He was already behind the truck, snapping a third set on Bobbie.

"What are you doing?" I yelled. "Hey—where are you going with her?"

Wordlessly, the figure pushed Bobbie up the blacktop. They passed on the shoulder side of the roadway, on the dark side from me. He was pushing her by the back of her shoulders and speaking low behind her ear. I doubted if she had seen his face yet. He put her in front seat of the Chevy truck and shut the door, then walked up to his patrol car, got in, and backed it up in a lurch so it was positioned behind the truck, although off to the shoulder. He got out and walked back over to where I lay, pulled out his revolver and shot twice over my head toward his own car. The patrol car's headlights shattered. Again I tried to roll into a sitting position. I couldn't see what he was doing now, and the cuffs held me fast.

He walked back to his patrol car. The Ford's grill was smoking, and the night was pitch-black. I heard him opening his trunk. A rattling sound came my direction. He walked up toward our Chevy truck and chained something fast around my bumper. Then he stood next to me. I moved to head-butt him, but he easily side-stepped me. Again he moved toward me, a chain in his hands, and I moved to swing into him, maybe take him down. A boot came into my ribs and I sucked in air. I felt his hands over my hands. Hot. Clammy. He drug me backward to the bumper of the Chevy truck and linked a chain around my handcuffs—the same chain that was tied to the bumper of the truck.

"Okay, Rowdy," the figure said, and I thought I recognized that voice from somewhere. "Let's go for a little drive." He pushed back the brim of his hat and a small red gleam of taillight caught his sideburns.

Only then did I fully realize who it was.

Crazy Ake jumped back in the cab of my pickup, put my vehicle in gear, and took up the slack in the chain. Bobbie screamed. The Chevy truck started down the highway with me dragging behind. I rolled on my back and tried to absorb some of the scraping with my hips. He went only about twenty feet before he hit the brakes and stopped. The handcuffs bit into my wrists and my body ached. I tasted blood from biting my cheek and heard the truck door open. Bobbie was screaming hysterically. "Please stop! Oh Jesus, please make him stop!"

Crazy Ake walked back to me and kicked me hard in the ribs. "You best know that's only a taste." He unchained the longer chain from my wrists and the back of the bumper and threw the chain in the bed of the truck.

I spat blood. "Taste of what?"

"A taste of torment. It's how I'm going to drag both you and your girlfriend along the highway the rest of the way to Cut Eye if you don't do exactly what I say. What'll it be, Rowdy? Answer quick, or I'll hook up the girl to the bumper too."

"We'll do whatever you say," I said.

"Right answer!" He yanked me to my feet and threw me in the bed of the truck, then locked another set of cuffs around the rail so I couldn't move and threw a tarp over me so I couldn't be seen by passersby.

I heard footsteps again in between Bobbie's screams and then heard a slap and a thud. All went quiet, and after that I didn't hear Bobbie scream again. The truck door slammed shut and the truck took off. We began to gain speed down the highway.

In my mind I counted Mississippis and tried to think of a plan. Five minutes passed. Ten minutes. Twenty. An hour passed. Two. Three. We hadn't changed direction, so when the truck slowed and stopped, I reckoned we were nearly back at Cut Eye.

The door opened and footsteps came around to the side and the tarp came off. A rough hand unlocked my cuffs from the rail. He grabbed the lapels of my jacket and dragged me out. I noticed by the headlights we were near the sign for the Murray Plant. I also noticed three large duffel bags tied fast to the rear of the truck's bed, which he must have placed there sometime earlier when he was talking with Bobbie. He clipped me to the truck's rail so I could stand, then hefted out one of the duffel bags from the bed of the truck, shucked off his deputy's clothes, and started putting on a dark-breasted twill suit and a pair of fancy shoes. He took out a can of pomade, slicked back his hair, and grinned. I could just see him in the light of the taillights.

"What did you do with her?" I said. "If you touched her, I'll kill you."

"Relax," Crazy Ake said. "She's still squirming in the front seat with a gag in her mouth. Something I bet you wished for a long time ago."

I spit his direction. He pasted me in the side of the head with his fist.

"You have no bargain in this, Rowdy. Absolutely none. So let me explain my plan and how you're gonna help me get rich. The sooner you help me, the sooner I let your girlfriend go free."

"She's not my girlfriend—and you better."

"First thing is you shut your mouth unless spoken to." He pasted me again, this time in the gut. Again I sucked air.

"Right now, it's a quarter after 10 p.m." He tossed the spent can of pomade into the weeds. "An hour ago four fellas began to play poker two miles from here at the home of Cut Eye's beloved mayor, Oris Floyd. I know you know him, Rowdy, so I won't explain why this is such a big deal. Nod if you follow so far."

I nodded.

"The benevolent mayor is hosting a small party tonight. He's flown in three of his richest friends. One is a Denton Bright, an oilman from Oklahoma. Another is Carl Stanford, a cattleman from San Francisco. I don't know the third fella's name, nor do I care. All I know is I've kept a close eye on Oris for some time now, and he only plays high stakes poker. Real high stakes. The pot tonight will be at least fifty grand. You following me? Nod if yes."

I nodded.

"Good. From here on out, you're on a need-to-know basis." He walked to the passenger side of the truck, opened the door, and yanked Bobbie out. "Say hello to your new partner in crime, Rowdy. She's a real looker, ain't she?" He undid her gag and ran his finger down the side of her face. Bobbie looked absolutely white.

"I'm sorry, Bobbie," I said.

"Oh, don't be sorry," Crazy Ake said. He undid her handcuffs and escorted her over to me. "A fine flower such as this is what makes our plan truly unique." He pulled out the revolver from his ankle holster and pointed it at her head. Bobbie's lips quivered but her stare remained fixed at the man.

"There's a better way of doing this," she said. "A way that doesn't involve killing. You could be a changed man if you wanted to."

Crazy Ake laughed. "Yeah! A much better way. In fact, forgive my indiscretions." He pointed the revolver at the ground. "I only wanted to ensure you knew what true fear felt like. We are not joking around tonight, young lady, and you need to sense the seriousness of our ambitions. I'm not a man to be trifled with, and I will kill if provoked. Nod if you understand me."

Bobbie nodded.

"Good," Crazy Ake said. "Because this is where it gets really fun." He held out the revolver to Bobbie. "Go ahead. Take it. It's reloaded with all six bullets again. Point it at me if you like, but I'd rather you put it in your handbag for safekeeping." He chuckled. "This is where I explain how this is truly a better way. You see, I don't need a gun to get what I want. You're asking why—am I correct?"

Tentatively Bobbie took the handgun from Crazy Ake. She looked at it, nodded, then pointed it at the ground.

Crazy Ake undid the handcuffs around my ankles and wrists. My muscles tensed. I wanted to rush at the man, but I knew him too well to fall for a trap, whatever it was.

"Before you both pounce on me," he said, "let me ask if you know where Pachuca is. Either of you—answer if you know."

"Just north of Mexico City," Bobbie said.

"Correct," he said. "By tomorrow at precisely 12 o'clock noon I will walk into a telegraph office in Pachuca, Mexico, present identification to the clerk behind the counter, and send a telegraph back to somewhere in Texas saying I'm alive, I've arrived safely, and all is well. Would either of you care to know to whom I'm sending the telegraph?"

"Get to the point," I said.

"Tsk, tsk." Crazy Ake was frothing at the mouth now. "I'm sending the telegraph to Sally Jo Chicory. You remember her, don't you?"

I grit my teeth. "What does she have to do with anything?"

"Sally Jo Chicory is how I stay alive," he said. "Because of her you both will not only not hamper my plan to get rich in any way, you will also help me, even protect me. I will become like a rose in your hands. One wrong move, and the petals fall from the flower."

"Talk plainly," Bobbie said. "You're speaking gibberish."

Crazy Ake held up his index finger. His eyes were round as dinner plates. "Patience, girlie—we're talking about what you both love most. You need to know that your father received a visitor this afternoon while you were both up visiting that nut ball at the state loony bin. Well, he did. It was the sheriff of Rancho Springs along with Sally Jo Chicory herself, and I hear that your father didn't take it as kindly as I hoped he would. You see, the sheriff of Rancho Springs could have hauled your father to jail on a kidnapping charge if he wanted. But I understand they're old and dear friends, so he let him be."

"Kidnapping?" Bobbie's eyes widened.

"Yes, kidnapping a poor, dear, five-year-old girl. Susannah Clugman, I believe is her name, although sometimes she's called Sunny. She really is a sweet girl."

"Touch my daughter and I'll kill you," I said.

"No, you won't kill me," he said. "Because this, too, is part of tonight's plan. You see, Rowdy, if you harm me, you will kill her yourself." He laughed. "And that is why a moment ago I gave this young lady my revolver, since I have no need of it anymore." He motioned to Bobbie. "Let me explain. I can see you're confused. The one thing Sally Jo Chicory has held all this time is Sunny's custody papers. The child legally belongs to her and her poor dead husband, Rance. God rest his soul. You might have sired the child, Rowdy, but you never had a legal right to Sunny—ever."

I growled in my throat. Somewhere under my skin I was praying like crazy, but even that praying felt like a growl.

"Sally Jo and the sheriff of Rancho Springs were so glad when Sheriff Barker released the girl into their care. And that's where the child went—straightaway back to Sally Jo Chicory's house. I believe you call it the 'pigsty'—but that's so unkind." Crazy Ake laughed again. "That's why I absolutely must get to the telegraph office at Pachuca, Mexico, by precisely tomorrow at noon." He paused and wiped froth from away from his mouth. "No, I sense what you're scheming, but both her and the child moved to an undisclosed location, and not even I know where she is at this exact moment. But this is the beauty of this plan—and no, it ain't original with me: evil men have been holding folks ransom since the dawn of time. See, if Sally Jo doesn't receive my telegraph saying all is well, then Sally Jo Chicory will slit Sunny's throat."

# TWENTY-SIX

D on't just stand there, Rowdy," Crazy Ake said. "You should
say something."
My limbs shook so hard I could barely keep standing. My
fists clenched and unclenched. My mouth opened and unopened.
I didn't know whether to hit the man or help him sit down and
get comfortable.

"There's another suit for you in that other duffel bag," he said.
"I think it'll fit. We can't have you showing up at Oris Floyd's
house looking like you were dragged behind a truck." He laughed
and looked up and down at Bobbie's figure. "What you're wearing
will do fine."

My limbs found movement and I grabbed the other bag,
turned my back on Bobbie for modesty's sake, undressed to my
skivvies, and put on the suit of clothes that Crazy Ake brought
for me to wear.

"Rowdy, you drive," he said. "I'll sit in the middle. Bobbie
you sit close to me on the other side. You know your way to the
mayor's house?"

I nodded.

"Good then." We slid in the truck. I started the engine and
put it in gear. We turned left onto the road that bore the mayor's
name and started heading east. The headlights cut a dense swath
of brightness in the dark. My head was running like a fast train,
but all I could think was that we needed to make Crazy Ake's

crazy plan work to save Sunny. We'd deal with the rest later.

"How we gonna get inside the mayor's house?" I asked.

"The plan's simple. Straight up the middle—the way I like it. His house is well fenced and he keeps three guards out in front, two in back, and two on each side, so there's no way we can bust our way in. That's where you and your honey pie are needed."

"Call her Miss Barker." My hands clenched on the steering wheel.

Crazy Ake ignored my attempt at a command. "The guards will know your face, so they'll let you pass. Tell them you've got some church business to discuss with the mayor and it couldn't wait until morning. They'll understand that. They won't even care that you've got a busted lip because you're known around town for your indiscretions." He elbowed me in the ribs. "All you need to do is get me safely to the door. Oris doesn't have a houseboy and always opens the front door himself. You ever been inside his house, Rowdy?"

"Never."

"Well that's a shame. Because I have. Plenty of times over the past three months. And my name's not Akan Fordmire anymore, either—at least not as far as he knows me. It's Daniel Q. Farnsworth. The Q stands for Quigley." He grinned like a cat. "I'm an oilman from Bartlesville. Least that's what the mayor thinks, so be sure to call me that all through this job." He pulled out a business card and handed it to me.

"Why do you need us to get you past the gate if he knows you already?" I stuck his business card in the front breast pocket of my suit jacket.

"So many questions, son. It's like this. I need to set him off track. Help him forget his focus. He and the boys will be looking at your girlfriend because that's what men do when a pretty girl enters the room. Plus, I need you along for muscle if circumstances turn ugly, and to help carry the bags when we make our getaway. I need Miss Barker here to carry something important for me, to ensure you work hard, and to add color to the job." He looked at his fingernails and feigned boredom. "Oh, I suppose I could pull another crew together, but I can't trust any other folks more than I can trust you. You know me, and you owe me your life. That's a winning combination as far as I'm concerned. Understand where I'm going with this?"

"I get the picture, yeah."

We were almost at the mayor's driveway. I slowed the truck and turned left. High pillars sat on either side of the road, each featuring a carved ram. A sign over top of the pillars read, "The Trophy Creek Ranch, Cut Eye, Texas." I pulled the truck up the first part of the driveway and stopped at the gatehouse, about a hundred yards in. A fella stuck his head out of the gatehouse, blinked a few times in my headlights, and held out his hand for me to stop. I recognized the man. I'd fought him a few times at the Sugar House but he didn't come to church. He tipped his hat and looked over each face in the truck.

"Reverend Slater. Bobbie. Sir. What brings you to the mayor's house this time of evening?"

I cleared my throat. "We picked up Mr. Daniel Farnsworth here at the airport a bit ago. He flew in from Bartlesville and needed a ride over. Gummer wasn't able to pick him up, so he asked us to do him a favor." I tried to smile. "Worked out well for us, because we've got some permit issues for the church septic field we need to talk to the mayor about anyway."

The fella squinted into the cab and eyed Crazy Ake. "Yeah, I've seen you here before. How are your oil wells faring?"

"Like rivers that never end," Crazy Ake said with a grin.

"That's good, Mr. Farnsworth, real good. Say, I'll need to ask both men to step outside the vehicle for a moment. It's rules, Reverend. I'm sorry. No weapons inside the house." The fella looked at Bobbie. "Ma'am, no need to involve you in this."

"No problem," I mumbled. I set the brake and climbed out. Crazy Ake slid out my side. The fella patted us both down and found none.

"Sorry for the inconvenience, fellas," he said. "Can't be too careful these days."

"No problem," Crazy Ake said. "No problem indeed."

The gatehouse guard nodded again to Bobbie. The revolver was still in her handbag. Crazy Ake and I climbed back into the truck.

"Go ahead," the fella said. He walked ahead of us and opened the gate.

We drove through the gate and up the rest of the long driveway. The front of the mayor's house was well lit by a huge wrought-iron chandelier and six sentry lights on poles. A circular fountain sprayed water high into the Texas air. The house rose three stories above ground and was constructed of alternating gray and red brick. Four high white-painted columns bordered the entryway, and the portico was roofed in a vast triangular shape bordered by ornamental carving. Oris Floyd didn't pay for all this on a mayor's salary, I knew that much.

We parked the truck, got out, and climbed the cement stairs leading to the two white and glassed front doors. Crazy Ake carried the two duffel bags like they were suitcases and he planned to stay the night. I grabbed the knocker and rapped hard. Wind whipped around the sides of the house. I shivered.

Two minutes later the door opened. Oris Floyd was dressed in his ever-present white suit pants but he wore no jacket and had his shirtsleeves rolled up. For a hat he wore a green poker visor.

"Well, well, this is a surprise," he boomed with a hearty voice. "A pleasant surprise indeed. Mr. Farnsworth—we weren't expecting you tonight, but you're always welcome at my table."

"Thanks very much, Mr. Mayor," Crazy Ake said. "You must not have received my telegraph. I had a business meeting end early tonight and thought I'd fly out to Cut Eye and enjoy some of your famous Texas hospitality. Mr. Lopez at the filling station wasn't able to give me a ride from the airstrip, so the good reverend and this lovely young lady were kind enough to bring me over."

"Ah. Come in, come in." Oris Floyd eyed Bobbie and me suspiciously, but he shook hands with Crazy Ake and they slapped each other on the back. He shut the door behind us and added in Crazy Ake's direction, "We've got a card game in the back and you're welcome to—"

"Oh—" Crazy Ake interrupted. "The reverend and Miss Barker won't be staying long enough for games. Miss Barker brought over a message for you, in fact. It's in her handbag." He looked sharply at Bobbie. "Miss Barker, give the mayor the message we discussed earlier."

Bobbie paused and stared hard at Crazy Ake. The mayor was grinning silently and staring at the top buttons of her blouse now. My heart pounded in my chest and I wondered if she understood what Crazy Ake wanted her to do. Sunny's life depended on her jumping into the act.

"Mr. Floyd." Bobbie's lips trembled, her voice barely above a whisper. "The message is that you're to turn around and get down on your knees." She stuck her hand into her handbag.

"What's that you said, sweetie?" the mayor said.

Bobbie pulled out the revolver and pointed it at the mayor. "You need a hearing aid?" Her voice was still low. "Do it now, and no one gets hurt."

The mayor's face fell.

"Miss Barker," he said. "What would your father think of your uncharacteristic behavior? All those Sundays you stood in the pulpit, telling all us about the love of Jesus, and now here—"

"Do as I say—" Bobbie's voice turned calm and she pointed the revolver between the mayor's eyes. "Or the next word out of your mouth will be your last."

The mayor obeyed.

Crazy Ake slipped handcuffs out of a duffel bag and around the mayor's wrists and ankles. He pointed at me and motioned to the hallway. "Through that door you'll find a room with a grand piano. Beyond that is his office. Behind his desk he's got a swivel chair with wheels on it. Go get it. Don't make a sound."

I obliged, walked quickly through the living room and into the mayor's office. Sure enough the chair was there. I carried it back to the entryway in case its wheels squeaked and set the chair down. A gag was already stuffed in the mayor's mouth. Crazy Ake and I hefted the mayor off his knees and into the chair.

"You push," Crazy Ake said to me.

The floors were polished oak, and I slid the mayor, wheelchair style, to the other side of the entryway and turned right into another hallway—this one longer than the first. The hallway's ceiling was high; the walls on either side were painted a pale blue and bordered with white trim. Mirrors hung on the walls every ten feet with high ceiling fans appearing in regular intervals above us. A long carpet lay on the floor and I didn't want to risk catching the lip of the chair's wheels on it, so quicklike I tipped back the mayor's chair to get him up and over, and the mayor passed by with ease. I glanced over at Crazy Ake. He looked positively gleeful. A tuft of hair was sticking up from his pomade-soaked head, and he walked with a jovial canter, as if his life had finally found its deepest purpose.

"Miss Barker, you were a real peach back there," Crazy Ake said, then patted the mayor on the back of his shoulder. "Say, I heard a good one the other day, Oris, you want to hear it?"

Oris Floyd growled from beneath his gag.

"Seems an old priest got sick and tired of all the folks in his parish confessing adultery," Crazy Ake began. "During one of his homilies on a Sunday he looked over his congregation and said, 'Y'all are getting too busy in this here town. If one single person more confesses to adultery, then I'll up and quit!' Well, all the folks in town liked the old priest real swell, so they gathered themselves when he wasn't around and figured they'd get smart and from then on use a code word—fallen—when anyone around town strayed from the straight and narrow. Everything went swell for years, but one day the old priest finally kicked the bucket." A trickle of foam appeared on Crazy Ake's lower lip and he wiped it away. "So they got a new priest. A real young fella this time. And right after he gets to town, he pays a call on the mayor." Crazy Ake paused, patted the mayor on the back of the shoulder again, and added, "That's what made me think of you. Anyway, the priest was real worried and he says to the mayor, 'Y'all need to do something to fix the sidewalks in this town, Mr. Mayor. You'd never believe how many folks confess to me about having fallen.' Well, the mayor started to guffaw, realizing none of the folks had filled in the young priest about their code word for messing around. But before the mayor could explain what was what, the priest wagged his finger at the mayor and said, 'Well, I don't know why you're laughing so hard, Mr. Mayor. Just last week your wife fell three times!'"

Crazy Ake chortled deep in his sideburns. The rest of us stayed silent—including Oris Floyd. At the end of the hallway we turned left, pushed the mayor in his chair another twenty feet, and faced a closed door.

"This here's the game room," Crazy Ake said. "Go on, Rowdy, open it slowly."

I opened the door.

In front of us sat two overstuffed chairs and a couch—all empty. The room's walls were lined floor to ceiling with shelves of books. A red carpet lay on the floor. At the far end of the room was a stone fireplace with a stuffed longhorn above the mantel. A card table sat in front of the fireplace with three men positioned around it all intent on their card game. They didn't even look up as the door opened.

"You want us to deal you back in, Mayor?" one of them called over his shoulder.

"That won't be necessary," Crazy Ake called back as he took the revolver from Bobbie's hand and pointed it toward the card players.

One of the men glanced our way, a man with a waxed mustache. He was heavyset and stood with a start, and the card table jostled as his knees hit its edge. Another man grumbled and swore, then glanced our way and stood up himself. The third took another drink from the glass in front of him, then realized the two men were standing. He glanced around him, then stood up wide-eyed and stared in our direction. All three were dressed in dark suits and smoking cigars. Two of them already looked tipsy.

"What do you want?" said one. We all stayed silent.

"You can't do this," said another. Again, none of us said a word.

"Who are you, anyway?" said the third.

"Just shut up and lie on the floor," Crazy Ake said. "Rowdy, cuff and gag them." He tossed toward me a duffel bag while keeping the revolver aimed at the men. Inside, I found six more sets of handcuffs and three bandanas. I gagged the men and cuffed their hands and feet, leaving them on the floor where Crazy Ake had instructed they lie.

"What now?" I asked.

"Take their loot, empty their pockets. It's simple burglary, Rowdy. Relax and make yourself at home. We've got some time to kill anyway. If we leave too soon, the boys at the front gate will get suspicious and we'll have a shootout on our hands." Crazy Ake walked over to the card table and poured himself a tumbler of whiskey. He kicked one of the fellas out of the way, twirled the revolver on his finger, sat on a chair, and stared glassy-eyed at the loot on the table. "How much would you say is there?"

Already I was going through the last fella's wallet, anticipating the question from Crazy Ake. The rest of the cash was already in one of the duffel bags. "Looks to be about fifty grand total," I said. "Same as you reckoned."

"Good," he said. "Let's take a search around the house—see what else we can find." From the other duffel bag he took out a long chain, the same one he'd dragged me with behind the truck, and strung the fellas together and then to a ring on the fireplace. They weren't going nowhere.

Crazy Ake giggled like a schoolboy at the start of summer vacation. He knew he owned us all. The three of us left the game room and wandered back down the hallway. I noticed a telephone near the entryway, but who could I call, what could anyone do? I kept up a rumble of prayer inside me and I knew from a glance Bobbie was doing the same. In a side room we found some silverware that looked expensive. "Too heavy," Crazy Ake said and passed them by. Another room held a porcelain vase that looked to be expensive. "Too much fiddle-faddle," Crazy Ake muttered, and we kept wandering from hallway to hallway, from room to room. Each room was filled with costly items, but Crazy Ake overlooked them all. Finally he asked, "Rowdy—if you were mayor of Cut Eye and had prime reason not to trust a soul, where would you hide your money?"

"I got no idea."

"You always were the dumb one," he said. "Miss Barker, how about you? Any smart ideas?"

Bobbie got a faraway squint in her eyes and I could tell she was trying to think like a criminal. "*Secretive like the color blue. The robber's den is papered with hue. By and by, all will be dead. All cash lies under a bed.*"

"Emily Dickinson?" Crazy Ake asked. "Or is it Charlotte Brontë?" He was smirking because he knew the names of a couple of poets.

"Radchenko," Bobbie said. "A loose translation from the Russian."

"Ah. Under the mayor's mattress it is. Sometimes the obvious answer is best."

We hiked upstairs and wandered around the rooms. The mayor lived alone except for his guards. I'd heard somewhere they all stayed in a bunkhouse toward the back of the property. Toward the south wing we found the mayor's bedroom. It was layered over in expensive tapestries. A gigantic four-poster bed squatted in the middle of the room. Crazy Ake walked around the mayor's bedroom, picking up items and examining them closely. He sorted through the man's dresser drawers. He splashed cologne on his sideburns from a canister on top of a side shelf. "Any luck?" he called to me.

I had the quilt off the bed already and the mattress turned over. It seemed so stupid, but this was the mayor we were talking about here. Some folks in Texas are so wealthy they don't know what to do with their money. Under the bed there was nothing but lint.

"Well, it can't be helped," Crazy Ake said. He shot Bobbie a dirty look and eyed the bed. "We do have an hour."

"Touch her and I'll kill you," I growled.

Crazy Ake walked over and slapped me gently twice on the cheek. "Don't worry, ya rascal—all that virtue won't go to waste. I'm seldom in the mood for untapped resources anyway, but I thought you might like a quick roll while we wait."

"I told you, it's not like that with her," I said.

"She's not one of the many, eh?" Crazy Ake laughed. "Or maybe she's not one yet?" Bobbie gave me a blank stare. That was something she and I had never talked about before—my background with women—that was one of the reasons I'd been steering shy of her all along. It didn't seem right for a fella such as myself to date someone as honorable as her.

"Let's get out of here," I said in Crazy Ake's direction. "You're making me sick."

Crazy Ake complied, and the three of us wandered back downstairs. We checked on the fellas—they were still bound and tied. Crazy Ake looked at his watch. "It's nearly two a.m. We'll give it to three and then leave."

There was nothing more to do. Bobbie and I sat on the couch. Crazy Ake wandered into the kitchen and came back with an entire grilled chicken, cold from the icebox, and a six-pack of beer. He didn't offer us any, nor was I hungry. I glanced at Bobbie. She shook her head. Crazy Ake drank two beers, devoured the rest of the meat on the chicken, tossed the carcass on the floor, and half closed his eyes. My mind was racing, always racing, trying to think of a way out of our predicament. I had nothing. We had ten hours to go before we reached Pachuca and fulfilled our part of the bargain. Until then, the man had us over a barrel.

Bobbie took my hand in hers, the same hand that half an hour ago held a revolver. It was a sign of her forgiving my past perhaps, or maybe a sign she was worried about our futures. She didn't belong with someone such as me. I was only trouble, all the time. I stared at our hands clasped together and I feared for those hands of hers—I did—the same way I feared for my own.

# TWENTY-SEVEN

When the clock on the far wall struck 3 a.m., Crazy Ake roused himself, stood, and shuddered as if a chill ran up and down his spine. "You folks awake?" he called toward us. Bobbie and I stood. Neither of us had been sleeping.

"The fat fella with the waxy mustache is Denton Bright," Crazy Ake said. "We'll be taking him with us but we need him ungagged, unbound, and full of whiskey first." He turned my direction. "Rowdy, there's three-quarters of a bottle of Jim Beam on the side table. Pour it down his throat. If he threatens to scream while you're pouring, remind him of the revolver I'm carrying."

I grabbed the bottle and walked over to the man. His eyes were round as saucers. "Sorry about this," I said as I undid his gag and began to pour. He didn't seem to mind too much with all the whiskey going in, and within ten minutes the bottle was empty and he let out steady snores.

"Get the chair," Crazy Ake ordered, tossing me the key to the man's handcuffs. "No sense breaking your back under all that girth. We can push him to the front door."

I undid the man's cuffs, rubbed some circulation back into his ankles and wrists, and loaded him in the chair. He was almost double the mayor's size and the chair scraped dully across the room, out the door, and down the hallway to the entryway. Bobbie and Crazy Ake followed. When we reached the front door, the girl opened it, looked both ways, and said, "Coast is clear."

"Good," Crazy Ake said. "We'll take the mayor's Cadillac. No sense us slumming any more than we already have." He cast a furtive glance at my old Chevy.

I hefted the man in a fireman's carry and lugged him outside. The mayor's Cadillac sat near the fountain. Bobbie opened the rear door of the car, and I rolled the man over and plunked him inside. To anyone looking in the window, it appeared the man was passed out drunk and we were merely giving him a ride. Crazy Ake grabbed the duffel bags and put them in the trunk. He sat in the backseat next to the fella, and Bobbie sat in the passenger's seat while I slid behind the wheel.

"Where to now?" I asked.

"Really, Rowdy?" Crazy Ake said. "Your head's as thick as that man is fat."

It wasn't a problem for me to unwire the Cadillac and get it started in a jiffy. I stuffed the wires up underneath the dash, put the car in gear, and headed back down the driveway. The fella at the gatehouse nodded and held out his hand for me to stop. I rolled down the window so we could speak.

"Mr. Denton had a few too many," I said with a nod to the backseat. "We're taking him back to his plane. Mr. Farnsworth flew in on a charter, so he'll be accompanying Mr. Denton back to Oklahoma. They've got some business together in that city. Mayor Floyd told us to use his Caddy for the trip so the men could ride in style. We'll be bringing it right back."

The fella nodded without a word, tipped his hat to Bobbie, and opened the gate. We drove through and down the rest of the driveway, hit the main road, and turned right. When we reached Highway 2 we turned south and headed through Cut Eye. Everything was quiet and dark, and no one was out yet this time of the morning. I hoped we'd pass the sheriff or at least Deputy Roy making an early round, but nothing stirred. The sheriff undoubtedly would be worried sick when he found out Bobbie hadn't come home last night from our trip up to Rancho Springs, but he was a solid sleeper and probably wouldn't be awake to discover the fact for another two to three hours at least.

We passed by the laundry mat and hardware store, the filling station and city hall, the mercantile, the café, the Sugar House Tavern with the school across the street, and the baseball fields. That was the town. Passed right through and I hadn't thought of a solution to our predicament. I glanced over at Bobbie. Her face was grave, her eyes shut tight as if in prayer. When we reached Lost Truck Road we turned left and headed east.

Workers were already out at the monstrosity and working the graveyard shift. The airstrip sat toward the rear of the construction site, and a large corrugated hangar had hastily been built next to it already. The entire site was gated and guarded, and when I pulled up in Oris Floyd's Cadillac, the fella at the gate shot me a snappy salute like I was an officer in the military. I rolled down the window.

"Just taking Mr. Denton and Mr. Farnsworth back to Mr. Denton's plane," I said. "Mr. Farnsworth is going to fly him home."

The guard nodded and we were through. We drove around the edge of the site and circled around to the airstrip.

"That's his," Crazy Ake said. "The Beechcraft Bonanza."

In spite of our dire predicament, I let out a low whistle. It was a honey of an aircraft—that much was sure. I'd read about these last month in a magazine at the barbershop. The Bonanza was brand-new for 1947. This one must have been right off the lot, and already it set the standard for stylish yet well-equipped private planes. Mr. Denton's plane was colored a shiny silver with a red nose and two red stripes down the side. A single prop sat out front. Two broad wings sat on either side like a regular plane. A strange V-tail wing configuration brought up the rear.

I remembered the theory of the V-wing, according to the magazine article. The two surfaces of the wing would reduce weight and drag compared with a regular three-surface straight tail design. This would make the Bonanza faster and more maneuverable in the sky, although some fellas had already nicknamed the tail the "doctor killer" due to a propensity to yield accidents, both on the ground and in the air.

"Leave the fat man here," Crazy Ake said with a thumb jerk toward Mr. Denton. "All we needed him for was to get us on the lot."

"You fly?" I asked.

"Second highest marks at Chanute Field. They trained me on the P-51 Mustang. If I can fly a fighter plane, I can certainly fly this lump of tin."

"How'd you end up in the mortar squad?"

Crazy Ake chuckled. "The colonel's daughter turned out to be fifteen." He tossed me the duffel bag—we hadn't opened this one yet. He carried the other two.

"Let's leave her here, too," I motioned toward Bobbie. "She got us inside the mayor's house, just like you wanted. She doesn't need to be involved anymore."

"No. That would never do," Crazy Ake said with a laugh. "You'd get lonely. Besides, she'd just run home to Daddy and tip him off to where I'm going. Climb aboard."

Time was ticking, so I opened the passenger door on the right side of the plane. It was positioned behind the low side of the wing. Bobbie felt safer sitting next to the door, so I got in first then helped her climb aboard. Crazy Ake climbed in after us and shimmied his way over us and up to the pilot's seat. He set the revolver on his lap. In front of him sat a dashboard full of gauges—altimeter, vertical speed, fuel, oil temperature, oil pressure, amperes—I only caught a glimpse of a few as I snuck a peak. There was only one steering column and it swiveled to either side.

The cockpit looked too snug up front for two large men to sit shoulder to shoulder and I figured Crazy Ake could fly the plane well enough by himself, so I sat in the back with Bobbie instead. It was snug in the back too, and our knees touched side by side. I helped her fasten her seat belt and fastened mine as well. Altogether the plane sat five, but the farthest rear seat had been removed and a small wet bar installed. The sign next to the window read in bold red letters: "Warning: verify door is properly latched before takeoff."

Crazy Ake began to flip switches. The Beechcraft's front prop turned and coughed and its engine sputtered to life. I'd never piloted a plane before; I didn't know what he was doing. Crazy Ake hit some more switches, tapped on the foot pedals a couple of times, and pulled out the throttle, I guessed it was. The plane started rolling down the field. At the end of the airstrip the plane turned around and stopped a moment. All at once the motor roared and the plane quivered and shook.

"Here we go," I said to Bobbie. Faster and faster we rolled until the plane gave a little jump and we were off the ground. I looked out the window and saw the hanger go streaking past. We were soaring through the air now and doing a climbing turn. I could see lights from the town of Cut Eye beneath us. Bobbie reached over, squeezed my hand tightly, and held on. I gathered it was her first time in an airplane.

The plane leveled off and we began to fly what I guessed to be due south. Crazy Ake hit some more switches and a vibrating sound was heard as the landing gear sucked back into the belly of the plane. It felt like we were riding in a car except we were high over what I guessed to be clouds. It was hard to tell exactly where we were because of the darkness all around us.

"Attention—attention. This is your captain speaking." Crazy Ake laughed as he yelled back to us. "Our trip's six hundred miles as the crow flies. The Bonanza cruises about 160 m.p.h. We should be at the telegraph office in Pachuca before breakfast. You like tequila with your scrambled eggs?" He laughed again and looked forward.

Bobbie and I said nothing. For some time we were quiet and my mind churned on various plans. When I played them all forward in my mind, none seemed to work. I stared out the window. The sky was black. Bobbie's eyes were closed.

In about an hour and a half, a streak of color began to show low across the western horizon. It showed as an intense red at first. The red stayed on the horizon and a band of orange lay out across it. In a few seconds the sky streaked with yellow rays. Darkness changed to blue, the scattered clouds became white, and all around us looked far off and immense, like we were hurtling along through heaven itself.

Bobbie opened her eyes, squeezed my hand tighter, and spoke. *"Who hast set thy glory above the heavens. When I consider thy heavens, the work of thy fingers, the moon and the stars, which thou hast ordained; what is man, that thou art mindful of him? and the son of man, that thou visitest him?"*

We were quiet for some time to come, both looking at the sunrise. Then I asked, "Was that Radchenko again—the Russian?"

She tried to smile. "King David. Psalm 8. Don't you ever read your Bible?"

"Not enough, I reckon."

Her voice was low over the engine, just low enough for me to hear her, and I saw her smile fade in the eerie light from the dashboard. "Rowdy," she said, "you ever wonder what Jesus was talking about when he told folks to turn the other cheek if they get hit?"

"I wondered about it a few times," I said. "That was tough teaching for me to reckon with while I was slugging it out at the tavern all those nights, trying to get all those fellas to come to church. I know some folks believe it means we should never fight nor protect ourselves, but I'm a man who's been to war. I've seen how unchecked evil can ruin innocent lives. So I confess I'm not in harmony with pacifist ways of thinking, no."

"I've thought about Jesus' words quite a bit," she said, "and, as a rule, I believe the Bible says what it means. Yet when you grow up in Texas and your Daddy's a sheriff, you learn to broaden some interpretations. I believe Jesus was telling folks to overlook matters of personal insult, not assault, because later on he told his disciples to buy swords. Whether those swords were so they could be classified as transgressors, or for them to protect themselves when he wasn't around, I'm not certain. But I do know one thing for sure—and that's regarding the direness of our circumstances at this moment."

"What's that?"

"Crazy Ake will not let us live. I'm not sure he'll let Sunny live, either. Not when we've come this far with him. We know too much now for him to ever let us return to our former ways of living."

A drop of sweat rolled down my forehead and I clutched Bobbie's hand. "No, you're wrong about that. We will live through this, and so will Sunny. We just need to help get him to Pachuca, then he'll let us go. I don't know how it's all going to turn out, but we're all gonna stay alive. Trust me on this. I didn't take a bullet in Holland just so I could die in Mexico." My heart hammered, and I hoped the words I spoke were true.

Bobbie was silent, her brow furrowed, then she said, "There's another verse of Psalm 8 that comes to mind, and it's not nearly as nice as what I just quoted."

"How's that?"

"*Out of the mouth of babes and sucklings hast thou ordained strength because of thine enemies, that thou mightest still the enemy and the avenger.*"

"What's that mean?" I asked. "All that talk about stilling an enemy?"

"It means," said Bobbie, "that if Crazy Ake hits your right cheek again, Rowdy, that Jesus wouldn't want you to turn to him your left."

# TWENTY-EIGHT

We were three and a half hours into the trip, flying low over the Sierra Madres, when Crazy Ake pulled out a bungee cord from the side compartment near the window, and tied the controls fast. We were flying low on purpose, Crazy Ake had explained earlier during one of his many rants, since it was harder for radar to pick up our location. With the plane now on a crude sort of autopilot, he turned around from the front seat and stared at us, the revolver in his left hand.

He didn't move or lunge. All he did for about five minutes was hold his gaze steady. The foam out his mouth was dribbling again although he hadn't told a story in at least half an hour, and I glanced out the window to gain our bearings and saw the craggy formations underneath us in the morning sunlight. The land looked to be weathered by long periods of sun and erosion. Large blocks of plateaus were lifted up out of the ground, and deep gorges were formed in the valleys between peaks of rock. The entire earth below looked angular and full of canyons.

"Well, it's time at last," he said finally while looking at his watch. "Look behind you in that big duffel bag—the one we ain't touched yet."

"Time for what?" I asked.

"Time for you to keep doing what I say. We can't waltz up to any old airport in a stolen aircraft. But I've been anticipating this all along. Exactly three minutes from now we'll come to an area of some deep outcroppings. The locals call it Cañón de Fresa—the Strawberry Canyon. We'll find a Ford pickup waiting for us at the bottom. The keys are inside, hidden under the seat. It's a straight shot on a dirt road south to Highway 85. That'll lead us all the way into Pachuca. When we get to Pachuca, we need to send a message to Sally Jo at the Rancho Springs telegraph office."

"She'll be at the Rancho Springs office?" I said. "How come you're telling us her whereabouts now?"

"As a gentleman and a crook, I am both unoriginal and cheap," said Crazy Ake. "When I ordered Sally Jo to drive around with Sunny all day, she wanted extra for gas money." He laughed. "That wasn't going to happen, so I told her just to go park in the shade, and then drive over to Rancho Springs at noon. I'm telling you this because I want you to know I'm a man of my word, rotten to the core though I may be. There's the thin chance one of us ain't gonna survive this next step of the plan, and although I'm no stranger to murdering folks, you were my cellmate once, and decent about it. Besides, I don't want the ghost of your dead daughter haunting me the rest of my life."

I was thankful for the slim revelation, but still I began to sweat, sensing what lay before us next. I needed to ask to make sure. "Just how you propose we reach a deep canyon while flying in an airplane?"

"We won't by flying in, of course, which should be no problem for an ex-paratrooper such as yourself. As for the young lady—" He glanced at Bobbie. "I'm afraid the first time jumping out of an airplane can come as quite a shock. Inside that last duffel bag are three parachutes, Rowdy. I packed them myself. Get 'em out."

I glanced at Bobbie. Her face was expressionless and she stared straight into Crazy Ake's eyes.

Leisurely, the man looked at his watch again. He turned forward and examined the gauges, then turned back to us. "In precisely sixty seconds, I'm going to drop this bird another two hundred feet and we'll all exit the plane. We need to exit the plane quickly because once we do, the plane will slam headlong into the hard side of the next mountain. That, again, dear friends, is all part of the plan. A burned plane means no bodies are found—and that's only good for us when the law gets antsy to look for the loot."

"What are we waiting for?!" My mind snapped into gear and my head was already craned around behind us in an effort to rummage the chutes out of the duffel bag. I passed one up to Crazy Ake, threw mine on, and helped Bobbie buckle hers.

"Rowdy!" Bobbie said, her face white. "I'm not sure I can do this."

I heard Crazy Ake back at the controls, muscling the plane lower in altitude. A long drone sounded as the plane dropped quickly. Time was wasting.

"Yes you can!" I said back to Bobbie. "It's just like when we jumped off the running path into the river. I'll place your hand directly overtop the rip cord. After you jump, you count three Missisippis in your mind, then pull the cord. You'll feel a powerful tug, but after that it's an easy glide to the bottom. I'll be right by your side the whole way."

"No," she said. Her voice trembled. "I don't think I can do this today. Maybe tomorrow."

"Plane's level!" Crazy Ake's leisurely tone vanished. "Twenty seconds to impact!"

He was wrestling to buckle himself into his chute, and I turned my head his direction a moment to judge his success. In a flash I saw him take the other duffel bag, the one filled with cash, lay it against his chest, and buckle it securely to him with two sets of handcuffs. "Ten seconds!" he yelled. With a charge, he shimmied over the seatback, kicked open the side door, and propped it open. The wind howled past the aircraft's opening. His body lay halfway overtop of us in his effort to reach the door. There wasn't much room in the backseat to begin with. A gob of froth stuck to his bottom lip. "Five seconds."

"Go!" I yelled. "Go!" Crazy Ake jumped first. I slapped Bobbie's chute to signal okay, pushed her out, then jumped myself.

In those first few split seconds after jumping out of the Beechcraft, nothing existed. No feeling of falling. No rush. No markers or indications of orientation. Just streaming straight down. In the whirl of air, I saw two images almost simultaneously—one by glancing up and the other by glancing down. The first was the plane slamming into the face of the mountain. The Beechcraft exploded in an orb of fire, as colorful as the sunrise we'd viewed a few hours earlier. The second was Bobbie's chute opening below me. The girl had found her courage, and I knew she was going to be okay.

We'd jumped so low, the ground was nearly upon us. I could see it rushing straight at me with the power of a freight train. I pulled my cord. Instantly I felt a pop and a jerk then looked up into the silk to check that all twenty-eight panels were still there. Blow too many, and you fall too fast. I swung back and forth, the only sound in my ears a rush of wind around the chute.

The ground hit. My legs buckled beneath me. I lost sight of Bobbie. I was tumbling, rolling, falling, bouncing. We'd all hit the ground at an angle against the side of a valley, and I had the good sense to clutch myself into a ball and raise my arms up against the sides of my head. Something brown and prickly whooshed by my face and I closed my eyes, bounced twice, hit my head against something hard, and saw black.

I was out for only a minute. Blood ran in my mouth and my sight line was blurry when I looked into the distance. The terrain was sun scorched and waterless, although somewhere within my hearing I heard the faraway burble of a brook. All else was silent. I couldn't fathom how strawberries ever grew in this grassless canyon, an arid wasteland so full of desolation and rock, if that's indeed where we'd landed—in Strawberry Canyon.

Gingerly I fingered my way along my legs and ribs. No bones felt broken although at the back of my head my hand passed over a large lump forming. My gaze shook, then became clear. I tried to stand, sunk to my knees, then tried again.

Far in the distance stood Bobbie. She was wrestling with the back of her chute, trying to free herself, and as I walked toward her she stepped out of the silk and walked forward a few steps, then went and sat on a small rise that overlooked a waterfall. Sure enough it was a brook, but a brook that tumbled through brown boulders. She gazed far off into nowhere, and I noticed how her hair was the color of honey. Her skin like a peach. She was quizzical and wide-eyed and looked like she could have been the mother of my child.

Crazy Ake was next to her in a jiffy. He was already out of his chute, too, twirling the revolver with his finger. I managed to make my legs keep working and ambled over, sat down a short distance away to catch my bearings, and looked at them out of the corner of my eye.

"Good—you ain't dead," Crazy Ake called. "Let's get going—time's wasting. At the bottom of those falls lies a road. Our truck sits on that road. Let's move."

Bobbie and I both stood up. I wobbled, but I asked her if she was okay.

"I could write a thousand poems," she said, "and never describe that feeling of jumping out of a plane. I'm fine, yeah, but you look like you could lay down a spell. How's your head?"

"I'll be all right."

Crazy Ake hiked behind us as we wound our way downhill around rocks and boulders. Sure enough, the truck sat parked where he said it would be.

He threw the duffel bag with the money in the back, opened

the driver's side door, pocketed the keys, and pulled out a rifle from underneath the seat. It was an M1, same as I was used to, and he checked the clip to make sure it was full, and tucked his revolver in his belt. He walked forward ten paces, drew a line in the sand with the toe of his boot, and walked back. Bobbie and I both stood near the truck.

"Well, you've both got grit," Crazy Ake said. "That was good to see—not that I ever questioned yours, Rowdy. But I'm afraid I need to ask you both one more question before we can proceed any further today, and I'm sorry I didn't tell you about this before, I truly am. But I doubt if you would have helped me get so far and so kindly if you knew this lay ahead."

"What question?" I asked. My voice was flat.

"A question of great importance," Crazy Ake said. "The question of loyalty. I need to know right now—without a shadow of a doubt—if you're both in or out."

He pointed the rifle our direction and motioned to the line in the sand.

Bobbie and I stared at him with quizzical looks, wondering exactly what he meant.

"This has always been about more than money," Crazy Ake said. "You know that. Money makes it all happen, but it's about me running the system, same as I did in jail—and I can't do that alone, particularly on the outside. I need my sergeants, Rowdy, same as I once had. You savvy what I'm saying? I know you do. I'm just not so sure your girlfriend does."

"Point your rifle down," I said. "I ain't never been one of your sergeants, and time's wasting besides. We need to get to the telegraph office quick."

Crazy Ake laughed and licked the foam from his lips. "Oh, I'll get to the telegraph office, I promise you. I'm a man of certainty, and it's a straight shot from here to there. But the big question is if you're truly a changed man. See—what I need now is a regular gang. There's plenty more of these jobs to be pulled—even some with pots larger than fifty grand—so what I most need now is a few friends I can fully trust."

"Friends?" Bobbie said. "We are not your friends."

"Well, that's what I'm sorting out, girlie," Crazy Ake said. "Now that we're in Mexico, I'm safe. You've both done your job, thank you much. You got me in and out of the mayor's house safely, and you got me onto the airstrip and into the plane. The law in Cut Eye doesn't know what direction we were going, and the Mexican authorities are doubtful to know about the heist yet. That means I'm a free man where I stand, and, sorry to say it, but you two have used up your usefulness." He glanced at his rifle and laughed. "Whenever I don't need a gang member, there's only one fate awaiting the deadwood. But you both did good, and I'm proposing a wide-open opportunity. I'll cut you in for thirty percent of the cash—that's fifteen thousand dollars today to split—more money than you'll see in two lifetimes of being reverends, and I'll cut you in on future jobs, too. I just need to know for certain whether I can trust you from here on out."

"Why would we ever trust you?" Bobbie asked.

"Not you trusting me, no," Crazy Ake said. "Me trusting you." He smiled and continued. "It's very simple. It's one thing to play along being a thief for one evening, Miss Barker, but I need to know if you're ready for a lifetime of wrongdoing. And you, Rowdy, you can't go back to Cut Eye and your new preaching job now, so you may as well throw in your lot with me once and for all. That's the offer. If you're with me, then there's big reward. If you're against me—" Here he looked at the line in the sand. "Then I'm afraid your adventures with the mighty Akan Fordmire have come to an end."

"Lay it out plainly," I said. "What do we need to do?"

Crazy Ake grinned wider. "Just swear allegiance."

"To the flag?"

"No," Crazy Ake said. "To me."

"No problem," I said. "I swear allegiance to Crazy Ake. Let's go to Pachuca." I opened the door of the truck.

Crazy Ake fired the M1 at my feet. The bullet zinged into the dirt near the front tire and I jumped. "Not so fast, Rowdy. You both need to be legitimate about the swearing. You gotta know the depth of what's at stake. All those months I spent in jail before I met you, Rowdy, I pored over books, you know. I ain't the only one here who's been to a university of sorts." He glanced at Bobbie with a sneer. "Day after day I read everything in the prison library—even books I reckoned were foolish. Books of mathematics. Books of poetry. The writings of Tertullian of Carthage. Of Pliny the Younger. The term those idealists threw around was 'baptism in blood,' didn't they, Miss Barker? Those ancient historians. Surely you must have studied that at your university in Dallas."

"Baptism of blood—" Bobbie scrunched her brow, a look that told me she was searching her mind for where she'd heard it before. Her eyes grew round with fright and she whispered, "That's a martyr's death."

"Yes sir, dying for the cause you believe in!" Crazy Ake bellowed. "James the Just—clubbed in the head. Perpetua and Felicitas—ripped apart by lions. Polycarp—burned at the stake for his beliefs. Applying hard pressure is the only way a fella can sort fact from fiction out of you idealists, or so I've studied. So here's what I propose. To join my gang on the south side of the sand, just stay where you are and swear a firm and unbending lifetime of allegiance to lawlessness and the devil and me. If you stay put then you live, and you live with big cash. But step to the north side of the line and that means you're holy rollers through and through and I can't trust you, so you'll get a bullet to the head from my rifle. What's it going to be? I'll give you thirty seconds to decide." He looked at his watch.

Bobbie looked at me. I looked at Bobbie. Neither of us made a move.

"Time's ticking," Crazy Ake said. "Rowdy, you're saying you're a changed man. But I don't believe that's true. You're just as incorrigible as you ever was. If you stay incorrigible, then you stay alive. We'll swing by Texas from time to time. You'll see your daughter again. You'll pay off your debts. You'll be rich. That's everything you ever wanted. And you, pretty little Miss Barker—why, your whole life is stretching out before you. There's so much you have yet to taste. Why . . ." He laughed heartily. "I bet you're even still a virgin."

I heard a rustle at my side. Bobbie was walking. She was already across the line, standing on the side of her death. She turned around and squared her shoulders toward Crazy Ake.

"Look, mister, I might have played along with your little charade back at the mayor's house. But that was only because I believed Sunny would die if I didn't. I'll never swear my unbending allegiance to you, and I'll never join your gang. In fact, I strongly recommend you reconsider your ways, Mr. Akan Fordmire—if that's truly your name. Death comes to all men, and after that comes judgment. It's not too late, even today, to save your soul."

Crazy Ake laughed, frothy and nonsensically. He wiped his eyes then looked at me and spoke with a chuckle, "Oh, that was precious. A real sermon for the damned. Time's up, Rowdy, what's it going to be?"

I was thinking all this time. Thinking in that split second. Thinking back to that good meal of bacon and eggs and hot coffee I'd sought so earnestly at the mission. The man behind the pulpit was speaking straight to me. He was showing the way for any man to change, and he didn't fiddle around with his words nor sugarcoat the facts. I'd been so hungry that morning. So hungry indeed. I walked across the line, and stood next to Bobbie.

Crazy Ake pulled the trigger.

I was watching his finger the whole time, and he was aiming to kill Bobbie ahead of me. I leaped in front of her, and the bullet meant for Bobbie drove into my body. Call me a coward, but I just couldn't bear the thought of seeing her go with my own eyes.

A second shot rang out.

This one I heard with my ears but didn't see. I was on the ground by then, gushing blood from my shoulder.

The next thing I knew, Bobbie was kneeling by my side, her snake gun in her hand.

"Oh, Rowdy," she said. "You been hit bad."

# TWENTY-NINE

T he body of Crazy Ake lay sprawled in the dirt near the tire of his truck.

The man was killed clean with one shot through his forehead. Bobbie's Daddy had taught her how to hit a bull's-eye back when she was thirteen. The girl had no problem shooting a snake in the head.

She had removed her gun from its place of concealment just after she was on the ground and was stepping out of her chute. In the bustle of silk and wind, neither I nor Crazy Ake had noticed.

"Rowdy!" she said and shook my mind alert. "Come on, we need to go!" She tugged at my shirtsleeve, trying to pull me into an upright position. "I don't know if I can stop this blood before you bleed out and die."

"What—what time is it?"

Bobbie glanced at her watch. "Just after eleven a.m. We got to get you to a hospital."

"No." My mind was getting fuzzy. "Just cut a strip off Crazy Ake's shirt and bind me up tight. We gotta get to the telegraph office first."

Bobbie was already on her feet, already ripping Crazy Ake's shirt apart. "I was hoping we'd have time to do both," she said. "How far to Pachuca?"

"You're the one who knows geography," I said. "I don't remember him saying so." I was standing now, wobbling on my feet,

262

trying to clear my head, the truck keys jangling in my hand. The lump on the back of my skull throbbed and I felt weak all over. My arm was covered in blood.

"Sally Jo's not actually a murderer, is she?" Bobbie said. "We're talking about her taking the life of a child."

I lurched toward the truck. Bobbie met me halfway and began to bind a tourniquet around my upper torso. "Knowing Crazy Ake, he built some sort of incentive into the plan for Sally Jo to take Sunny's life," I said. "He might have been cheap, but he was serious in his plans. We can't take any chances."

We were at the truck now. Bobbie piled in on the passenger's side and I slid behind the wheel. She gave a little start and slapped the dashboard.

"What was I thinking?" she said. "You're almost dead. I'm driving."

"If you think you're driving, you've got another think coming."

"Don't argue with me, Rowdy. Time's wasting. If I can drive a jeep, I can surely drive this. Slide on over. I'll run around to the other side—quick."

I stared at the girl, then obeyed.

Bobbie started the truck and put it in gear. We bounced down the dirt road. Sure enough, in about two miles we hit blacktop. Another mile passed and a sign read, *Carretera Federal 85*, which I gathered to be Mexican Federal Highway 85.

Bobbie floored the truck. Sagebrush flew by us on either side. The road was flat and straight, the ground next to the highway chalky and white, and the Madres Mountains soon looked distant in the side mirror. Mile after mile passed and soon the sun began to rise directly overhead.

"What time is it?" I asked. Blood dripped on my seat.

Bobbie looked at her watch. "Quarter to noon."

"Can't this thing go any faster?"

The outskirts of Pachuca were nearly on us now. Traffic picked up and our truck slowed. The car ahead of us put on its brake lights and came to a stop. Bobbie drummed her hand on the steering wheel. "We gotta figure out where the nearest telegraph office is," she said. "Do you speak any Spanish?"

"Only a mite from talking with Gummer."

She leaned on the horn and squirmed in her seat. "Oh, this will never do." She veered off to the shoulder and accelerated. We tore through the dirt. Cars honked at us. Someone yelled our direction through our open window. Bobbie steered the truck along the shoulder at full throttle until we came to a small store and screeched on the brakes.

"Time?" I yelled.

"Three minutes to noon."

She parked the truck and she flew inside the store. I followed at a slower pace, wobbling and clutching the walls.

"¿Cómo estás?" she was already shouting to the man behind the counter. "Where's the nearest telegraph office? Quick!"

He stared at us and shrugged his face blank.

"Telegraph!" Bobbie said. "You know—telegraph-o." She tried to mimic poles and wires.

"Ah, telégrafo," the man said. "Si. Al lado."

Bobbie glanced back at me. I hadn't made it farther than the doorway. I stared back at her. "Al lado? Al lado—what does that mean?"

"Al lado," said the man. "Si . . . uh . . . ¿Cómo se dice . . . *next door-oh?*"

"Next door?!" we both said.

Bobbie flew out the door and around the corner to a laundry mat. The door banged against me a few seconds later and I shuffled inside to the counter. "Telégrafo!" Bobbie was saying to the proprietor. "Please! We need to send a telegraph immediately!"

"Two minutes to noon!" I shouted, glancing at a clock on the wall.

"Si," said the proprietor. He shuffled around behind the counter. "I speek a bit of Engleesh. Who to send to?"

"To Sally Jo Chicory in Rancho Springs, Texas. Please! We're in a terrible hurry."

"Si." The man didn't appear to hurry at all. Neither did he seem fazed by the amount of blood I was dripping on his floor. "And who is thee telegraph from?"

"From Akan Fordmire," I called out. "No—wait. From Daniel Q. Farnsworth of Bartlesville, Oklahoma."

"What ees message?" The proprietor had a pencil now. He wrote down all the information.

"'All okay. Stop.' That's it."

"That ees all?"

"Yes, that's all! Please send it. It's an emergency."

"Your identee-fication, please, Meester Farnsworth." The proprietor looked at me.

I drew a blank.

"We don't have any identification," I said. "We lost it—we were robbed."

The proprietor sighed. "El Señor Farnsworth. I am so sorry, but you are forbeedden by law anywhere in this city to send a telegraph weethout identification."

"Please!" Bobbie said. "I'll vouch for this man. He might look like raw hamburger, but he's telling the truth. We need to send this telegraph immediately. If we don't, a child will die."

The proprietor gave us a confused look.

"Ten seconds!" Bobbie shouted.

"Surely you have a passport, Señor Farnsworth," the proprietor said. "Something weeth your name on it. A driver's license. A birth certificate. Even a printed business card will do."

Bobbie slapped my good shoulder. "The business card!" she cried. "Your jacket pocket!"

I thrust my good hand into my pocket and slapped the card

down on the table. The proprietor flipped some knobs and dialed some dials. He clicked in Morse code on the receiver.

"Your message has gone through," he said. "That is one peso. Will you be waiting for a reply?"

Bobbie and I looked at each other. "We don't know," I said.

"Never mind," he said. "A message has just returned." Carefully he wrote down the message as he listened to the electric clicks. Slowly he turned from his table. Gravely he looked at us. "I am sorry, Señor and Señorita. The news does not look in your favor."

"What does it say?!"

The proprietor cleared his throat. "All plans canceled. Stop. Sally Jo."

# THIRTY

They kept me in a Mexican hospital for two weeks until I healed enough to be shipped home by train. Bobbie spent the first night pacing the halls in the hospital, all the while checking in on me while trying to reach her father by phone. Around midnight she finally got through, and he and the sheriff from Rancho Springs soon had Sunny safe and sound and took Sally Jo Chicory in for questioning. The sheriff called the hospital in the morning and then drove down to Pachuca, stayed the night in a hotel, and took Bobbie back to Texas with him the next day. She didn't want to leave me in my aggravated state, but I said go, just go.

U. S. federal agents soon came to interrogate me in the hospital as did members of the Policía Federal, who were wondering about a dead body and a crashed plane and why I'd shown up with a bullet wound and a lump on my head. All the money in the duffel bag, I turned over immediately. They were already working with Sheriff Barker and had Bobbie's story, just like they soon had mine. Fortunately they soon had Sally Jo's story too, for she spilled the truth and confirmed our stories in exchange for a plea bargain. They reduced her charge from attempted murder to extortion and kidnapping. She'd be going away for a long time to come, and I heard the rest of the girls in her home for up-and-coming prostitutes were soon placed with sound-minded adoptive families around the state. So that was that.

Oris Floyd got his fifty grand back and was able to disburse the funds among his poker friends, yet he grumbled and complained to any and all who'd listen that he'd been roughed up in his own home, that was true. But in the end the story all got sorted out to everyone's satisfaction. Bobbie and I were quickly cleared of all charges for our part in the night's events, and Bobbie said she never doubted it would happen that way. Not for a moment, she didn't.

———————

I kept a low profile around Cut Eye right up until the morning of my trial as March 1947 dawned clear and bright. Mostly I just healed up from my bullet wound, kept preaching and visiting folks, and doing what I'd come to consider my calling.

A warm breeze wafted through the open window of the parsonage that morning. My one-year anniversary of being the reverend at the Cut Eye Community Church was all but a week away. One year and I'd survived just fine. One year and I was still a reverend of sorts—as reverend as a man like me was ever going to be.

Sheriff Barker was set to escort me to the trial, which would be held over in the courthouse in Brewster County on account of them having better facilities. I'd decided earlier to spill the beans to the prosecutor about all my misdeeds—I wanted to wipe the slate of my conscience clean when it came to the law, so among the long list of charges to be read against me later in the morning were robbing the banks of Rancho Springs and Cut Eye, participation in the assault of a uniformed federal employee (seeing that Crazy Ake had walloped the bank guard in Cut Eye), fleeing the scene of a crime, damaging federal property, violating parole, disorderly conduct, general recklessness, speeding, endangering citizens, and doing it all with weapons in hand.

While waiting for the sheriff to arrive, I cranked out five sets of twenty-five push-ups, then went to the woodpile and did another five sets of twenty-five overhand pull-ups, chopped wood for a while, then went back inside.

Despite this undoubtedly being a difficult day ahead for me, I couldn't help but look around my surroundings and grin. By then the parsonage had grown into a domicile worth living in, I do declare. The church's building program had finished in February. As part of the program, the walls of the parsonage were insulated and re-sided. A fresh coat of paint stood out on both the exterior and interior walls. They'd even built a bathroom with a shower to the side. After my exercising, I grabbed a towel, went inside and closed the door, and turned on a cascade of hot water. The water poured out lavishly and I soaked and scrubbed under the faucet, then climbed out, dried myself off, and lathered and shaved.

The suit waiting for me was freshly cleaned and my shirt was well ironed. I dressed, tied my tie, and put on socks and my church-going shoes. The clock over the mantel chimed at 8 a.m. Right on time. I walked over to the church building and paused before going inside.

Everything within the church's grounds sparkled fresh and new. The walls of the main building had been redone both inside and out. A fresh coat of paint everywhere announced all was well. The foundation was re-poured, solid, and set. The septic field was in, and there was real running water and flush toilets in a new wide lean-to at the back of the building.

Before the sheriff arrived, I had one last task to do as reverend. I realized it might be the last chance I got to do this for a long while, and so I walked over to the bell tower, took the rope with both hands, and pulled with all my might.

The church bell resounded clear and inviting, as it had been doing each morning ever since it had been oiled and re-roped. I'd gotten in the habit of ringing that bell and purely enjoyed the strong sound of it, I did. The melody rang out all over the county. Folks told me they heard it from miles around—and they liked it fine.

Emma Hackathorn heard it in the mercantile. Her engagement to Gummer Lopez was in place, and their knot-tying ceremony was set for early June. Her children were excited to receive their new daddy into their home, and so was Sunny. My daughter was back living with the Hackathorns, back where she belonged—at least for now. It wasn't as hard as we all thought for me to regain full and legal custody from Sally Jo Chicory, which I'd done as soon as possible.

Cisco and Augusta Wayman heard the bell sounding at the Pine Oak Café. They were both back in the place they loved so much, both cooking up a storm. Cisco had his bad spells on occasion, but whenever he did he went upstairs to his bedroom and lay down, and the spells passed within an hour or two. He was still a sad man in many ways—and I didn't try to stop him none for feeling the depth of what he felt. The man would undoubtedly grieve for his lost son for the rest of his days, and that was doubtless the way things should be. The grief had become part of Cisco Wayman, it had. He felt it in a strong and powerful way, a different way, yes, than what his wife felt, but remindful of a different time and place, of a better world where young men grew up strong and proud and were never called to fight the world's wars of horror.

They heard the bell over at the Sugar House Tavern. Ava-Louise heard it upstairs in the brothel, and Luna-Mae heard it behind the bar where she worked. Every Sunday I saw them sitting in church. They were both making strides, they were. Still working their old businesses, but coming along nonetheless in their spiritual journeys. Both gals were learning more about the ways of a fisherman from Nazareth, a man born as a babe in a straw ox manger, a man who could change their lives if they let him. A man who'd changed mine.

Deuce Gibbons heard it at his house and shop south of town. He quit working odd jobs for Oris Floyd and began his own construction company to take advantage of all the additional building projects going on in the area. He enjoyed his time on the deacon board and seldom visited the Sugar House anymore, except when a good fight was expected to break out.

The widow Mert Cahoon heard the bell over at her new apartment in town. In addition to her secretary duties, she was still selling her canning and quilts. Still working her mail route, and still driving the school bus. And she was still secretary of the church. That was for certain. Most days when I saw her at the office she greeted me with a smile. Right after she told me I was late—and late again!—that is.

They heard the bell at the new casino and tavern and hotel and restaurant. The monstrosity was nearly built and set to open next October. Oh, they had their supporters and their detractors. On one hand, folks said change was good for business. On the other, folks said a business like that was nothing needed in this state. But the monstrosity was happening like it or not, and there was no way of stopping it, and that made Mayor Oris Floyd exceptionally happy, which worked out to everyone's advantage all around.

They heard the bell at the jailhouse where Deputy Roy was still convinced I was an evil influence on the town.

They heard it at the laundry mat and lumberyard.

They heard it at the livery and feed store, and Oris Floyd could even hear it far up at his house northeast of town.

I rang that bell and I felt at home. This was my job, my calling, and I finished ringing the bell just as the sheriff showed up.

"You ready for this, Rowdy?" he said.

"I am."

"Okay," he said. "Let's go face the day of your reckoning."

———

Well, in the evening after the day of my trial, they held a party for me at the Pine Oak Café so the town's folks could stop by and say hello, shake hands all around, and celebrate the verdict. My trial was exceedingly short—far shorter than expected—and when the gavel fell, my sentencing was done right on the spot, and it turned out to be a grand total of one year's probation. That was it.

There was no question of my guilt—at least to a few of those charges. They could have put me in the chair and set it to fry, or at least thrown me away for thirty years, but after all the evidence from the facts and witnesses got legally sorted through, all I received in the end was the Texas State judicial system's equivalent of a slap on the wrist. Now it may have been due to the extenuating circumstances surrounding the first crime, or because I was an unwilling accomplice for the second crime, or because I was the fella who returned the stolen money from both bank jobs, but I reckon I'll never ascertain why my judge proved so lenient. When a man receives such mercy, I suspect there's far more that goes on behind the scenes than can ever be told.

Augusta Wayman cooked up a real buffet spread for the party. She held nothing back and the theme was all the food folks in Texas like to eat. The first table was laden with appetizers. There were armadillo eggs and beef tacos, black bean dip and broiled brunch grapefruit. There were thick cheese enchilada puffs and a big bowl of smoky cocktail links with corn dip. Another bowl contained spicy marinated shrimp flown in that morning from the Gulf coast, and another bowl held mushroom rolls. And that was just for starters.

Another table was solely devoted to beef main courses. There was beef chili and cowboy brisket and flank steak with pineapple salsa. Next to that sat a platter of grilled flank steaks and alongside of that was a plate of tamale-and-frito-pie, and there were barbecued spareribs and barbecued burgers and then came the chicken.

Oh, there were barbecue wings and hot-and-spicy wings and chicken and dumplings and turkey potpie. There was skillet chicken and lime chicken burritos and honey barbecue baked chicken and plain old fried chicken and hash. There were salsas and pickles, relishes and salads, sauces and marinades, and soups and stews. After that came dessert.

There was but one dessert.

Augusta called it Peach-Lime Cornmeal Shortcake, and she described the ingredients in the same easygoing motion as she lay down plateful after plateful to all who came near. "Four cups fresh peaches—canned if it's all you can muster." She dabbed her forehead with the corner of a serving towel. "One tablespoon fresh lime juice. One cup cold heavy cream." The shortcake flaked in all the right places, still warm from the oven. The peaches dripped over the side, serious in their syrup. Another layer of fruit followed underneath with cream so buttery everyone who ate it swore it came straight from the cow that morning. Another solid foundation of shortcake held it in place from the bottom up, and when I ate mine I cleaned my plate and sat back and loosened my belt. I'd arrived in the culinary sweet spot, and I didn't want to ever leave.

As I patted my belly and wished I could fit in another piece, I reflected back on the trial, how more than twenty men from the town of Cut Eye testified on my behalf. They said that through my leadership and by the influence of the Word of God and the power of the Spirit, they'd become better men. More than fifteen gals testified on my behalf too, even the three elderly ladies from the church who insisted—under oath—that I was still preaching heresy. But they'd gotten accustomed to my strange ways of ministering and wanted me back in the pulpit as soon as possible, they did.

My year's probation would need to be served in close proximity to a jailhouse and a lawman, insisted the judge. That meant each week I needed to check in with the jailhouse, and only with a lawman's permission could I travel more than a hundred miles away from my hometown. Halligan Barker stepped right up and volunteered to be my probation officer. We would keep right on meeting each week as part of my continued job functions, he explained to the judge.

Later, when I asked Halligan what my continued job function was going to be, he said, "Exactly what you're doing now, of course. What'd you expect? It ain't easy to hire a new preacher in Texas."

At the party, Gummer called everyone together and announced that he had a gift for me. He knew all along I wasn't going to fry, and so he'd been working on it in his spare time. It was parked right out in front, and he took me outside with the crowd of townsfolk following along behind.

Gummer's gift was another DUKW. He had bought it cheap at a surplus auction, and the huge, green, six-wheel-drive vehicle was as ugly as the day was long and exactly like the other DUKW I drove—except for one thing. Gummer had sawed off the trailer hitch.

"So you cannot haul any more large German guns," he said in his clipped accent, and everybody laughed at the trouble I'd seen.

---

Well, I didn't want to travel more than a hundred miles away from Cut Eye anyway, even if I had the chance. Since I wasn't going to jail for the rest of my life, that meant that Sunny could come and live with me at the parsonage if she wanted to.

Emma and Gummer and I worked out a plan. We agreed it was good for my daughter to be around other children, particularly if they were Hackathorns, so she'd eat breakfast with me and then spend the rest of each day with Emma and the gang while I worked. We'd eat dinner together again at the café, Sunny and me, and then she'd sleep each night in the front room in the parsonage, the one with the cots and crib in it. Although I was taking the crib out and putting it in storage. For now, anyway. A man never knew what the future might hold forth.

Sunny liked that idea real fine, she told me, in words as clear as any child ever spoke. She was looking forward to beginning kindergarten in the fall. And on the evening I asked her about coming to live with me, she asked, "Why would I live with my uncle?" So I explained some things to her, enough for now. And when she found out I was her real daddy she hugged me tight for a long, long time.

# EPILOGUE

Early one morning near the end of May 1947, two months after my trial, Bobbie and I drove in her jeep east along the Grayson-Gregg Road, which lies a couple miles south of town off of Highway 2.

The sun was not yet up and the road turns into gravel before long. Few folks ever travel this direction. I slowed the jeep to 20 and kept a sharp lookout for any deep ruts that were made in last spring's heavy rainstorm, the storm that filled the river with rage and began the trajectory of my change from incorrigible paratrooper to country preacher, seemingly so long ago now.

Bobbie talked while I drove, and I gave the occasional grunt of affirmation. She chatted about nothing and everything—it seemed more monologue than conversation—and all the while she kept looking to her right, far away from me, southward out over the cool fields of prickly pear cacti that dot the rolling hills of the lower Edward Plateau.

Tucked in the back of the jeep was a picnic breakfast hand-packed the evening before and sent our direction with love from Augusta Wayman. It seemed everyone in town was urging me to strike the right mood and say something while I still had the chance, anything that might prompt Bobbie to change her mind about leaving. Course, they knew it was hopeless. They all knew Bobbie feared Jesus, and they were learning to respect the ways of a mysterious God, just like I was learning, particularly when God seems to be directing two folks together or keeping them apart.

At mile thirty Bobbie whapped me with the back of her hand on my accelerator knee and nodded ahead toward the distance.

"There," she said. "Just over that rise. Up ahead is what I wanted you to see, Rowdy. Stop the car and we'll walk the last bit."

The sun's rays were coloring the skies of the eastern horizon now, straight in the direction we were driving, and I pulled the jeep over, switched off the headlights, and pulled the key out of the ignition. She reached up to the red ribbon in the back of her hair to make sure it wasn't mussed, then brought her hands down and smoothed the pleats of her dress.

She was wearing this blue-checked country job that looked mighty swell on her willowy frame. The dress tapered around her waist, and she was keeping the skirt of the dress tucked underneath her legs to keep it from billowing in the breeze of the open jeep. She fluffed out the skirt, then sat perfectly still until I remembered my manners and shuffled around the front of the jeep and over to her side, gave her my hand, and helped her out.

Not like the girl ever needed help from me, I thought. I'd come to know this girl as a true sassafras, that she was, a right capable and free-thinking girl. Yet she didn't let go of my hand when we started walking away from the jeep neither, and I certainly didn't let go of hers. Bobbie's hand felt warm and small inside mine, and I wondered how long it might be before she remembered her propensity toward independence and let go. I decided to speak first, while I still had a shot, and cleared my throat.

"Mert wants to know if you're still bound to go to Haiti and be a missionary."

Out of the corner of my eye I watched for Bobbie's reaction. She was still looking far off to the right, far off away from me, and she said simply, "So, Mert wants to know, does she?"

We walked a few more steps and I cleared my throat again and added, "Well, she's not the only one."

Oh, for ever so many years I've always been so confident with the opposite gender. I've never been the fella to clear his throat before speaking, never been the one to mince at words. But with Miss Bobbie, and what I needed to lay on the line this morning, all was different. Sure, I knew the plan. I knew it well. I'd been thinking it through, wandering around it, scratching my head and pondering if anything might be different. But it was no use.

When the spring was over in a few short days the girl was still headed off to language school in Dallas for all of next year. Her particular course of study began earlier than most—at the start of June, not the start of fall—so as to stretch in a longer frame of studying. The university was a fourteen-hour drive away, maybe more like sixteen, and surely we were bound to see each other at holidays when she came home, but it wouldn't be much.

Worse yet was when that next year was over her plans were now set more firmly than ever. Those plans involved a train ride from Texas to Florida, and from Florida a boat ride south to Port-au-Prince where she was already contracted to work as a nanny in an orphanage. That was another year of her being away. Maybe two, if they liked her work and extended the contract, which they was sure to do. Dang her competence. Worst of all yet was that it might even be more time away—maybe a lifetime. Going to Haiti for an indeterminate stretch of time was what God was laying on Bobbie's heart to do, and I wasn't one to fight against God no more.

"So . . . uh," I said, "what I'm asking directly is that when you reckon your time in the orphanage is over . . . uh, whenever that is . . . if things might change for you then."

"Well," Bobbie said—and here she glanced my direction, then quickly looked the other way again, out to the fields, far away from me. "I guess any plans can change."

Oh, she was a sassafras. A real sassafras. We were silent for another ten paces and we'd nearly crested the hill when Bobbie let go of my hand and stopped abruptly.

"The surprise is just over there," she said. "I should have brought something to tie your sight with. You need to close your eyes the rest of the way, Rowdy—promise me you'll keep your eyes shut tight until I say when. Promise. Okay?"

I inhaled sharply. I knew no man who hankers for surprises. But I nodded anyway and in faith scrunched tight my eyes. She grabbed hold of my hand again to guide me the last steps. Together we walked to the top of the hill.

"Open," she said.

On the other side lay an ocean of coreopsis blooms as far as the eye could see—that brash yellow flower that looks like a black-eyed Susan. Everywhere I looked was carpeted with bright and golden yellow; a sprinkling of red gaillardia mixed in with the blooms, and scattered underneath were smudges of green prairie grass. With the sun coming up, everything was haphazard and crazy and untamed and stunning, and I marveled at how such a sight of beauty ever grew in the desert. There must have been a spring nearby to water this one particular field and provide it with so much color. I looked at the field a long, long time, and then I looked at Bobbie.

She was already looking at me.

I closed my eyes and pulled her close and breathed her in. Both her hands were held up around my chest and she clenched her hands and gave me a little pound with her fists, her body tense in my arms. Then she settled down and settled in, and she wrapped her arms around me in return.

This time I kissed her first. I didn't know if a girl like Bobbie Barker could ever truly love a man like me, even changed as I was, but this time she didn't slap me nor turn away, but instead kissed me right back. All this kissing made me more certain things would work out one day between this girl and me. I would marry her when the time was right. I just didn't know when.

"I'm still going away," she murmured in the midst of my mouth.

"I know," was all I said.

# AUTHOR'S NOTE

*Meet the man who inspired the character of Reverend Rowdy*

Over the past six years, I've interviewed World War II veterans for various nonfiction projects, mostly related to the Band of Brothers (E Co, 506th PIR, 101st A/B), the elite group of paratroopers who jumped into Normandy and fought their way through Europe.

During the process, I discovered the story of a man named Wayne "Skinny" Sisk. Not much is known about him and he's deceased now, although he's mentioned a few times in historian Stephen Ambrose's book *Band of Brothers*. I attempted to contact Mr. Sisk's relatives but was never able to track them down. Nor is anyone in Easy Company still in contact with them that I know.

From talking with other veterans who knew him, I learned that Skinny Sisk was generally thought of as "Easy Company's best yet most incorrigible paratrooper." It isn't known exactly how he was incorrigible, but we know that Skinny had a genuinely warm streak through him as well.

We know he was well liked because, a few years back, I wrote a book about Shifty Powers, the sharpshooter in the company. Shifty was the warmhearted family man whom everyone in the company loved and respected, and Shifty's son in real life today is named Wayne, in Skinny Sisk's honor. So if Shifty Powers thought well of Skinny Sisk, then Skinny Sisk was genuinely a good-hearted guy, incorrigible as he may have been.

From Ambrose's book, we also know that Skinny was one of

the first privates in Easy Company who trained at Camp Toccoa. Skinny had a good sense of humor and broke the tension during the flight to Normandy by asking the men in his plane, "Does anybody here want to buy a good watch?" (which brought a roar of laughter to the men). Once, while on the march on the Cotentin Peninsula, the men traversed by the body of a dead man whose hand was sticking out in the air, and Skinny shook hands with the corpse. While on a special mission in Austria immediately after the war's end, Skinny helped track down and execute a high-ranking German officer.

Ambrose recorded that after the war Skinny had a hard time shaking his war memories. Skinny turned to alcohol, that generation's drug of choice, and was often seen drunk and hungover.

Then in 1949, Skinny experienced a genuine spiritual conversion when his four-year-old niece shared the gospel with him. Skinny repented, chose to follow Jesus, and was later ordained into pastoral ministry. He wrote to his commander, Dick Winters, "I haven't whipped but one man since, and he needed it."

The Reverend Skinny Sisk lived and ministered in West Virginia. He died in 1999.

The example of Skinny Sisk inspired the creation of this novel's main character, Rowdy Slater. Every other detail about Rowdy's life has been fictionalized, including the company he fought with, and none of the specifics of Skinny's life were used in this novel. Other than the mention of Colonel Robert Sink as commander of the 506th Parachute Infantry Regiment, every other character, plot line, and conversation in the book is purely fictitious.

Still, I began this novel with one big story idea and question in mind—an elite paratrooper becomes a minister. Here's a man used to solving problems with a rifle or his fists . . . *What sort of wild-hearted minister might such a man make?*

# THE HISTORICITY OF DIALECT

*Why Rowdy speaks the way he does*

I've always been fascinated by classical novels such as *The Adventures of Huckleberry Finn*, *To Kill a Mockingbird*, and *The Catcher in the Rye*, which all recounted stories in the dialect and spoken attitude of the respective day. As Mark Twain wrote in an explanatory note to *Huck Finn*, "The [use of dialects has] not been done in a haphazard fashion; but painstakingly, and with the trustworthy guidance and support of personal familiarity with these forms of speech."

The same is true for Rowdy Slater. Here was my protagonist—born in a small town in western Texas, educated to tenth grade, a manual laborer in Roosevelt's CCC camps, a paratrooper in an elite army unit, a prisoner in a military jail, a drifter, an outlaw, and finally a student of Scripture. I envisioned Rowdy as an older man, leaning against the mantel of a fireplace, dictating this book. He would say, "Well, years ago, this is how it all began . . ." And then I asked myself, How might such a man talk and write?

To create Rowdy's speech patterns, as part of the process of researching this book, I pored through almanacs, visited cities and towns in Texas, researched jail systems, read dozens of nonfiction books and novels, studied innumerable war and Western movies, and spoke to Texas pastors. Central to my research was interviewing WWII veterans.

Rowdy's army experience posed a unique challenge. When divisions such as the 101st were created, men were brought together from all across America and from all walks of life. Rowdy would have been exposed to this smorgasbord of dialects for the nearly three years he was in the service.

Below is a sampling of some speech patterns from WWII veterans.

### Use of double negatives:

J. B. Stokes: "I wasn't at Toccoa where they'd formed up. But I didn't have no trouble with the guys."

### Swapped verbs:

J. Anderson: "When we got to the north end of Peleliu, we was put on amphibian tractors again."

### Colloquialisms:

Clancy Lyall: "Swimming in that nasty [Sabine River in Texas] are water moccasins and copperheads. Dad threw me right in. I doggied out of that place like you never saw."

### Using "aggravation" to describe trouble:

Bill Wingett: "I certainly didn't have any aggravation with the Indians."

### Use of larger words despite lack of schooling:

Hank Zimmerman: "I didn't have much schooling. I had to quit school, which I hated. I didn't want to quit but my old man told me to go out and get a job. My old man was a tyrant. . . . I was working at Phelps Dodge. There were a lot of promises of good things to come that never materialized."

### Continuous present tense ("ing" verbs):

Rod Bain: "I was minding my own business as a student when suddenly we were in a world war with no apparent limitations."

## Use of "reckon" to mean guess or judge:

Dewitt Lowrey: "My family was pretty close. I don't reckon we could have had a better mother. But she also had a temper and knew how to use a switch."

## Use of "real" as an adjective (instead of "really")

Darrell Powers: "We were going to take the town, but we got there real late and didn't have time to do it before dark."

## Upbeat and optimistic language:

Robert Van Klinken [in a letter home]: "Say Johnny, I bought another guitar the other day. Gave 30 bucks for it. It sure is a honey."

## Humorous, self-deprecating language:

Sid Phillips: "We were so stupid, we'd never heard of Parris Island [the Marine Corps Recruiting Station in South Carolina]. I think that recruiting sergeant told us we'd have a short training at a beautiful resort. We were rapidly sorry within the first few hours that we were there."

## Sentences beginning with "well":

Sterling Mace: "Well, if you can't play ball, you don't stay with the ball team. So they sent me over to the post troops, which is a different duty every day."

Note also that many of the WWII vets I've spoken with mix expletives in with their speech, although the expletives are used more for emphasis than to actually curse. I figured that Rowdy would filter the cussing out of his speech patterns due to his new profession.

# THANKS

Deborah Keiser and the team at River North Fiction. Greg Johnson and the WordServe Literary Group. Early readers H. C. Jones, Robert Craddock, Karen Sue Clark, Elizabeth Jones, and Becky Kimball. The men of Easy Company, 506th PIR, 101st and their families. The Marines of K/3/5, H/2/1, and D/1/7 and their families. The University of North Texas libraries. Clint Whitwer. Matt Weeda. The people of Dallas, Houston, Austin, Plano, Bonton, Galveston, (and Texas in general) for your hospitality during research trips. Mike and Judy Albin, Graham and Dorothy Brotherton, Paul and Renay Fredette for your vision in sponsorship. Mary Margaret, Addy, Zach, and Amie-Merrin for your love.

# ABOUT THE AUTHOR

**M**arcus Brotherton is a journalist and professional writer, the author or coauthor of more than twenty-five books. Many of his books center on the veterans who fought in World War II, what they stood for, and their struggles and triumphs upon returning home. Notable nonfiction includes *Shifty's War*, *A Company of Heroes*, and the oral history project *We Who Are Alive and Remain: Untold Stories from the Band of Brothers*, a *New York Times* bestseller. *Feast for Thieves* is his first novel.

Marcus was born in 1968 in Canada, the son of a minister father and a journalist mother. He studied theology and writing and earned a bachelor's degree from Multnomah University in Portland, Oregon, and a master's degree from Talbot Seminary at Biola University in Los Angeles. He served in pastoral ministry in rural church settings for nearly a decade before turning to a career in writing full-time. Marcus lives with his wife and children in Bellingham, Washington.

Read his blog: www.marcusbrotherton.com.

# river north

*Thank you! We are honored that you took the
time out of your busy schedule to read this
book. If you enjoyed what you read, would you
consider sharing the message with others?*

- Write a review online at amazon.com,
  bn.com, goodreads.com, cbd.com.

- Recommend this book to friends in your
  book club, workplace, church, school,
  classes, or small group.

- Go to facebook.com/RiverNorthFiction,
  "like" the page and post a comment as to
  what you enjoyed the most.

- Mention this book in a Facebook post,
  Twitter update, Pinterest pin, or a blog post.

- Pick up a copy for someone you know who
  would be encouraged by this message.

- Subscribe to our newsletter for information
  on upcoming titles, inside information
  on discounts and promotions, and learn
  more about your favorite authors at
  RiverNorthFiction.com.